On deck all was chaos. Every wave that slammed over the ship's side threw me down.

Reaching the stub of a broken mast, I managed to stand and look around. One side of the hull was bashed in. The bow was awash and coming apart. Ignoring us, their only passengers, the crew had hurried into lifeboats. "Please!" I cried out. "Wait for my family!" There was no answer as the last boat descended into the sea.

A Background Note about
The Swiss Family Robinson

The Swiss Family Robinson is set in the late 1700s. The story is told in the form of a journal kept by the father. In this journal, he writes down the events in the lives of the family.

The family—mother, father, and four sons—have left their home in Switzerland and are on their way to settle in a colony. The ship they are traveling on is loaded with supplies for the colony—tools, equipment, furniture, farm animals, seeds, fruit trees, and so forth. The Robinson family are the only passengers on the ship.

The ship is caught in a violent storm that drives the ship far off its course. When the story begins, the storm has been going on for six days.

The Swiss Family Robinson

JOHANN WYSS

Edited, and with an Afterword,
by Bill Blauvelt

 THE TOWNSEND LIBRARY

SWISS FAMILY ROBINSON

TP **THE TOWNSEND LIBRARY**

For more titles in the Townsend Library,
visit our website: **www.townsendpress.com**

All new material in this edition is
copyright © 2006 by Townsend Press.
Printed in the United States of America

0 9 8 7 6 5 4 3 2

Illustrations © 2006 by Hal Taylor

Townsend Press, Inc.
439 Kelley Drive
West Berlin, New Jersey 08091
cs@townsendpress.com

ISBN-13: 978-1-59194-056-2
ISBN-10: 1-59194-056-7

Library of Congress Control Number:
2005930218

Contents

Afterword

CHAPTER 1

Shipwreck & Desertion

Our ship had been storm-tossed for six days. The raging sea had increased in fury each hour until, by the seventh day, all hope was lost. Constant struggle had exhausted the men. Their yells of frustration and anger had turned to prayers for mercy, with strange and often silly vows to behave better if spared. We had no idea where we were, no way to navigate. The masts had splintered. New leaks opened faster than any crew could have mended them.

We huddled below in our cabin, as if to shut out the sounds of doom. My heart sank as I looked upon my wife and my four terrified young sons. "Dear children," said I, "if the Lord wishes, He can save us. If not, remember that we will all be reunited in Heaven."

My dear wife, Elizabeth, looked bravely up from her tears. The boys clustered around her, and she began to reassure them in calm tones. I led us in prayer, and each person prayed aloud in turn. Fritz, the eldest, prayed for the rescue for his dear parents and brothers, with hardly a thought for himself. My children's simple, honest prayers gave me heart: I felt they would be answered.

Amid the roar of storm and breakage I suddenly heard the cry of "Land! Land!" At that instant, the ship trembled with a dreadful *crash!* The impact tossed us across the cabin; we heard the sounds of splintering timber and water roaring in. The captain's voice rose above the devastation: "Lower the boats! We are lost!"

"Lost!" I exclaimed. Then, for my family's sake, I forced cheer into my voice. "Take courage, my boys! Land is near, and we shall do our best to reach it. God helps those that help themselves! Stay with your mother while I investigate." With that I went above.

On deck all was chaos. Every wave that slammed over the ship's side threw me down. Reaching the stub of a broken mast, I managed to stand and look around. One side of the hull was bashed in. The bow was awash and coming apart. Ignoring us, their only passengers, the crew had hurried into lifeboats. "Please!" I cried out. "Wait for my family!" There was no answer as the last boat descended into the sea.

I could only watch the crew row away. Calling to them was a waste of breath. In those

heavy seas, they could not have returned even if they had suddenly remembered their duty. We were deserted.

Even so, I saw reasons for hope. The ship's stern was jammed between two high rocks, partly above the waves that were battering the bow to pieces. My family's cabin was in the stern, safely above the waterline. Through the pelting rain, I could make out a line of rocky coast. My heart leaped, yet I was deeply concerned as I returned to my family.

Five pairs of eyes looked to me for news. I forced a smile. "Courage, dear ones! Although our good ship will sail no more, neither is she likely to sink; she is wedged. Land is in sight.

Tomorrow, if the storm eases, I see no reason we cannot get ashore."

My children's spirits rose immediately. Such trust they had in my words, such optimism! They acted as though our escape was certain. The ship's position also helped; while we could still feel the impacts of waves, they no longer tossed us like stones in a box.

My wife saw through my forced cheer, though, and I answered her questioning look with the grim truth: we were abandoned. Her brave reply inspired me. "We must find some supper," said she. "We will need all our strength tomorrow. No use being hungry as well as abandoned."

Night drew on with no letup in the storm. Each crash announced new damage to our ship. I thought of the lifeboats; I doubted the crew had survived.

"God will help us soon, won't He, Father?" said my youngest child, Franz.

"You silly little thing," said his brother Fritz, too sharply. "It is up to God to decide what and when to do for us. We must have patience."

"Well said, Fritz, had you said it kindly," I said. "You often speak more harshly to your brothers than you truly feel. Let your words reflect what is in your heart."

After my wife prepared a hearty supper, my three youngest went directly to sleep. Fritz, who was old enough to understand our danger, kept watch with us. After a long silence, he spoke: "Father, we could make swimming belts for mother and the boys. Since you and I can swim, those might enable us all to reach land."

"Your idea is so good," I answered, "that we will do it right now, in case something happens tonight." We found a number of empty flasks and tin canisters, which we connected with rope to make floatable belts. My wife put hers on, and I wakened my younger sons to equip them. I then gathered up matches, tinder, knives, cord, and other small useful items. If the vessel fell apart that night, and we reached shore, we would have a few tools.

Now Fritz joined his brothers in sound sleep. My wife and I kept watch all night, dreading some fatal shift in the wreck with each new sound.

When the day finally came, the storm had passed. We went on deck—or what remained of it—to see blue sky and a lovely sunrise.

Only then did my boys discover that we were alone. They all spoke at once:

"Papa, what has become of everybody?" "Are the sailors gone?" "Have they taken away the boats?" "Oh, Papa! Why did they leave us behind? What can we do by ourselves!"

"My good children," I replied, "we must not despair. The men may have abandoned us, but God will not. Let us all do our best. Does anyone have a suggestion?"

"The sea will soon be calm enough for swimming," said Fritz.

"Very well for you, because you can swim," exclaimed Ernest, my second eldest, "but think of mother and the rest of us! Why not build a raft and go ashore together?"

"It would be difficult to build a raft to carry all of us," I answered, "but it's the right idea. First, though, let us all look around for useful items."

Away we all went. I checked on supplies of food and fresh water, while my wife and young Franz went to care for the animals, who were in a pitiful state. Fritz hastened to the arms-chest. Ernest searched for tools.

My second youngest, Jack, headed for the captain's cabin. The moment he opened the door, two huge dogs bounded out in great joy, bowling him over. He cried out in surprise and protest, and the dogs apologized as dogs do, licking his face where he lay. I laughed, but warned him: "Remember, these are animals. They may be hungry. Be careful." Jack nodded. "Even so," I continued, "I'm glad you weren't angry with them. They can not help their nature."

When we reassembled in the cabin, we all displayed our treasures. Fritz had two guns, a belt with pouches, powder-flasks, and plenty of bullets. Ernest produced a can of nails, a pair of large scissors, an axe, and a hammer; his pockets were full of carpentry tools. Little Franz opened a large box, eager to show us the "nice sharp little hooks" it contained. His brothers smiled scornfully.

"Well done, Franz!" I cried. "These fish hooks, which you—the youngest—have found, may be the most important find. Fritz and Ernest, you have chosen well too."

"Will you praise me too?" said my dear wife. "I have found no tools, but I can give you good news. Some animals are still alive: a donkey, two goats, six sheep, a ram, and a cow and a fine sow, both pregnant. I was just in time to save them from starving. I milked the goats, though the milk will not keep in this dreadful heat."

"Excellent," I said. "My friend Jack, however, has presented me with a couple of huge, useless dogs, who will eat more than any of us."

"Oh, Papa! They will be of use!" protested Jack. "They will help us to hunt when we get on shore!"

"No doubt they will, Jack, if we ever get on shore; but I'm not sure how we will."

"Can't we each get into a big barrel, and float there?" he asked. "I have often sailed like that around the pond at home."

"A fine idea, my son!" I cried. "Ernest, give me your tools. Then let us gather the largest barrels we can find!"

We soon dragged four large barrels out of the hold onto the lower deck, which was barely above water. I sawed them across the middle, converting them into tubs. After this hard work, we sat down to a lunch of goat's milk and biscuits. We also had wine, with that of my sons well diluted, as was the custom in our country.

My eight tubs now stood in a row near the water's edge. I was satisfied, but my wife was not. "I shall never," she said, "be brave enough to get into one of these!"

"Do not be too sure of that, dear wife, until you see the finished craft." I sorted through the ship's lumber supply and found some long, thin, flexible boards. These I nailed together in a long, narrow boat-shape. I then nailed the tubs to this frame, all in one long row of eight, to produce a sort of narrow boat. We tried to launch it and got a bad surprise: it was too heavy to move, even by all heaving together.

"I need a lever," I cried. "Run and fetch a capstan bar!"

Fritz ran to the capstan, a great horizontal wheel normally used to raise the anchor, and removed one of the heavy spoke-like bars. I sawed a spare mast into rollers, then put the capstan bar under our boat's bow and pried upward. Thinking quickly, my sons slipped a roller under the boat without my orders.

"Father," inquired Ernest, "how does that thing let you do more than all of us together?"

"Using this lever, the further I can stand from the object, the more weight I can lift," I explained in haste. "But now we must hurry. We can have a longer talk about mechanics on land."

I tied a long rope to our boat's stern, then to the ship's side, and heaved the boat so that two more rollers could fit underneath. Again we all pushed and our gallant craft slid swiftly into the water. It was narrow and tipsy, so we nailed a pair of boards across it and attached empty barrels on each side, similar to the outriggers used to make sea canoes stable. Even so, we would have to distribute the weight very carefully.

I boarded our boat, both to test it and to cut away some wreckage blocking its exit. The boys brought oars and wanted to jump in, but it was too late in the day to try for land. We did not care to spend another night aboard the wreck, but we had no choice. My wife had prepared a good dinner, and we ate heartily after the day's hard work.

Before nightfall I made everyone put on a swimming-belt. I persuaded my wife, with difficulty, to change her dress for a sailor's clothing; surely she would find it more comfortable. She finally gave in and left for a short time. When she came back, she wore a seaman's shirt and trousers, blushing scarlet. At home she would have considered this indecent, for in Switzerland women always wore dresses. We all told her she looked splendid, however, and her embarrassment faded.

Nothing was left but to try to sleep. Tomorrow would be the crucial day.

CHAPTER 2

Attempting Landfall

We rose early, filled with anticipation. After our prayers, I turned to my family. "My beloved ones, with God's help we will escape. Put out food for the poor animals we must leave behind, for we may yet save them. Then collect everything useful you can think of."

The boys gathered a great array of valuable items. From the collection I selected sail canvas to make a tent, a chest of carpenter's tools, weapons and ammunition, rods and fishing tackle, an iron pot, a case of ship's biscuit, and another of beef gelatin to make soup. We loaded these in the most balanced way possible, and knelt again to pray before embarking.

The moment had come. Each of us climbed into his or her tub. The roosters and chickens began to protest the desertion. "Let us bring them!" I exclaimed. "If we cannot feed them, we can eat them!" Amid much squawking and flapping, we packed ten hens and two roosters into a tub and covered it with chicken wire. My wife went to set the ducks, geese, and pigeons free. The pigeons winged for shore, while the others took to the water. She returned from her task carrying a pillow-sized bag. "This is my contribution," she said, throwing the bag to little Franz. I thought it was a cushion, perhaps to keep him from being tossed about.

All was ready; we cast off and rowed away from the wreck. My good, brave wife sat up front; next was Franz, a sweet-tempered boy of nearly six. Then came Fritz, a handsome, spirited young fellow of fourteen; the two center tubs contained the valuable cargo; then came our impulsive Jack, age ten. Behind him was twelve-year-old Ernest, my second son, very intelligent but a bit lazy. I took the stern as captain and steersman. Fritz and Jack rowed. Everyone wore a float belt and carried something useful in case things went wrong.

We left the two large mastiffs, Turk and Juno, on the wreck. As we began to move away, the two dogs set up a great howl of complaint. We felt badly about leaving them, but they were far too large to ride. When their howls did not bring us back, both dogs sprang into the sea. This I regretted, for I was sure it would be the end of them, but I underestimated their will. They caught up and swam alongside us, keeping up easily. At one point Turk rested a forepaw on an outrigger, and Jack moved to push him off. "Stop!" I ordered him. "God has given us these faithful companions. It would be unkind and foolish to deny them their chance."

Our passage was safe but slow. The nearer we approached the shore, the less inviting it looked. At first we could see only barren rocks, suggesting a future of misery and want. Many casks, boxes, and bales of goods floated on the water around us. Fritz and I managed to secure a couple of barrels, and we towed them alongside. Nearly anything they contained might be useful.

Soon we began to see green grass and trees beyond the cliffs. "I see tall palms," said Fritz.

"Maybe they're coconuts," observed Ernest. The thought of the refreshing milk cheered us all.

"I wish I'd thought to bring the captain's telescope," I said.

"Look here, Father!" cried Jack, drawing a little spyglass out of his pocket.

"Fine work, Jack!" I exclaimed. "This makes up for your unkind impulse toward the dogs." Through the spyglass, I saw that the coast to our left was much more inviting. Unfortunately, a strong current was carrying us right toward the frowning rocks. The ducks and geese were ahead, paddling toward the mouth of a small stream. I steered after them, taking us into a small bay with smooth, shallow water.

The ground sloped gently up from the low banks to the cliffs, and we had an easy time landing the boat. Everyone sprang gladly out but little Franz, who lay packed in his tub like a little pile of supplies. His mother had to lift him out.

The dogs had beaten us ashore and met us with leaps and loud barks of joy. The birds made nearly as much noise, as did the flamingoes and penguins whose world we had invaded. I welcomed the noise, for the birds might furnish good dinners.

As soon as we could gather our children on dry land, we knelt to offer thanks and praise. All hands then got to work unloading, and, oh, how rich we felt!

The ducks and geese made themselves at home in a nearby swamp. We let the chickens fend for themselves while we looked for a good place to pitch a tent. There was a hole in the cliffside rocks, into which we thrust a pole; we braced it with another planted in the ground and stretched the sailcloth over it. We pegged the bottom of the cloth to the ground, adding our heavy chests and boxes to the edge. The boys then ran to collect moss and grass for bedding while I set up a fireplace. When I had the fire going, I filled the iron pot with water, then gave my wife several cakes of the beef gelatin. She established herself as our cook, with little Franz as helper.

Franz misunderstood the purpose of the gelatin. "Papa, why are you melting glue? What are you going to make next?"

"This is to be soup for your dinner, my child. Do you think these cakes look like glue?"

"Yes, I do!" replied Franz, "And I don't want glue soup! Mamma, shouldn't we have meat instead?"

"Where can I get it, dear?" she said. "We are a long way from a butcher's shop! But these cakes are made of beef broth, boiled to a jelly. They keep well at sea and can be dissolved into a nice soup for sailors, who mostly get salted meat and hard biscuits."

Fritz loaded a gun and went exploring along the coast. Ernest went down to the beach. Jack went scrambling among the rocks in search of shellfish. I was looking for a good spot to land the two heavy, awkward barrels we had towed alongside when I heard Jack shout for help. I hurried toward him, hatchet in hand.

I arrived to find the little fellow standing in a deep inlet, screaming in pain. When I got closer I saw why: a huge lobster had him by the leg, and Jack could not kick him loose. I waded in and pried the lobster off, and we brought it onto land.

Jack's spirits speedily recovered, and he took the lobster in both hands. It gave him a severe blow with its tail; he flung it down and hit it with a large stone. "Don't be childish, my son," I said. "Yes, the lobster hurt you, but you intend to eat the lobster, so that's fair. Next time, be more mature."

My son picked up the lobster more carefully, then ran triumphantly toward the tent. "Mother! A lobster! A lobster, Ernest! Where's Fritz? Careful! He bites!" All crowded round Jack and his large prize. Ernest wanted his mother to add the lobster to the soup, but she declined, preferring to cook one dish at a time.

Jack's inlet offered a convenient place to roll the barrels up on shore, so I beached them and returned to camp. "Jack, when we are ready to eat the lobster, you shall have the claw that bit you," I promised.

"I found something very good to eat also," said Ernest, "but I would have got my feet wet."

Jack grimaced. "All he saw was some nasty mussels," said he. "Who wants to eat trash like that? Lobster for me!"

"They were stuck to the rocks," answered Ernest calmly, "so I am sure they are oysters, not mussels. Mussels lie in the sand like clams."

"Ernest, bring some of these oysters back here in time for our next meal," I said. "And in the future, don't be afraid to get your feet wet. It hasn't harmed Jack or me."

"I can also bring some salt," said Ernest, "for I saw much of it lying in the crevices of the rocks.

It tasted good and was probably produced by seawater evaporating in the sun."

"Extremely probable, learned sir," I cried. "If only you had actually brought some back rather than merely speculating. Go now and get some."

It was indeed salt, which my wife strained to make it fit for the soup. After tasting the soup with the stirring-stick, she announced, "Dinner is ready. But where's Fritz?" she continued, a little anxiously. "And how are we to eat it without plates and spoons? We should have brought some."

"My dear, one cannot think of everything at once. Let us hope that's all that we've forgotten."

"But we can't lift the boiling pot to our mouths," she said. This was true. We all sat perplexed for a moment, then burst into laughter.

"Oh, for a few coconut shells!" sighed Ernest.

"Oh, for half a dozen plates and silver spoons!" I joked.

"Oyster shells would do," said he, after a moment's thought.

"A superb idea! My boys, get some oysters and clean out the shells. And no complaining about the spoons lacking handles."

Jack was soon knee-deep in the water collecting oysters. Ernest followed, but stood on dry land gathering up the oysters Jack threw him. He also pocketed a large mussel shell for his own use.

Just as they returned, we heard a shout from Fritz in the distance. We answered joyfully, but he appeared with his hands behind his back, looking glum. "Unsuccessful!" he said.

"Better luck next time, my boy," I replied.

His brothers had looked behind him. "Oh, Fritz!" they exclaimed. "A small pig! How did you shoot it! Let us see it!" Eyes sparkling, Fritz showed off his prize and told us what he'd seen.

"The other side of the stream is beautiful country, and the shore slopes down gently to the sea. All sorts of useful things have washed up from the wreck. Let's go and collect them. And, Father, shouldn't we return to the wreck and get some of the animals? We could have cow's milk! If we move across the stream, she will have good grazing, and we will have more shade. And, Father, I wish—"

"Stop, my boy!" I cried. "All in good time. Did you see any trace of our shipmates?"

"No sign," he replied.

"But the pig," said Jack, "where did you get it?"

"I found several on the shore," said Fritz. "They are very curious little animals that hop rather than walk and like to rub their snouts with their forepaws. I would have liked to catch one alive, but I was afraid to come away with nothing."

Ernest had been carefully examining Fritz's prize. "This is no pig," he said. "See, its teeth are more like a squirrel's. In fact," he continued, looking at Fritz, "your pig is an agouti."

"Listen to the great professor lecturing!" laughed Fritz. "Now he will prove that a pig is not a pig!"

"Ernest is right," I said. "This is indeed an agouti, a pig-like animal that nests under trees and lives on fruit. Its meat is dry and has no fat. Europeans don't care for it, but some places it is considered a delicacy. But, Ernest, the agouti does grunt like a pig."

While we spoke, Jack had tried in vain to pry open an oyster. "Watch this," I said, placing an oyster on the fire. It opened immediately.

"Now," I continued, "who will try one?" All hesitated, for the inside of the oyster looked unappetizing. Finally Jack made a face, closed his eyes tightly, and gulped one down. We each did the same, some grimacing, then dipped our shells into the pot—not without a few scalded fingers. Ernest drew out his long, smooth mussel shell, which made a much easier soup-scoop than the shapeless oyster-shells. He dipped up some soup and put it down to cool, looking smug.

"Do not think yourself so clever," I said. "Your cool soup will feed the dogs, my boy. Take it to them, then come and eat like the rest of us."

Ernest winced but silently placed his shell before the dogs. They lapped it up in a moment. He returned, set another helping of soup down to cool, and we all went on with dinner.

So did the dogs. We heard eating noises and looked to find Turk and Juno feasting on the agouti. The boys all began to yell, but the dogs kept eating. Fritz threw a rock at them, and when that failed he took his gun and ran over to rescue the carcass. Before I could stop him, he struck one dog so hard that he bent his gun. The poor beasts ran off howling, followed by a shower of stones from Fritz. He shouted so fiercely that I feared he might kill them.

I ran after him. "That was terrible," I told him. "Look what your temper has done. You have hurt one of the dogs, maybe seriously; you have frightened your mother and ruined your gun, all in a moment's rage. You are the oldest and must set an example, so don't act this way."

Luckily, Fritz was a good boy whose temper cooled swiftly. "Will you forgive me, Mother?" he asked, back at the fire. "I should not have acted so."

"Of course, my son," she said, and calm was restored.

By this time the sun was sinking, and our birds gathered round us to pick at fallen crumbs of biscuit. Then my wife reached into her mysterious bag and brought out some oats, peas, and grain, which she began to feed to them. She also showed me some vegetable seeds she had brought. "Very thoughtful," I said, "but please don't give food that we can eat to the birds. We can bring plenty of soggy biscuits from the wreck to feed them."

After dark, we loaded our guns, prayed, and prepared to sleep. The children remarked at the sudden nightfall, which convinced me we must be near the equator. As I explained to them, the nearer the equator, the less twilight there is.

Before sleep I reflected. We were marooned but safe. We had a few useful items and the hope of more. With hard work and divine blessing, we might await our rescue in relative comfort. With that thought, I closed our tent and joined my family in sleep.

CHAPTER 3

Our First Venture

*T*he night was as cold as the day had been hot. But thanks to our tent, we slept well after our hard day's work. The rooster woke me up at sunrise, and I awoke my wife to talk privately. We agreed that our first duty was to search for the sailors. Investigating the local resources was also important. "After breakfast," she said, "perhaps you and Fritz should go exploring along the coast. The younger boys and I will see what we can accomplish around here."

Her plan made sense. I went to the boys. "Wake up, my sons," I cried cheerfully. "Come help your mother with breakfast."

"All we have is soup," she said, smiling.

"Jack, where's your fine lobster?" I asked.

"I put it in this hole in the rock, Father, so the dogs wouldn't eat it," he said.

"Very sensible," I remarked. "Even my impulsive Jack learns wisdom. Good thing it's so large; it can be food when we go exploring."

That last word sent the children wild with delight, leaping and clapping for joy.

"Steady there!" I said. "We can't all go. This will be too dangerous and tiring for you younger ones. Fritz and I will go. We will take Turk and leave Juno to guard you. Fritz, prepare the guns and tie up Juno."

At the word "guns" poor Fritz reddened in shame. He tried in vain to straighten his weapon. I let him work on this for a while. Then I gave him permission to take another gun, satisfied he had learned half of his lesson. A moment later he tried to collar Juno, but the dog remembered how Fritz had treated her the night before and growled a low warning. Turk did likewise. They would not come until I called them myself.

Fritz went to his mother in tears, asking, "Mother, I want to give them my breakfast biscuits." With her consent Fritz took the food to the suspicious dogs. Fortunately, dogs are not vengeful. Juno accepted the food and allowed Fritz to pet her. But Turk was still wary and stayed back.

"Give him a claw of my lobster," cried Jack. "I was going to give it to you anyway, for your journey." Fritz did so and won Turk over. Then we each took a gun, a small hatchet, and a game bag. Fritz stuck a pair of pistols into his belt. We packed the rest of the lobster and some biscuits, along with flasks of water. Almost all was ready.

"Stop!" I exclaimed, "we have forgotten something very important."

"Surely not," said Fritz.

"Surely so," I said. "What of our morning prayer? We must not forget our faith." After we prayed, I cautioned my wife and younger children to stay near camp. When I was satisfied that my sons would do so, Fritz and I said our good-byes. We were nervous but excited at the prospect of exploring a new land.

Our first obstacle was the stream with its rocky banks. I could see no signs of regular crossing until we moved upstream. This pleased me because it meant our camp was in a relatively isolated spot and therefore likely safe. Fritz and I moved upstream until we came to a large waterfall, then a shallow spot with enough large rocks to let us cross. This put the sea on our left. Away to our right was a long line of cliffs and rocky hills dotted with clumps of trees. The long, tangled grass made for slow going.

We had scarcely gone fifty yards when something rustled behind us. We stopped in alarm. Something was moving through the grass. We could not tell what. Fritz turned coolly, trained his gun on the movement, yet held his fire. Out rushed trusty Turk, whom we had forgotten. My thoughtful wife must have sent him. Fritz lowered his gun and smiled. "You behaved wisely and bravely," I told him, "not to fire without being sure of your target. Well done."

"Thank you, Father," answered Fritz, still embarrassed at his lapse the day before. "But this exposes a danger. What if a fierce beast were to sneak up on us here?"

"Well observed, my son," I replied. "We would be far safer on the beach." We hastened down to the open seashore. The view was lovely: a background of hills, tall grass above the tide-line, and groups of trees here and there. We searched the smooth sand for any trace of our unfortunate companions but found no foot-prints. "Shall I fire a shot or two?" asked Fritz. "That would bring them, if they heard it."

"If there are any hostile inhabitants, it would bring them too," I replied. "No, let us search carefully but quietly."

"But why, Father, should we bother about the sailors? They left us to die. I don't care to see them again."

"Because we are not like them, my boy," I said. "Think of the help they could give us in building a house of some sort, and perhaps other ways. Finally, remember that they took nothing with them. They may be starving."

"But Father, we are wasting our time with almost no hope of helping them. Why aren't we returning to the ship to save the animals, who may help us?"

"When you have many tasks to choose from, always choose the one that gives the clearest advantage," I answered. "Saving a human life is a higher calling than comforting a few animals who have plenty of food. Also, the sea is calm and will not dislodge the wreck."

We pushed on into a pleasant grove stretching down to the water's edge and sat down under a large tree to rest. A tiny stream splashed past us. A thousand brightly-feathered birds flew overhead. As Fritz and I gazed up at them, my son jumped up. "A monkey!" he exclaimed. "I'm almost sure I saw a monkey." He sprang around the tree, stumbling over a small, round, hairy object. He picked it up and handed it to me, saying, "A round bird's nest! I have heard of these."

"You may have," I said, laughing, "but this is a coconut. We'll break the shell, and you will see the nut inside."

With some difficulty we split it open, but the inside was dry and crumbly. "What?" cried Fritz. "I always thought a coconut was full of delicious sweet liquid, like almond milk."

"At first it is," I replied, "but it dries to a hard kernel. When the nut falls on good soil, the seed bursts through to form a new tree. Now let's try to find a better one."

That was not easy, for coconuts fall only when they are overripe. We finally found one with liquid inside. It was a bit oily and rancid, but we could find no better. Feeling refreshed, we decided to save our lunch for later and marched on. A dense thicket overgrown with vines gave way again to seashore with an open view. The forest swept inland, and here and there were some odd-looking trees. Fritz noticed them and exclaimed, "Father! Look at those strange shapes hanging down!"

As we got closer I recognized them as calabash trees, dotted with gourds of all shapes. "In some parts of the world people make spoons, bowls, and bottles of such gourds; people even cook food in them," I explained.

"That is impossible," returned Fritz. "The fire would burn through the rind."

"They don't put the gourds on the fire. First they clean out the gourd, then they split it. A half is filled with water, then with fish, or whatever. The cook then adds red-hot stones until the water boils. This cooks the food without damaging the gourd."

"That is very clever. I'm sure I would have thought of it, had I tried," said Fritz.

"Perhaps so," I said, and left it at that. "Let's prepare some of these and take them home."

Fritz took up a gourd and tried to split it equally with his knife, but the blade slipped and made a jagged cut. "Spoiled!" he exclaimed, throwing it down. "And it looked so easy to split!"

"Patience," I said. "Those pieces are still useful. Try to make a couple of spoons from them, while I make a dish." I then took out a piece of string, which I tied as tightly as I could around a gourd. I tapped the string with the back of my knife until it penetrated the outer shell, then drew the string as tight as I could. The gourd fell, divided just as I wished.

"How clever!" cried Fritz. "Where did you get that idea?"

"I read about it in travel books," I smiled.

"It certainly makes a good soup-plate," said Fritz, examining the gourd. "But how would one make a bottle?"

"Even easier," I said. "Cut a round hole at one end, then scoop out the interior. Then drop in some stones and shake it to loosen any remaining debris, and that would complete the bottle."

"But that would be more like a small barrel, Father."

"True, my boy. For best results, you must plan ahead. To give a gourd a neck, for example, you bind the top while it is still young. All but the tied part will swell as it grows." As I spoke, I filled the gourds with sand and left them to dry, meaning to return for them on our way back.

For three hours or more we advanced, keeping a sharp lookout for any trace of our companions. We stopped at a point where a bold, steep hill stretched away into the sea as a peninsula. The rocky summit looked easy to reach, and would offer us a fine view, so we climbed up. Before us stretched a wide, lovely bay, fringed with yellow sands, enclosed by two shadowy ridges of land. The surface was a sheet of rippling water that reflected the glorious sun.

The scene inland was as lovely, yet Fritz and I both felt a shade of loneliness. It lacked one key element: there was no sign of human beings, either our shipmates or others.

"Remember, Fritz," I said, "that we had already chosen to become settlers. God certainly granted our wish! We didn't expect to be quite so alone, but let us trust in God, and try to live comfortably here. Be glad we all survived and washed up on a fertile island." I mopped my forehead and continued, "A hot one, too. Let's find some shade before we broil."

We descended through a dense thicket of bamboo-like reeds, working our way toward a nearby clump of palm trees. This was hard work, and dangerous, for it would be easy to step on some poisonous snake. I sent Turk ahead, then cut a reed, thinking it might be more useful against a snake than my gun. A thick juice seeped from one end. I tasted it and found it sweet and pleasant. It was sugar cane.

I wished Fritz to discover this, so I advised him to cut a cane for his defense. His reed split, covering his hand with thick juice. He took a careful taste, then another, then exclaimed,

"Father! This is sugar cane! Let's take a lot home to mother!"

"Gently," I said. "Cut some if you like, but no more than you can conveniently carry."

In spite of my warning, my son cut a dozen or more of the largest canes and tucked them under his arm. We then pushed through the canebrake to the clump of palms. As we entered it, a troop of monkeys scrambled into the treetops, seeming to make fun of us.

Fritz raised his gun. "No!" I objected. "Never kill any animal without need. A live monkey up in that tree is more use than a dozen dead at our feet. Watch."

I threw a few small stones in the monkeys' direction. The monkeys began to pick and hurl all the coconuts within reach.

Fritz was delighted, perhaps because we managed to dodge all the missiles. He rushed forward to pick some up, and we pierced them for the milk. The taste was not exactly pleasant, but it quenched our thirst. Much tastier was the solid cream lining the shells, which we scraped off and ate. Fritz put some of the milk in his flask.

After this delicious meal, we gave Turk the lobster. After he devoured it, he began to gnaw the ends of the sugar canes, and to beg for coconut. I slung a couple of the nuts over my shoulder, and Fritz picked up his burden for our homeward march.

He soon found it a heavy one. He began to shift the canes from shoulder to shoulder, then carried them under his arm, and finally stopped short with a sigh. "I had no idea," he said, "that a few reeds would be so heavy."

"Patience and courage, my boy," I said. "Let us each take a fresh one, then we'll fasten the bundle crosswise with your gun." We savored the sugary juice as we pressed on.

"I can hardly wait to see Ernest's face when he drinks this coconut milk," commented Fritz.

"By then it will probably be vinegar. The sun's heat will ferment it."

"Vinegar! How horrid! Let me see," cried Fritz, hastily pulling the cork from the flask. The contents came out with a loud *pop* and a foamy spray, like champagne.

"There!" I said, laughing as he tasted this new luxury. "Moderation, Son. I'm sure it's delicious, but if you drink too much, you will feel it."

"Father, it's wonderful! Try some. Vinegar, indeed! This is like excellent wine."

This unexpected treat gave us new energy, so on we went, picking up the gourds we had left. A little further on, Turk suddenly darted away from us toward a troop of monkeys playing around on the ground. He had been hungrier than we realized. Before we could stop him, he was tearing a monkey to shreds.

His luckless victim was the mother of a tiny

little monkey, trembling in the grass as he watched his mother's tragic fate. Fritz rushed to the rescue, but was far too late to save the mother.

No sooner did the tiny monkey catch sight of him than it leaped to his shoulders in a single bound. Fritz's curly hair was an excellent handhold. My son screamed and leaped around to dislodge the creature, but it only clung tighter.

I laughed so much that I wasn't any help to Fritz. "He seems determined to adopt you," I suggested, chuckling. "Perhaps he senses that you will someday be a fine father."

"Or rather," Fritz said, shaking his head back and forth, "the rascal guesses that I'm too softhearted to mistreat an animal that has begged my protection. But Father, can we talk about his motives after you help me get him off? He's yanking my hair."

At last, by coaxing the monkey with a bit of biscuit and gradually disentangling its small paws from Fritz's curls, I managed to relieve poor Fritz. He looked with interest at the baby monkey in my arms, no bigger than a kitten.

"What a jolly little fellow!" he exclaimed. "May I try to raise it, Father? Coconut milk would probably do until we can bring the cow and goats. If he lives he might be helpful, for I have read that monkeys know which fruits are safe to eat."

"He's yours," I said. "After all, you made a

brave effort to save the mother's life. You must train her child carefully, or he will cause us a lot of mischief."

Meanwhile Turk was devouring the unfortunate mother. Fritz wished to make him stop, but I could not deny Turk his meal. Besides, Turk stood three feet high and was immensely broad-shouldered, as mastiffs are. He likely outweighed me, and a starving dog the size of Turk could be very dangerous to the family. We had no wish to watch him eat, however, so we loaded up and resumed our march.

As we walked, Fritz said, "I'll have to find a way to protect this monkey from Turk."

"Don't worry," I said. "Although Turk will attack strange beasts, he will soon regard your little monkey as a member of our family. Heaven has given us dogs and horses as our allies, and a mounted man with a pack of trained dogs can face any wild beast in the world—even a lion or a pack of hyenas."

Thoughtfully, Fritz replied, "What a pity that the horses died during our voyage, and left us with only a donkey."

"He is large and strong," I said. "If we can get him safe on land, he may do for us what a horse would. We already know we can provide him excellent pasture to thrive on."

The tiny monkey sat on Fritz's shoulder. I helped to carry his canes, and we were some distance along before Turk overtook us, licking his chops. He took no notice of the monkey, but the tiny creature scrambled down into Fritz's arms. Fritz found this so inconvenient that he came up with a plan.

Calling Turk in firm tones of authority, Fritz seated the monkey on the dog's back and secured it with a cord, then put a second string round the dog's neck for reins. Putting this into the comical rider's hand, my son said, "Having slain the parent, Mr. Turk, you can now carry the son."

Neither liked this arrangement at first, but they soon accepted it. Before long the monkey rode along like a human out for a pleasure ride. "We look like a couple of traveling showmen on their way to the fair," I said. "The children will have quite a laugh!"

Before long we approached the rocky streambank close to camp.

Juno was the first to detect our approach, barking her loudest. Turk answered in his own deep voice. His little rider panicked, slipped out of the cord, and took refuge on Fritz's shoulder. Finding himself free, Turk dashed forward to meet Juno. One after another our dear ones came running to the opposite bank, cheering our return. It was a happy reunion indeed.

It did not take the boys long to find the monkey. They launched an unanswerable barrage of exclamations and questions: "A monkey! A monkey!" "Oh, how splendid!" "Where did Fritz find him?" "What can we give him to eat?" "What is this bundle of sticks?"

I let the excitement die down a little before speaking. "I am glad to see you all safe. Our expedition was a success, except that we found no trace of our shipmates."

"If it is God's will that we be alone here," said my wife, "let us rejoice that we are all together. I have been worried sick over you two, but now that you are finally back, I know my fears must seem foolish. Now please let us take those heavy loads, and then tell us your adventures!"

Jack shouldered my gun, Ernest took the coconuts, and little Franz carried the gourds. Fritz distributed the sugar canes among his brothers, handed Ernest his gun, and replaced the monkey on Turk's back. Ernest soon found his load too heavy, and his mother offered to help. When Ernest gave up the coconuts, his elder brother exclaimed, "Ernest, are you going to hand over those coconuts without even tasting them?"

"What? Are they really coconuts?" cried Ernest. "I thought they were bowls! I'll carry them, please, Mother."

"No, thank you," replied my wife with a smile. "I would not want you to be overburdened."

"But I can throw away these useless sticks and carry the coconuts easily."

"Worse and worse," said Fritz. "Did you ever hear of sugar cane?"

The words were scarcely out of his mouth when Ernest began to suck at the end of the cane, but without result. "Here," said Fritz, "let me show you the trick." Poking a hole so that air could enter, he soon had all his brothers extracting the luscious juice. My wife was delighted; the sugar would be good for cooking, and with the new dishes we could eat more like civilized beings.

We would soon try them out, for my family had prepared a delicious meal. Two forked sticks were planted in the ground on either side of the fire, supporting a rod with several tempting-looking fish. A goose—or so I thought—hung from another rod while the gravy dripped into a large shell. Franz gave the spit another turn, proudly claiming it was his job to keep dinner from burning. In the center sat the great pot full of delicious soup. On top of it all, one of the barrels was open, and it contained Dutch cheeses.

My wife had overseen a tremendous amount of worthy effort, and Fritz and I were hungry, but I was about to beg her to spare the poultry until we could breed more. She sensed my anxiety and explained, "This is not one of our geese, but a wild bird Ernest killed."

"Yes," said Ernest, "a penguin, I think. It let me get close enough to knock it on the head with a stick. Here, I saved its head and feet to show you; notice the narrow, down-curved bill and webbed feet. It had funny little useless wings, and its eyes looked so solemn that I was almost ashamed to kill it. Do you agree that it must have been a penguin?"

"Without a doubt, my boy," I answered. Before I could say anything more, my wife called us to dinner. Fritz now remembered his delicious wine and gave the flask to his mother to taste.

"Try it first yourself," I said. Fritz did, and I saw from his face that it had turned to vinegar. He explained to his mother.

"Never mind," said my wife. "We already have wine, but no vinegar, so this is excellent. Mixed with the fat from our roasting bird, it will make a delicious sauce." Indeed it did, masking the penguin's fishy flavor and enhancing the fish. We did full justice to this impressive meal, using our gourds for the first time. For dessert I produced the coconuts.

"Here is better food for your little friend," I said to Fritz, who could not get the monkey to eat bits of our food. "The poor little animal has only had its mother's milk. One of you, fetch me a saw."

After extracting the milk from the natural holes in the coconuts, I carefully cut the shells in half to provide several more bowls. Fritz dipped a handkerchief in the milk, and the baby monkey sucked eagerly at it.

The sun was now rapidly sinking, so we prepared for sleep. After our prayers, we lay down on our beds. The monkey crouched down between Jack and Fritz. We were all soon fast asleep—but not for long.

Our dogs' barking awakened us, and we heard the fluttering and cackling of the birds. Fritz and I sprang up, seized our guns, and rushed out into the middle of a desperate battle.

Our gallant dogs were surrounded by a dozen or more large jackals. These fierce, wild dog-like creatures, while not as large as our mastiffs, were not small. Turk and Juno had fought well, to judge by the four jackals already dead, but the rest continued to attack. Fritz and I sent bullets through the heads of two more. The rest fled. Unsatisfied, the dogs chased and caught another jackal, which they quickly killed and began to devour.

Fritz wished to save a jackal to show his brothers in the morning, so he dragged his dead target to a concealed spot near the tent. I told him that if our dogs were still hungry, we must let them have this last jackal. But they were already satisfied and curled up to sleep. We did the same.

CHAPTER 4

Back to the Wreck

*M*y wife and I awoke to the crowing of roosters. Without disturbing the children, I asked her advice. "It is urgent that we return to the vessel. It is full of useful supplies and animals, which we may lose forever if there is another storm. At the same time, we also need a better shelter and a place to store our things. I can't decide what to do first. Which do you suggest?"

"We must have patience," she replied cheerfully. "I think that the wreck should come first. Let's wake up the children and get to work."

Fritz, first up, ran out for his jackal. Finding it cold and stiff from the night's chill, he set it up on its legs in front of the tent and then stood by to watch the fun.

The dogs were the first to detect their remarkably lifelike "enemy," and moved to dispose of it, but Fritz called them off. The noise brought the younger children out.

"A yellow dog!" cried Franz.

"A wolf!" exclaimed Jack.

"It's a striped fox," said Ernest.

"The learned Professor apparently does not know a jackal when he sees one," said Fritz.

Ernest looked closer. "I really think it's a fox," he said.

"You must know better than your father," retorted Fritz, "for he thinks it's a jackal."

"Enough arguing," I said. "None of you are far wrong, for the jackal is related to the dog, wolf, and fox."

The monkey had come out on Jack's shoulder but hid in the tent at first sight of the jackal. Jack soothed and comforted the frightened little animal. We had our prayers, then a breakfast of biscuits and cheese. Ernest went down to the shore to look for shellfish and soon returned with a few oysters. "If only we had some butter," he said.

"Ernest, your constant 'ifs' annoy me. 'If' neither hunts, gathers, or fishes, and so brings us no food. Now sit down and eat your biscuit like the rest of us," I said.

"I would prefer it with butter," he said, pointing to a large barrel. "Father, that is a keg of butter. I noticed some oozing out."

"Well done, Ernest," I said. "I will open the keg." I cut a small hole, so as not to expose too much butter to the air. Soon we were toasting our buttered biscuits. But something seemed strange. After a moment I realized it was the dogs—or rather, the lack of dog activity. They lay very quiet, so I inspected. Each had several deep, painful wounds, especially about the neck. They were licking each other where they could not reach with their own tongues. My wife dressed the wounds with butter.

"We must remember to look around the ship for spiked dog collars," said Fritz. "That would give them an advantage."

"Yes!" exclaimed Jack. "If mother will help me, I can make spiked collars."

"Then try, my son," I said. "Now, Fritz, we must go to the wreck."

"I will help you, Jack," said my wife, "because I'm curious to see what you plan. All of us must invent as many things as we can. There is no better use of our time."

"Well said, my wife," I added. "Now: Jack, Ernest, Franz, listen to me. Stay together, and obey your mother. Let's ask a blessing." After we prayed, I worked out a set of signals with my wife while Fritz readied the boat. I set up a flagpole, with a strip of sailcloth as a flag. So long as all was well ashore, it would fly. If we were needed, she was to lower the flag and have the boys fire three shots. If I wished news of shore, I would hoist a white flag of my own. When we had arranged a few other signals, I took my dear wife in my arms.

"We may have to spend the night on the wreck," I told her.

"If you must," she said. "I will feel better when you return, but we will manage."

With some effort we broke our embrace and I prepared to embark. We took only guns and ammunition. Fritz, however, had brought his monkey, hoping to get it some milk. My three young sons and my brave wife waved us off to sea.

Not far from shore, I felt a river current grab our boat. It was carrying us directly for the wreck, leaving us with little to do but remain in the current until we were nearly there. A bit of hard rowing soon had us through the gap in the hull. There we tied up and disembarked.

Our first task was to care for the animals, who greeted us with joyful barnyard sounds. They were not starving, but we put out fresh food and water. Fritz placed his monkey by one of the female goats, and she let the little chap nurse in his chattering, grinning way. My son and I got some lunch, then sat down to plan.

"We should attach a mast and a sail to our boat," said Fritz. "That current will not help us get back to shore."

"What makes you think of this now, when we have so much else to do?" I demanded, grumpily.

"I had a hard time rowing us through the opening," he answered. "Our boat will be very heavy when we embark, and I'm not sure I'll be strong enough to row us to land. Since the current will not help us, perhaps we can make the wind take its place."

"Good reasoning, my boy," I replied. "Even so, we mustn't overload the boat. Better to make more trips than risk capsizing or throwing valuable things overboard." I chose a small mast and set it up in a tub, using boards and ropes to brace it up. We found a spare sail and hoisted it to our new mast. "You were quite right, Fritz. Having done this first, we can do far more afterward."

Fritz beamed. "Thank you, Father. We should have a banner for our mast. How about this red streamer?" He showed me a bit of red cloth. I thought it was childish but harmless, so I smiled and nodded. I got to work adding a rudder, which would make for easier steering than the oar I had been using. Fritz examined the shore with his telescope and announced that the flag was flying.

It was now too late to return to shore that evening, so we signaled our intent to remain on board. We then started unloading the stones we had used to weight the boat, replacing them with cargo to take ashore.

The ship had sailed with all the supplies needed for a colony, so the difficult part was to choose wisely. Fritz was sure we could return for more, but I was not. First we loaded a large amount of powder and shot, adding three excellent guns and an armload of swords, daggers, and knives. We loaded a large stock of kitchen-utensils, plus some silver plates and a case of good wine from the captain's cabin. Next was the food supply. We grunted over heavy armloads of preserved meats, beef gelatin, hams, sausages, a bag of grain, and many other seeds and vegetables.

I then added a barrel of sulfur for matches and as much string, rope, and sailcloth as I could find. Fritz recommended we take some hammocks and blankets, and we filled the rest of our space with nails, tools, and farming implements. Our boat rode so low in the water that we were fortunate to have a calm sea.

As night drew on, a large fire ashore showed us that all was well. We replied by hoisting four ship's lanterns, and two shots acknowledged our signal. If another storm struck in the night, I doubted that the ship could survive it, so we decided to sleep in our small boat. Praying God to keep our dear ones safe ashore, we retired.

Fritz slept far better than I did. I could not stop worrying about my wife and children, alone with only two wounded dogs to protect them. This entire experience would force my young men to grow up faster than I had ever intended. If there were trouble in the night, I could only hope that Jack and Ernest would step up to the challenge. Perhaps leaving them alone ashore was the only way to teach them this, but I could not be easy about the risk.

I greeted daybreak with joy and anxiety, and Fritz and I immediately went on deck. Through the telescope I saw the flag still waving on shore. Better still, my wife came out of the tent and looked our direction. I hoisted a white flag, and the shore flag dipped three times: all was still well. What a weight that sight lifted from my heart!

"Fritz," I said, "my next concern is for the animals on board. Let's try to take some of them with us."

"Could we make a raft," he suggested, "and tow them ashore?"

"How are we going to get a cow, a donkey, and a sow to board a raft, much less stand still on it? We might get the sheep and goats aboard, but I have no idea how to get the rest ashore."

"We could tie a long rope around the sow's neck," Fritz proposed, "and just throw her in the water. We could tow her."

"An excellent idea for the pig," I replied, "but I'm not sure about the others, even if I felt they could swim that far. In any case, the pig is the least important to keep." I had an idea, but I wanted Fritz to invent a solution, so I kept quiet.

"Well," he said, "the only other thing I can think of is to make them swimming belts like the children's."

"A good idea!" I said. Fritz smiled, thinking I was kidding. "I'm serious," I added. "This may save them all. Let's begin with a sheep."

I caught a fine ram, fastened a broad piece of cloth round its belly, and attached some large corks and empty cans. Fritz and I flung the bleating animal into the sea, and it bobbed up to the surface. Success!

"Hurrah!" exclaimed Fritz. "This will work!" We got to work equipping the other animals. The cow and donkey were hardest; cans and cork were not enough, so we lashed some empty barrels to them. When we had attached a rope to each and put a float on the loose end, the whole herd was ready for the voyage.

We brought the donkey up first, protesting and lashing out at being led so near the edge of the deck. Once there, we both gave him a sudden heave overboard. He brayed furiously as he sank into the water. We were relieved when the frightened animal's head and back floated above the surface a moment later. The cow, sheep, and goats followed him one after the other. We now had a barnyard in the sea, but it was not quite complete.

The sow came last, and she seemed determined not to leave. She kicked and squealed so fiercely that I feared we might have to leave her. Earlier we had needed to muzzle her just to keep from being bitten while we fitted her for sea; now, as we wrestled her, we were glad we had left the muzzle on. It took all our strength and cleverness to shove her overboard. But once in the water, the energetic old lady outswam the rest to shore.

Now we gathered up the ropes and set sail for shore with our herd in tow. Fritz had been right: without the sail, we could not possibly have rowed such weight all that distance. But thanks to the sail, we had leisure to eat a lunch of biscuits. Afterward, I took up my telescope and tried to see what our dear ones on shore were doing.

A sudden shout from Fritz got my attention, and I turned to see him with his gun at his shoulder. The huge dorsal fin of a shark was headed for one of the finest sheep. The shark turned, exposing a stretch of white belly. Fritz's shot echoed across the still water. Our enemy disappeared, leaving a trace of blood on the calm water.

"Fine shot, my boy!" I cried. "I hope you won't always have to shoot such dangerous game." His eyes sparkled. He reloaded and kept watch, but the shark did not return. Soon the breeze carried us to the safety of shore, so I let loose the animals to make landfall on their own while I piloted us to a good landing place.

There was no immediate sign of my wife or children, but a few moments later they came running with shouts of joy. After the first exchange of questions, we got to work removing the swimming belts, which were very awkward for the animals on shore. My wife marveled at them. "How clever you are," she said.

"Fritz behaved with great credit," I replied. "The belts were his idea, and he saved at least one of our beasts from a terrible death." I then told them of his calm bravery against the shark.

"Fritz, I'm tremendously proud of you," said my wife. "You are thinking and acting like a man, and I feel safer." I saw Fritz stand straighter. My wife's wisely chosen words had meant much to him. She continued, "Even so, I will now dread these trips even more, if there are sharks in the water."

Fritz, Ernest, and I began unloading, while Jack tried to free the poor donkey from his cumbersome swimming-belt. The animal would not stand quiet, and the knots were too tight, so Jack mounted up and rode the donkey toward us.

"There is no time to fool around, Jack," I said. "You can practice riding later. Now get off and come help us."

"But I've been working all day," said Jack as he dismounted. "Look here!" He pointed to a broad yellow belt around his waist, with a couple of pistols and a knife sticking out. "And see what I've made for the dogs! Here, Juno! Turk!" The dogs bounded up, and I saw that each wore a nail-studded leather collar—a bad surprise for any attacker.

"Well done, my boy," I said, "but how did you make them? Did you have help?"

"Except for sewing," my wife said, "he did it

himself. As for the materials, Fritz's jackal supplied the skin, and the needles and thread came out of my wonderful bag. You men have yet to learn how many useful things are in that bag. It is fortunate you have a woman along."

"For many reasons," I agreed with a warm smile. Fritz, however, was not impressed and held his nose. "Really, Jack," he said, "you should have cured the hide first. It smells disgusting. Don't come near me."

"It's not the hide that smells," Jack said sharply. "It's the nasty jackal that my oldest brother himself left lying in the sun."

"Stop arguing," I said. "Jack, help your brother drag the carcass to the sea. If your belt still smells, then take it off and dry it better."

With the offending corpse gone, we finished unloading our boat and started for our tent. I saw no dinner preparations, so I said, "Fritz, go get us a ham."

"Ernest," said my wife, smiling, "let's see if we can conjure up some eggs."

Fritz got out a splendid ham and carried it to his mother in triumph, while Ernest set before me a dozen white balls with leathery coverings.

"Turtles' eggs!" I said. "Well done, Ernest! Where did you get them?"

"We can talk about that while we eat," replied my wife. "For now, let's see about getting dinner ready."

While she set to work, we returned to the shore and brought up the rest of the cargo. The sow ran away, but we herded the rest of the animals toward the tent.

Dinner was quite different from our first night's fare. My wife had improvised a table of a board laid on two casks. She had spread a white tablecloth, with knives, forks, spoons, and plates for each person. We had a bowl of good soup, followed by a large omelet with ham slices; then cheese, buttered biscuits, and a bottle of the captain's wine.

While we feasted, I told my wife our adventures, then asked about hers.

"There is not much to say about yesterday," she said. "I spent most of it worrying and watching for signals. You can't imagine my joy first thing this morning when I saw your signal. While my sons were still asleep, I tried to think of ways to improve our situation.

"'We can't stay here,' I thought. 'The sun is terribly hot, with no shade except the tent, and it's even hotter in there. Surely we can find a better place than this.'

"By now the boys were up, with Jack busy skinning Fritz's jackal. He had an ingenious idea to line the collars with canvas, so the nail heads would be covered. The hide was very moist and smelly. I gave him needles and thread to sew it. When I saw how hard and cheerfully he worked,

I felt sorry for him and finished the sewing myself. He then asked me to help him finish a belt of similar material. I did, but told him he had better figure out how to keep it from shrinking. Ernest had a good idea: stretch the skin flat on a board to dry in the sun. Jack did so.

"I gathered my young men and said, 'We must not waste this day. Shall we go exploring?' They all cheered, so I started packing food. Jack and Ernest carried guns while I took charge of the water flask and the hatchet. My dear husband, you were wise to teach our young sons to shoot at an early age. That training may save us one day. The dogs came, of course. Turk seemed proud to lead the way.

"We soon crossed the stream and reached the hill with the lovely view that you described. For the first time, I felt hopeful. I saw a little wood in the distance, and we headed that way along the beach. As we got close, we had to go through that tall, thick grass. While we were beating our way through, a great rushing noise startled us all. It was some large and powerful bird taking off. By the time either boy could aim, it had flown far away.

"'What a pity!' exclaimed Ernest. 'If the bird hadn't flown so fast, I would have gotten him.'

"'No doubt,' I said. 'If your target would always give you time to get ready, you would be a fine hunter.'

"'But I had no idea anything was going to fly up at our feet!' he complained.

"'Game animals will not send you advance notice,' I told him.

"'What was it?' asked Jack.

"'It was huge, maybe an eagle,' answered little Franz.

"'Fine logic. It was big, so it was an eagle,' Ernest said, in scorn.

"'Let's see where he was sitting!' I said. Jack sprang toward the spot, and a second, larger bird took off with a great beating and flapping. The boys all stared upward. I laughed, saying, 'Well, we will never go hungry with you great hunters on the job!'

"In the grass, we found a crude sort of nest, empty, with broken eggshells nearby. We could see the grass waving as the little birds escaped. 'Come see, Franz,' said Ernest, 'why this could never have been an eagle. Eagles do not nest on the ground, nor can eaglets run just after they hatch. That is a trait of game birds like turkeys, pheasants, bustards, and quail. You saw the white bellies, red underwings, and mustache-like feathers over the beaks: qualities of the Great Bustard.'

"'You are better with your eyes than your gun,' I said. 'In any case, I'm glad we didn't hurt the bustard's family.'

"We were getting close to the pretty wood. Many birds fluttered and sang high in the branches, but I asked the boys not to shoot any of them. It was a grove of the most marvelous, enormous trees, only a dozen or so, with huge roots well above the ground forming strong arches. I gave Jack some twine and told him to scramble up and measure one of the trunks. It was eighteen yards around.

"'Then it is slightly less than six yards thick,' said Ernest, 'nearly seventeen feet!'

"'Your mathematical ability is impressive, my Son,' I said with a smile. Ernest went on to explain his calculation while we looked around for fruit. We found none, but the ground was well shaded and carpeted with soft greenery.

"We had a wonderful midday meal amid these glorious trees. If only we could build a home up in their branches! I decided that we had explored enough, but that we should search the beach for any debris from the wreck. Jack persuaded me to wait until we finished his belt and collars. If you can believe it, the child had been carrying the stretching-board all this time. Finishing them was easy, and Jack put his belt on and strutted around while Ernest collared the dogs.

"We found the shore strewn with many things, probably useful but too heavy for us to lift. We rolled some barrels above the high-water line, and dragged a couple of chests higher on the beach. While we did this, the dogs were pouncing on the small tide pools, eating something.

"'They're eating crabs,' said Jack. 'No wonder they haven't seemed hungry.' Sure enough, they were catching little green crabs—but those didn't satisfy them. Just as we were about to leave the beach, we saw Juno digging up and eating some round items. Ernest investigated: they were turtles' eggs.

"'Then let's share in the booty!' I cried. Juno had other ideas, and it wasn't easy to get her to share, but we gathered up a couple dozen eggs. While we did so, we saw a sail approaching the shore in the distance. We weren't sure what—or who—it was. We hastened back to the landing place. What a relief to see that it was you!

"Now, I hope you approve of our efforts, and that tomorrow you will be so kind as to pack everything up, and take us away to live in that beautiful grove."

"You want to live in a tree, my wife?" I asked with a tolerant smile. "If we had wings, or a balloon, that would work out nicely."

"Laugh all you want," she answered, "but jackals wouldn't bother us at night in a tree; neither would anything else. At home in Switzerland I have seen tree houses, quite sturdy, with staircases to reach them. Why couldn't we build one?"

"I will consider it," I said, "and maybe we'll figure out a way. In the meantime, we've had a long day and a nice dinner. Let's have our prayers and go to bed."

We had a long, satisfied sleep, but there was much to decide the next day.

CHAPTER 5

A New Home

*M*y wife and I awoke at daybreak and resumed our discussion about the tree house.

"I trust you understand the difficulties involved," I began. "In the first place, I am reluctant to leave this safe spot. See how secure it is, guarded on all sides by these high cliffs, accessible only from one path. From here we can easily reach the ship with all its goods. Suppose we stay here until we have landed all possible supplies?"

"I agree with you to some extent, dear husband," she replied, "but you and Fritz are away all day, in the shade or at sea. You don't suffer from the daytime heat as we do. As for the cargo, a lot of it has drifted ashore. I would rather lose the rest than sit here and worry myself sick, as I do every time you even mention going to sea."

"You have a point," I continued. "What if, after moving to this place you like, we make this our supply depot and retreat in case of danger? I could easily make it safer, by blasting away some of the rock with gunpowder, but we will need a bridge to get all our gear across the river."

"By the time you finish this bridge, I will be broiled alive," cried my wife impatiently. "Why not just carry everything ourselves and wade across? The cow and donkey could carry a lot."

"They will have to," I said. "If you will work on bags and baskets to carry things, I will start work on the bridge. We will eventually need it anyway, because we have no idea how the stream will behave in all seasons. And a bridge is safer anyway."

"Wonderful!" cried my wife. "I do like the idea of storing the supplies and gunpowder here, though, where I don't have to sleep next to them."

"Our most dangerous possession, and our most useful," I said. "We will be very careful, and someday I'll hollow out a powder magazine in the rock."

We woke our children and told them of the decision. They were delighted and began calling the move "our journey to the Promised Land" and complaining about the time "wasted" building a bridge.

To get boards for the bridge, I would have to return to the wreck. Ernest and Fritz went with me. I let Fritz steer us into the helpful current. As we passed the small island at the entrance to the bay, a tremendous flock of sea birds rose into the air, screaming and crying. The noise was deafening.

Fritz wanted to take a shot at them, but I told him not to. Why had so many gathered on such a desolate little island? I set our sail to catch the breeze and had Fritz steer that direction. The birds were settling back down. Presently Fritz shouted, "I see! They are feasting on a huge monster of a fish! Father, let's have a closer look!"

We landed a short distance from the dining flock. After tying the boat to a large stone, we crept carefully toward the birds. It was indeed a monstrous fish, with hundreds of birds greedily battling for a taste. "This wasn't here yesterday, Father," said Fritz. "I wonder how this creature got stranded here."

"Fritz, it must be your shark!" cried Ernest. "I believe I can see where you shot him!"

"I think you're right, Ernest," I said. "Look at those jaws, and those teeth—thank God we were saved from them! Let's try to get these greedy birds to spare us some sharkskin. It is very rough, and when dry, it makes a good file."

Ernest took his gun's ramrod and charged manfully into the flock, striking left and right, killing several of the birds and driving off the rest. Fritz cut some broad strips of sharkskin. The shore of the islet was littered with useful boards, so we began to gather them up into a raft to tow behind us. There were so many that we no longer needed to visit the wreck at all. Instead, we set sail for shore.

As we sailed, I directed Fritz to nail part of the sharkskin flat on boards, and the rest onto the rounded mast. "Is that a good idea, Father?" he asked. "It will dry bent and crooked."

"I want it that way," I answered. "We can smooth wood with it." Before long we reached shore. Lowering the sail, we soon had our craft safely moored to the bank.

No one was in sight, so we gave a loud *hall-loooo!* We got the same in response, and soon my wife and young sons came running from behind the high rocks, each with a small bundle. They had not expected us so soon, so we explained the reason. They opened the mysterious bundles to display a large number of crawfish, which tried to scuttle away in every direction. This caused much laughter as my sons tried to round them all up again.

"Have you ever seen such splendid crawfish, Father?" cried Jack. "We must have hundreds. Just look at those claws!"

"Did you discover them, Jack?" I asked.

"No, it was Franz. We went down toward the stream to look for a good place for the bridge. He was picking up pretty rocks, some of which he thought were gold," Jack explained. "Then he cried out to me: 'Jack, Jack, come see the crabs on Fritz's jackal!' That's where we dragged the carcass, and sure enough, it was swarming with these. Will they be good to eat, Father?"

"They will be excellent, my boy. We can thank God for providing for us every day. A good job finding these, Franz. And Jack, as you so unselfishly gave credit to your brother, you deserve to share the praise with him." Both sons beamed.

When we had all shared our day's adventures, my wife started boiling the crawfish while the rest of us went to bring our lumber ashore. After some thought, I improvised a rope harness for the cow and the donkey to enable them to drag the boards to the edge of the stream.

Jack showed me where he thought the bridge should be, and I could see no better place; the banks were close enough together, steep, and of about equal height. "I wish we had a surveyor's table," I said. "How do we figure out what length of boards to use?"

"Tie a string to a rock, throw it across, then pull it back and measure the length," suggested Ernest. We did this and determined that the boards must be twenty-four feet long. At this point my wife called us to lunch. During the meal she showed off her accomplishment: two large canvas bags. She explained that she had no needle large enough to sew them, and had to bore each stitch hole with a nail. We all praised her clever work.

After lunch, we were eager to get back to our engineering. With the help of a pulley from the wreck, and the cow and donkey, we soon had our first board across the stream. The rest was easier; we added more boards, braced them with cross-pieces, and soon had a functional bridge.

Nothing could exceed the children's excitement. They danced on the wonderful structure, singing and shouting. I didn't join them, but I shared their feelings of triumph. Once this died down, we returned to our tent for dinner and rest. We had prepared the way for our most important undertaking yet, and we all slept quite well.

The next morning over breakfast, I gave my sons a little speech. "Remember," I said, "though you have begun to feel safe here, we have much to learn about this place. There could be many dangers, so be careful. No charging off on your own, Jack. Ernest, you mustn't linger to study everything. And now, all hands to work!"

Camp was a beehive of activity. Some collected food supplies; others packed and loaded kitchen utensils, tools, ropes, and hammocks onto the cow and donkey. My wife pleaded for little Franz to have a seat on the donkey. And she did not want to leave our birds alone even for a night.

She also insisted on bringing her bag of surprises. I agreed to try to satisfy these requests, if it could be done without overloading our animals.

The children ran to catch the chickens and pigeons. This resulted in much chasing, fluttering, and cackling, but not a single bird captured. After a few chuckles, my wife called her sons back, then scattered some grain inside the open tent. When the birds came, she dropped the curtain, making it easy to tie all the birds together. We loaded them onto the cow, who stood completely still while we piled item after item on her back—even the chickens. I covered the birds with some curved hoops and sailcloth to quiet them down. Our patient cow looked like she had a small wagon on her back.

The sow had refused to come and would have to fend for herself. Franz sat on the donkey, amidst bags and bundles of all sorts and sizes. His curly head rested on the precious magic bag. What we could not carry, we shut up tight inside the tent. At last we were ready to depart, well equipped and in high spirits.

Fritz and his mother led the way. Franz came next on the donkey, with the cow close behind. Jack herded the goats, one of whom also had a rider: the baby monkey, whom Fritz had named Knips. The little fellow tried Fritz's patience with his constant movement and playful tricks. Ernest served as shepherd, and I brought up the rear, with Turk and Juno constantly running back and forth as though they were my aides.

As we crossed the bridge, who should follow us but our grumpy old sow! Finding herself alone, she had come on her own, squealing and grunting her disapproval.

Soon we had no choice but to travel along the beach, for the tall grass was slow going and made it difficult to keep track of the animals. Only the dogs' help kept us from losing any. We were making good progress along the sand when Turk and Juno suddenly dove barking into the thick cover on our right. The barking soon gave way to howls of canine pain.

I was certain that some dangerous animal was at hand. I watched each of my sons react in his own way. Fritz cocked his gun and advanced, balancing boldness with caution. Ernest drew back, but shouldered his weapon. Jack hurried after Fritz without thinking to unsling his gun. Before I could catch up, I heard Jack shouting excitedly, "Father! Come quickly! A huge porcupine!"

Sure enough, the dogs were rushing round and round a porcupine, with a few quills in their muzzles. Each time they came near, the creature made a rattling noise and bristled up its spines. The poor dogs had never before encountered anything that hurt when they tried to grab it.

While we watched the creature's curious defense, little Jack stepped up with a pocket pistol and shot it dead. Brave action soon gave way to boyish glee as he called for help carrying his prize, which would not be easy. We got a lot of bloody fingers until Jack thought to tie his handkerchief around its neck. He dragged it off to show his mother the prize. "Mother! Look what I shot! Father says it's good to eat! You should have seen how it terrified the dogs, putting up its spines. What a fearful creature!"

I had said nothing about eating it, but he might be right, so I didn't mind. Ernest examined it carefully, giving us a lecture on porcupines. I let him talk for a moment before interrupting with: "Jack, weren't you afraid the porcupine would throw its quills at you, like darts?"

"Of course not," he answered, "That's only a fable!"

"A fable!" I said. "Look at your mother, pulling five or six quills out of each dog!"

"The dogs ran on the quills when they attacked. See, those are the shortest quills, and were very loose in the skin. The longer quills bent aside."

"Perfectly right, my boy," I said, "it is a fable. But shall we leave behind this prickly trophy of yours?"

"Oh, please, Father, let's take it! It's good to eat!" cried Jack.

To please my eager son, I wrapped the porcupine in cloth and added it to the donkey's load.

The rest of our march was uneventful, and soon we came in sight of our new home.

My wife had accurately described it. The place was calm and beautiful, and the trees were enormous. She glowed when I said, "A house among those branches would be the safest and most charming home in the world."

We unloaded the cow and donkey, tying their forefeet loosely together to keep them near. After hobbling the sheep and goats in the same way, we turned the birds loose and sat down on the soft mossy grass to make plans.

Fritz left us for a moment in mid-discussion. Soon we heard two shots, after which he returned proudly carrying the body of a spotted wildcat. He showed it to each of us in turn. "Well done, Fritz!" I said. "That saved our chickens from a bad night. We must be on the lookout, in case others are nearby."

"How odd it seems," remarked Ernest, "that God creates hurtful animals like this."

"That is because His wisdom and ways are far beyond us," I counseled my son. "What we do not understand, let us accept and trust as His will. Animals maintain a balance in nature by preying on each other. Look at cold countries, where they have no cloth. Without the furs of bears, arctic foxes, wildcats, and such, how would the people live?"

"Seal skin is also valuable," said Ernest.

"It is," I replied, "and seals prey on fish, as dogs once did on land animals. Fritz, tell us how you got him."

"I saw something moving among the branches," he said, "and went softly around the tree with my gun. When I saw that it was a wildcat, I fired. It fell but was only wounded and furious. When it tried to climb the tree, I finished it off with my pistol."

"Good thing it tried to escape rather than going for your throat," I said. "This is a fierce, bloodthirsty animal called the margay, or tiger-cat. Sooner or later it would have preyed on our animals."

"What can I use this beautiful skin for, Father?"

"I would cure it very carefully. From that long, handsome black and yellow tail, make yourself a hunting-belt. As for the rest, better preserve it until you find a use for it."

"How can we use my porcupine?" cried Jack, excited.

"The quills will make good needles and perhaps tips for arrows. From the rest, I would try to make some defensive armor for the dogs. They may yet face worse enemies than jackals and wildcats."

"Great idea, Father!" shouted Jack in glee. "Just like the dogs in boar hunts back home!"

Of course, I would have no peace until I got

my boys started. Soon each had his prize fastened up by the hind legs, skinning his kill. Meanwhile, Ernest was fetching large flat stones to form a fireplace, and Franz gathered sticks, as their mother was anxious to prepare a meal.

I was examining the nearest tree. "What sort of tree do you think it is, Father?" asked Ernest. "The leaves look like walnut leaves."

"There is a resemblance, but walnut trees don't have roots like these. More likely they are mangroves or wild figs, which are known for arching roots well above the soil," I replied.

Just then little Franz came up with a large bundle of sticks, and his mouth full of something. "Oh, Mother!" he cried, "this is so good!"

"What did you eat?" she exclaimed in a panic. "Don't swallow it! It might be poisonous! Spit it out this minute!" From the tiny mouth she extracted pieces of a small fig.

"Where did you find this?" I asked.

"There are thousands lying in the grass over there," said my little boy. "They taste good. I thought poison was nasty. Will they hurt me? The pigeons and chickens are gobbling them up, Papa!"

"No cause for alarm, dear wife," I said. "These seem to be fig-bearing mangroves. But in the future, Franz, never eat anything without showing it to me first, no matter how good it seems." I turned to the other boys and added, "If birds and monkeys eat a fruit or vegetable, we probably can as well." Taking the hint, they coaxed Franz to give them some figs, which they offered to Knips. The funny little creature accepted one from Jack, turned it over, sniffed and smelled it, then popped it into his mouth. The boys all laughed and clapped, praising the little monkey's good taste.

With my wife's mind at rest concerning figs, she got to work on dinner. We gave the margay's carcass to the dogs. Part of the porcupine we put on the fire to boil; the rest we saved for roasting. To my wife's delight, I made her new needles from the thickest quills. I also began to think of proper harnesses for our animals, but too many other matters demanded attention.

At the top of that long list was housing. The ideal tree would have many widely spread branches far overhead, to better support the weight of six people and their home. When we had chosen the best one, I thought about how we would get up to it. We must make a rope ladder, of course, and throw it over a branch. A sturdy enough ladder to hold us would not be easy to throw so high, though. While showing Jack and Fritz the next tasks in curing their hides, I mulled this over.

When lunch was over, I prepared our sleeping space. First I slung our hammocks from the roots of the tree, then covered the arching roots with sailcloth to keep out the chill and most of the insects. My wife got to work on harnesses for the cow and donkey so they could help us haul materials tomorrow.

I took Fritz and Ernest down to the beach to get suitable wood. In the beginning we found only rough, unusable driftwood. Then Ernest noticed a number of bamboos half buried in the sand. These were perfect, so I cleaned off the leaves and cut them into six-foot lengths, then bundled them up.

Next we hunted for reeds hard enough to make into arrows. I saw a likely patch of them in a nearby clump of trees. We entered cautiously, in case the woods contained something dangerous, but Juno rushed ahead. Suddenly there was a great flapping as a flock of flamingoes erupted from the edge of the trees. Fritz quickly shouldered his gun and fired, bringing down two, the rest sailing away in a perfect pattern of rosy pink and white.

One was quite dead, but the other had only a slight wound in the wing and ran off across the swampy ground. Juno took out after it and soon brought the protesting bird to my feet. Fritz and Ernest were delighted. "What a handsome bird!" Ernest exclaimed. "Is it badly hurt? Let's tame it and let it run with the chickens and pigeons."

"Its plumage is brighter than that of the dead one," remarked Fritz.

"Yes," Ernest said, "this one is full grown, while the other is younger. See what long legs it has, like a stork, and its great webbed feet. The flamingo is equally at home on land, air, or water."

"Then let's take it home to mother," Fritz said, "and see if it's at home in the cooking pot."

Fritz and Ernest then carried the birds and bamboos to the tree. I cut the hardest reeds I could find. Then I cut down two of the tallest canes to use in measuring the height of the tree. Back in camp, my wife liked the dead flamingo better than the live one. "Are you going to keep this big, hungry thing?" she asked. "We hardly have a surplus of bird feed."

"Luckily," I replied, "the flamingo will not eat grain, but will be quite satisfied with insects, fish, and little crabs. Now let me tend its wound." I dressed the hurt wing with some wine and butter, noting that it was not broken. Then I took the bird to the stream and fastened it to a stake with a long cord. If its wound healed, kind treatment might tame the flamingo.

While I served as veterinarian, my sons tried to determine the height of the lowest branch of the chosen tree. Unfortunately, the canes were far too short for this. When I saw what they were doing, I came over and said, "My boys, for this you need geometry. It enables us to measure even the height of tall, distant mountains."

Using a rod of known length, I measured out a certain distance from the base of the tree, marked the spot, then estimated the angle from the spot to the branch. After doing some mathematics, I made a confident announcement to my astonished children: we would be living thirty feet above the ground. Therefore, our ladder must be slightly longer.

Telling Fritz to collect all our rope, I sat down and made half a dozen arrows from reeds and flamingo feathers. I then took a strong bamboo. This I bent and strung to form a bow.

The boys were delighted and begged to have the first shot. "No, no!" I said. "This isn't meant as a weapon. The arrows don't even have points. Elizabeth," I called to my wife, "is there a ball of stout string in your wonderful bag?"

"Certainly," she replied. "I think that was the first thing I put in." Reaching deep inside, she drew out exactly what I wanted.

"Now, boys," I said, "I am going to fire the first shot." I fastened one end of the string to an arrow and aimed at a large branch above us. The arrow sailed over the branch and fell at our feet, draping the string over the branch.

Now for the rope ladder. Fritz had obtained two forty-foot coils of rope. Laying these out side by side, he cut the bamboos into two-foot pieces to make rungs. I tied knots in the ropes and passed the rung-ends through, while Jack fixed each end with a nail driven through the bamboo. When the ladder was finished, I used the line I had shot over the branch to hoist a strong rope across it. From there it was simple to hoist up the ladder, staking it firmly to the ground. The end of the other rope we tied to a stake also, until we could secure the ladder at the top.

The boys were all eager to be first. "Jack is the lightest except Franz, who is too small. Up with you, my boy, and be careful."

My agile Jack quickly scrambled to the top. "Three cheers for the nest!" he exclaimed, waving his cap. "What a great place to live! Come along here, Fritz!" His brother was soon by his side, hammer in hand, nailing and tying the ladder to the branch; this freed our rope for other tasks. Next I took an axe and climbed up for a good look around. The tree would serve well, for its branches were so strong and close we need only clear away a few obstructing branches and lay boards across.

I now called for a pulley, which my wife fastened to the rope we had used to haul up the ladder. It was crowded in the branches, so I told the boys to go down. I fastened the pulley to a strong branch above me, to use for hauling up lumber the next day, and made a few other preparations. I worked well into the evening moonlight, until I was too tired to go on and climbed down.

While I had been working in the tree, my

wife had been busy making two fine, complete sets of harness. She had also prepared a bountiful feast: a roast shoulder of porcupine, soup made from its broth, cheese, butter, and biscuits. When we had eaten this fine meal, we herded up our four-legged animals, letting the birds do as they liked. We built the cooking-fire up high to keep away any dangerous animals and lay down to rest.

The children were soon asleep in their hammocks, but I was full of anxious thoughts, one right after the other. Only in the early morning hours did my mind finally allow me to rest.

Early the next morning we were up and about our various tasks. My wife milked the goats and cow while the boys fed the animals. With this all done, I took my sons, the cow, and the donkey down to the beach to get bamboo, solid driftwood, and ship wreckage. We harnessed the animals to the heavier beams, and carried the lighter ones ourselves. Before long we were back at the tree, ready to build a home.

Fritz and I climbed up to clear the building area. We lopped off all useless branches, leaving a few about six feet above the floor from which to sling our hammocks and others still higher to support a temporary roof of sail canvas. One by one, my wife tied the boards to a rope, enabling Fritz and me to raise them up with the pulley. We put these side by side across the branches to make

a smooth solid floor, then built a wall on each side. The great trunk protected us from behind, and the open front let in the fresh sea breeze. We threw the canvas across the higher branches and secured it. Later we would build a more permanent roof, but this would do for now.

We then hauled up and installed our hammocks and bedding. With a few hours of daylight left, we cleared leaves and chips off the floor, then climbed down to make a table and a few benches from the rest of the wood. Exhausted,

Fritz and I lay down on the grass to rest and wait for dinner.

My wife soon called us, "Come and taste flamingo stew, on the lovely table you have built, and tell me if you like it. Ernest suggested it would be better stewed than roasted."

Laughing at the idea of Ernest turning scientific cook, we sat down. The birds gathered to pick up the crumbs, while Knips skipped about from one to the other of us, chattering and mimicking us. My wife was overjoyed to see the sow show up and gave her all the extra goat's milk. "It would sour by morning anyway, and this way, perhaps the sow will come back every night," she explained.

"True," I replied, "but we must find another use for that milk. Next time Fritz and I return to the wreck, we will bring a butter churn."

"Must you really go again to that dreadful wreck?" said my wife, shuddering. "You have no idea how nervous those trips make me."

"We must, I'm afraid," I replied, "but not for a day or two. Come, it's getting late. Both we and the chickens need to roost." We lit our watch fires, and, leaving the dogs on guard below, climbed to our new home. Fritz, Ernest, and Jack raced up the ladder. Their mother followed very cautiously; perhaps she had not fully considered that her housing idea would require her to climb up a high rope ladder. If she had second thoughts, she overcame them enough to reach the top. I took little Franz on my back, untied the bottom of the ladder from its stakes, and climbed slowly up.

Now for the first time we all stood together in our new home. Feeling safer than ever since we had landed, I drew up the ladder. In evening prayer, I thanked God for all the good that had come to us, and we retired for the night.

CHAPTER 6

Ernest and Me

*T*he next morning all were up early. The children sprang about the tree, full of energy. "What today, Father?" they cried.

"Rest, my boys," I replied.

"Rest?" they repeated. "Why?"

"Because it's the Sabbath," I replied. "The Bible says to rest on the seventh day."

"What, is it really Sunday?" said Jack. "All right, I won't do any work. I'll practice my archery, and we'll have fun all day."

"That's not how you spent Sunday in Switzerland," I said.

"Well, we can't go to church here, and there's nothing else to do," answered my son.

"We can worship here as well as at home," I said.

"But there is no church, no pastor, and no organ," said Franz.

"Our Creator made this beautiful tree for us. Its leafy shade is all we need," I said. "We will honor Him here. Now, boys, go down and set the table for breakfast."

The children, one by one, slipped down the ladder.

"My dear Elizabeth," I said, "we will devote this morning to God. After hymns and prayers, I'll recite some Scripture, then interpret a parable for them. They can have free time afterward. In the evening, when it cools, we'll take a walk." She agreed wholeheartedly.

After breakfast, the family assembled around me on the soft grass. We sang hymns and prayed. Then I told the parable of a great, wise king whose subjects rebelled against him. Rather than crush them, this great king offered to forgive the rebels, and the kingdom once again prospered in peace. "And so, my children," I finished, "when you are unhappy, remember the gift of Salvation, and be glad for the blessings you have."

I ended the service with a short prayer. After a thoughtful pause, we separated to do as each of us pleased.

With Jack's help, I began tipping some arrows with porcupine quills. Franz asked me to make him a little bow and arrows, while Fritz asked my advice about uses for the wildcat's hide. "I wish we had some glue to hold these quills in place," said Jack.

"Oh, Jack! Mamma's soup is sticky enough!" cried Franz. "Shall I run and ask for a cake of it?"

"No, silly. Look for some real glue in the toolbox," said Jack.

"He'll find some there. And you're right; glue would work better than the soup," I said. "But Jack, you ought to respect your little brother's ideas more. Look at the useful things he has discovered—crawfish, figs, and more."

Just as Jack was apologizing to little Franz, we heard a shot overhead. Two birds fell dead at our feet, and we saw Ernest among the branches. "How's that for a shot?" he said, climbing down. He brought me the birds for identification. One was a sort of thrush, but the other was a small type of dove called the ortolan, considered delicious eating. Many more had come, apparently to eat the just-ripening figs.

By this time Jack had tipped a good supply of arrows and was practicing his archery. I finished the bow and arrows for Franz, including a quiver. Off he went, very pleased with himself. "He looks like an innocent little Cupid," his mother said with a smile.

Not long after, she called us all to lunch. As we ate, I proposed that we begin naming local landmarks. "We'll feel more at home," I explained. "It'll also avoid confusion. It's cumbersome to say 'the little island at the mouth of our bay where we found the dead shark,' for example, or 'the forest where we found coconuts.' Let's start by naming the bay where we landed. Who has an idea?"

"Oyster Bay," said Fritz.

"Lobster Bay," cried Jack, "in memory of the one that bit my leg!"

"I think, in gratitude for our escape," observed his mother, "that we should call it Safety Bay." Everyone approved. Other names soon followed. Our first home we called Tentholm. The islet in the bay became Shark's Island. We named the reedy swamp Flamingo Marsh. Naming our leafy home was harder, but after some debate we settled on Falconhurst.

The rest of the names came swiftly. The first hill we climbed: Prospect Hill. The rocky height where we looked for a sign of the sailors: Cape Disappointment. The large stream flowing past Tentholm we named Jackal River.

After lunch, the boys kept at their projects. Fritz prepared the wildcat's hide. Jack asked me to help him make Turk some porcupine-skin armor. After scraping the inside clean and dry, we trimmed it, made holes for string, and tied it to the patient dog's body. We thought him quite handsome, but Juno was confused. Turk had changed his smell and look, as though he were no longer fully a dog. After one sniff, she rejected his friendly gestures and kept her distance. Now that Turk was almost invulnerable, I made Jack a helmet from the remaining hide and had the joy of watching him march around all-important and proud.

As evening drew on, I led my family in a pleasant walk through the nearby woods. We ended our Sabbath with a hymn and prayer, and climbed up to sleep with peaceful hearts.

The next morning, I proposed a trip to Tentholm by way of the stream. My three older sons and I each carried a gun and game bag, while Franz carried his bow and arrows. My wife alone went unarmed, carrying only a jar to get butter. Fritz wore his margay-skin belt, and Jack had on his new helmet. Turk scouted ahead in his new armor; Juno still kept a suspicious distance. Knips tried to assume his usual perch on Turk, but a landing on the porcupine-skin armor made him think better of it. The little fellow bounded over to ride Juno. The flamingo, which was already taking a liking to us, came along on its long, stately legs. What a curious sight we were!

We strolled on in the cool morning air, following the stream. The boys and dogs roamed ahead of me. Presently I heard a joyful shout. Soon the boys came running, Ernest in the lead with a plant in his hand. Panting but excited, he held it up to me. "Potatoes! Potatoes, Father," he gasped out.

"Yes," said Jack, "acres and acres of potatoes!"

It was indeed a potato. "My dear Ernest," I said, "this is a superb find. Potatoes grow quickly and easily, and keep very well. Our risk of starvation has just dropped."

"But come and look at them," said Jack. "There are thousands!" We hurried to the spot, and indeed there were many. "It would have been hard to miss them," he said as we feasted our eyes.

"Very likely," replied Ernest, smiling, "except that you probably wouldn't have recognized what they were."

"Maybe not," said Jack, "so you take the honor of the discovery, and I'll be the first to collect a supply." With this, he began digging and soon had a game bag full. The monkey begun to imitate him, and soon had a similar heap beside him. We all followed suit, filling every bag, pouch and pocket with a large supply. Some wished to return at once to Falconhurst with our heavy load, to taste our new find, but I overruled this and led us back onto the march. We soon reached the head of our stream, where it fell from the rocks above in a beautiful, splashing cascade and crossed into the tall grass on the other side.

Here the tangled reeds made tougher going, but the landscape beyond was lovely. Rich tropical vegetation grew on all sides: tall palms, luxuriant ferns, brilliant flowers, graceful vines, spiny cactuses. The wealth of herbs included aloe, jasmine, and vanilla. We also found Indian peas and pineapples. The boys ate so much pineapple my wife had to caution them against becoming ill.

While they were busy, I examined the nearby shrubs and made a great find of my own—the karatas bush. "Come here, boys," I said. "Here is something even more useful than pineapples. This plant with the beautiful red flowers is a karatas. Its leaf filaments make good thread, and the leaves are good to crush and put on burns. The inside can be used to help start fires, or even to bait a fishhook. Ernest!"

When he looked up, I asked, "Suppose you had been wrecked here without matches, flint, or steel. How would you make a fire?"

"By rubbing two pieces of wood together," he answered.

"Try it," I said, "but start early in the morning, ready to work with blistered hands until nightfall. Watch this," I added, breaking a dry twig from the karatas. I peeled away the bark, laid the middle on a stone, and struck two rocks together over it. A spark soon flew onto the pithy middle, catching it on fire. The boys were delighted. I collected some of the leaf filaments and presented these to my wife.

As we walked on, the boys pelted me with questions about every plant and shrub. I finally had to cry uncle. "Enough!" I exclaimed with a smile. "I've never seen even a fourth of these before. Not even the most learned naturalist could identify them all, much less their uses." Even so, I discussed those I did know, and so we passed the entire trip to Tentholm.

Upon arrival, we were glad to see that all was safe. I opened the butter keg for my wife. Fritz collected ammunition while Jack and Ernest ran down to the beach to capture the geese and ducks. This proved difficult, for the birds had grown shy. After some fumbling, Ernest came up with the clever idea of tying some pieces of cheese to long strings. These he tossed into the water near the birds and when they grabbed for them, he pulled the food back. He soon led them ashore and joined his brother in tying them together.

While Ernest and Jack were rounding up the rebel birds, Fritz and I got a fresh supply of salt. This we packed on Turk's back, taking off his armor. We fastened the birds to our game bags, happy there were not too many, for geese and ducks are heavy birds. Once we were loaded, we closed up our tent and started homeward along the seashore.

A cheerful, pleasant walk soon brought us back to Falconhurst. While my wife prepared a delicious dinner of potatoes with milk and butter, I clipped the birds' wings and set them loose on the stream.

Night soon came, and we climbed our tree and went to bed.

I awoke early and roused Ernest, in hopes of

curing his laziness. After a little stretching and yawning, he got up, and I told him the plan: we would go on an expedition together and let the others sleep. He received this cheerfully and helped me to hitch a large, broad tree branch to the donkey. I had a plan to help us move larger loads.

As we went toward the beach, I remarked to Ernest, "I suppose you didn't much care to be woken up and put to work at this early hour."

"I don't mind, Father," he said. "I know I can be a bit lazy, but I'm glad to go with you. I meant to shoot some ortolans this morning, but there will be plenty of time afterward. I think my brothers will hunt them, but without much success."

"Why not?" I asked.

"They will probably use the wrong sort of shot, and are likely to shoot up into the branches and leaves, which is very hard," he replied.

"Son, you are good at thinking and observing, and I'm proud of both," I said. "Now you should try to get better at deciding, especially in emergencies. In such situations, by the time you consider everything carefully, the emergency may grow worse."

Our work on shore didn't take long. I selected the wood I wanted, and we laid it across the branch. I picked up a small chest from the sand and set that on the pile. Ernest and I filled our arms with all the wood we could carry, and we started for home.

We heard the boys popping away at the birds as we drew near. They hurried to meet us and were most interested in the chest. While I let them open it, I explained our absence to my wife. "I wish you wouldn't go off like that without telling me," she said. "It makes me nervous." She liked my sledge idea better: "We can bring my keg of butter from Tentholm! Wonderful!" As for the chest, it was only a sailor's, containing nothing but wet old clothes.

The boys showed off several dozen birds. Over breakfast they told how they had killed them, including failures and successes. Ernest had correctly guessed the mistakes they would make but had not calculated how quickly they would improve and learn. They wanted to continue, but their mother said we had shot enough birds. "And is there any way we could trap them instead of shoot them?" she asked. "We can't keep using up ammunition at this rate."

I agreed and told my sons to set their guns aside for the moment. I took Franz and Jack and showed them how to weave the karatas leaf threads to make snares. Then I got Fritz and Ernest to help me build a sledge.

All were hard at work when there was a great flapping and cackling among the chickens. We hurried in that direction, but Ernest noticed Knips slipping away from the flock as if up to mischief. My son gave chase and soon caught Knips in the act. He was eating a newly laid egg, with several more hidden in the grass nearby. My wife was delighted to see the eggs, for the hens had not yet given us any. We resolved to tie Knips up in the morning until the eggs had been collected.

Soon after, Jack was setting the new snares among the branches and found something very encouraging: a pair of our pigeons building a nest. Since this would mean more pigeons, I cautioned the boys against shooting near our tree and to be careful where they put the snares. Jack spoke for all when he said, "We like the snares, Father, but we also like to shoot."

"We have only so much powder and ammunition," I said. "We have to ration it."

"I have an idea," said little Franz. "Let's plant some powder and shot in the ground, and grow our own!"

His brothers roared with laughter, and I had a hard time not joining in. I said, "Ernest, now that we've had our laugh, tell him what gunpowder really is."

"It isn't seed, Franz," explained Ernest. "Gunpowder is made of chemicals mixed together. You can't grow it like grain, any more than you can plant bullets like peas or beans."

In the meantime, I went on with my carpentry. To shape my sledge with the front ends upward, I used already-curved wood from the ship's bow. Two such pieces made the runners, and I nailed short bars across them. Our sledge was ready.

When I finished, I saw that my wife and younger sons had been plucking more than two dozen of the game birds. They had impaled them on a long, narrow spike to roast. "We can't eat that many," I objected.

"We don't plan to," answered my wife. "I'm half-cooking them, so we can preserve them in the butter keg. We may be glad to have them some time in the future."

"You're right. We'll go get the keg after lunch," I promised.

"Good. While you're gone, I'm going to do some washing. And speaking of washing, would you start arranging regular baths for the boys?" I agreed, and early in the afternoon Ernest and I were ready to start for Tentholm. Fritz presented us each with a neat margay-skin belt pouch. We harnessed the cow and donkey to the sledge, then took Juno and headed for the beach.

We reached Tentholm without event. After removing the harnesses, we began to load the sledge with the butter keg, a powder chest, a barrel of cheese, bullets and small shot, tools, and Turk's armor which we had left behind the day before. This engaged our whole attention for some time.

This finished, we meant to seek a good place to bathe—but the cow and donkey were gone.

We headed toward the bridge and saw that they had crossed it to get at better grazing. I sent Ernest after them and went down to the swampy ground at the edge of the bay to cut a large bundle of reeds.

When I came back, Ernest and the animals were absent. I stalked toward Tentholm to find out what was the matter. There I found my son napping on the ground as both animals worked their way toward the bridge.

"Get up, lazy!" I exclaimed in annoyance. "What did I tell you to do? Look at the animals—they're about to go back across the river!"

Ernest awoke unruffled. "No fear of that, Father," he answered. "I took a couple of boards off the bridge. They can't get across."

I couldn't help laughing at his clever method of avoiding work. "Even so," I told him, "you could have been doing something else useful. Now go collect salt or something while I take a bath."

When I came back, much refreshed, again there was no Ernest. I was wondering whether he was still gathering salt, or perhaps had resumed his nap, when I heard him calling out, "Father! I've caught a huge fish, but I can barely hold him!"

Hurrying that direction, I saw him lying in the grass near the mouth of the stream, holding on for dear life to a fishing rod. The fish was trying to get away, or failing that, to drag Ernest along. I quickly took the rod and gave the fish some line, leading it gradually into shallower water. Ernest ran in with his hatchet and killed it. What a catch! It was a salmon, weighing at least fifteen pounds, a wonderful prize to take home with us.

"Great job, Ernest!" I said. "See what you can achieve when you stay at work? For now, at least, you are cleared of the charge of laziness. Let's carry it to the sledge, where I'll clean and pack it, while you go and take a bath." This done, we harnessed our animals to the sledge, replaced the boards on the bridge, and headed for home.

This time we took the inland route. As we were passing along a grassy thicket, Juno suddenly barked and plunged into the bushes. With a great, swift flying leap, out sprang the strangest-looking creature I had ever seen. I fired and missed as it landed in cover. Ernest, behind me, held his fire and watched carefully. Juno was confused, and sniffed around, but my son saw movement in the nearby grass and crept up. When he was sure of his target, he fired at the spot with calm accuracy, and the new creature went down.

Our quarry looked even stranger on close inspection. It was the size of a sheep, with a mouse-like head and grayish skin. It had long rabbit-like ears, a tail like a tiger's, and tiny squirrel-like forepaws. Its hind legs were huge. We stood in silence for some time, for it resembled nothing I had ever heard of.

"Well, Father," said Ernest at last, "this is the weirdest creature I've ever seen. They'll get a laugh out of it back at Falconhurst!"

"You've had a lucky day," I said, "but let's try to figure out what it is. Examine its teeth, please."

My son obeyed. "It has four sharp incisor teeth, Father, two upper and two lower, like a squirrel."

"Ah! A rodent, then. What rodents can you remember, Ernest?"

"I don't know them all, but there are the mouse, the marmot, the squirrel, the hare, the beaver, the jerboa—"

"The jerboa!" I exclaimed. "Now we're onto something. This is jerboa-like, but far larger. It must be a kangaroo, an animal discovered first by Captain Cook in Australia. It carries its young in a belly-pouch. Congratulations on being the first to find one in New Switzerland!" I added, laughing at the name I had invented.

Adding the kangaroo to our heavy sledge-load, we resumed the march. Progress was slow and we arrived late but got the usual bright welcome. Four pairs of inquisitive eyes turned toward the sledge loaded down with unexpected things, but we too had reason to stare in surprise.

Franz wore a long nightshirt, trailing far behind him like a miniature ghost. Jack had on a huge pair of baggy trousers belted up around his chest. Fritz, buttoned up in a heavy sea coat down to his ankles, looked like a walking travel bag. There was much joking and laughter as my wife explained. "I was washing all day, and while their clothes were drying, the boys decided to dress up in the things they found in that sailor's chest. They decided to leave them on for your amusement," she finished with a smile.

"It worked," I said, "but it's also too bad we have so few clothes of our own from the wreck. They will soon wear out."

Everyone was very interested in what we had brought, especially the large salmon and kangaroo, but Fritz treated Ernest's kangaroo in the dismissive way of someone who is envious. This disturbed me, but I could also see that my eldest was struggling with these unworthy feelings, so I didn't criticize him. I was very pleased when he soon reasoned out his feelings and joined pleasantly in the conversation, saying, "You have had quite a day's sport together! It will be my turn next, won't it, Father? There is nothing to shoot near here, and it's been a dull day."

"But you were doing your duty, my dear son," I said, in words meant for a boy but the tone I would use with a grown man. "I left the family in your care, and they are safe and happy. Excitement may bring a boy happiness, but duty brings a man satisfaction." I saw understanding in his eyes and left the matter there.

With night drawing on, we hurried to butcher the kangaroo, preparing part to cook soon and preserving the rest for later. After the animals were fed, we made quick work of my wife's broiled salmon and potatoes. Every heart was thankful as we said our prayers and climbed to our well-earned rest.

CHAPTER 7

Bread

*B*efore breakfast the next morning, I worked to preserve the kangaroo's hide. After we ate, I told Fritz, "We're going to the wreck today. Get everything ready."

I called out to Ernest and Jack to give them some parting instructions, but they had disappeared shortly after breakfast. "We need more potatoes. Perhaps they went to get some," guessed my wife.

When they returned, I was a little annoyed with them for running off without permission. But they had at least had enough sense to take Turk with them. That was safer, but I didn't like the idea of my dear wife and little Franz left alone.

Fritz called out to say that all was ready, and off we went. On our way to the bridge at Jackal River, a sudden movement startled us. We halted and reached for our guns, only to find Jack and Ernest bursting from cover, delighted that they had surprised us. "We're ready to go too, Father," said Jack. "We'll be a big help!"

While I couldn't bring myself to scold my two merry rogues, neither could I grant their wish. "You boys can't come this time," I said firmly. "I need you to take care of your mother and little brother. Since you've come this far, you can do some work. Collect a load of salt and take it straight home. Once you're home, you mustn't run off again without telling your mother. And please tell her that our work will require us to spend the night on the wreck."

As my sons accompanied us toward Tentholm, I felt a pang of guilt. I had meant to tell her this before leaving, but I knew how she would react. The raft I wanted to build would take more than a day, and it would be a nuisance to have to return to shore. By good fortune, Jack and Ernest had given me a way to break this news to Elizabeth without confronting her objections.

We soon reached shore and boarded our tub boat. "Goodbye, boys. Take care of yourselves!" shouted Fritz as we shoved off.

The current carried us straight to the wreck, and we were soon scrambling aboard. A raft would enable us to land all the useful things that were too big or heavy for the tub boat. We gathered up twelve empty water barrels. After making sure they were closed, we pushed them overboard and arranged them in rows of three. We built a flat frame on top of the barrels, then laid boards across, finishing with a low wall around the edge.

By evening our raft was in fine shape, but it was too late to load up and start for shore. We got dinner from the ship's stores, then spent the night on comfortable spring mattresses. What a great luxury after our hard, narrow hammocks! The next morning, we loaded the mattresses first. We then loaded all our personal belongings from our cabin; then all the furniture, doors, window frames, bolts, and locks in the captain's cabin. Then came the officers' chests, and the carpenter's and gunsmith's chests—these last were immensely heavy.

With plenty of space left, we poked around for other cargo. The ship's mission had been to resupply a distant colony, so nearly everything aboard was useful to us. A large chest of tableware would surely delight my wife. Deep in the hold were a number of young fruit trees, carefully packed and labeled: apple, pear, chestnut, orange, almond, peach, apricot, plum, cherry, grapevine. We found blacksmith's tools, plumbing equipment, lead, paint, grinding-stones, cartwheels, shovels, plows, and even a disassembled sawmill. There were sacks of corn, peas, oats, and wheat.

We had a hard time deciding what to take. The next storm would probably destroy the ship, so the decision was crucial. The grain and fruit trees went first. We loaded a compass, fishing lines, reels, rope, and a couple of harpoons. Remembering the shark, Fritz rigged the harpoons as if going whaling, much to my laughing approval.

By early afternoon we were ready to sail. With the raft in tow, there was more potential for accident. Fortunately, the sea and wind favored us, and we were able to spread the sail.

We were making fine progress when Fritz spoke up. "I see something odd floating in the distance," he explained. "Can I have the telescope?" After he looked, he handed me the glass.

"It's a sea turtle. Appears to be asleep," I said.

"Let's steer toward it, Father!" Fritz exclaimed. I did so, to give him a nearer look. Had I known his intentions, I might have gone the other way. The sail blocked my view of Fritz's actions, but I felt a shock, then the sound of line going through a reel.

Before I could call out, there was a second shock. To my dismay, I felt our boat being hauled rapidly through the water. "Fritz, what in the world are you doing?" I cried out. "If he dives, it'll sink us!"

"Got him!" crowed Fritz. "Got him for sure!" Amazingly, he had managed to harpoon the turtle, which was now paddling away. A giant sea turtle is slow on land but swift and powerful on water. I hurried forward to cut the line.

"Father! Wait!" he pleaded. "I promise to cut the line myself if we are in danger! Let's catch it if we can!"

I frowned. "My son, if we lose all our goods, this turtle will cost us dearly—he may even drown us! For heaven's sake, be careful! I will wait a few minutes, but cut the line at the first sign of trouble!"

As the turtle began to make for the open sea, I hoisted the sail again. It was one thing for the turtle to tow our entire rig; it was another for him to battle the wind. He soon tired and headed for land.

Under wind power and turtle power, we flew shoreward, but far to the left of our usual landing place—rather near Falconhurst, in fact, and not an ideal spot. Our boat grounded out some distance from land. The exhausted turtle tried to escape, but I leaped overboard and finished it with my axe. Fritz fired his gun and shouted with glee, in hopes of bringing the family down to meet us, and soon they came.

The raft and cargo were of great interest, but my wife's chief pleasure was having us home safely. As expected, she was not pleased at our overnight absence.

It was important to get some goods unloaded before nightfall. The boys went for the animals and sledge while I anchored the boat and the raft with some iron blocks we had brought. The turtle was so huge that we could only bring the saplings in that load.

Back at Falconhurst, the first priority was to

get some turtle meat. My wife had misgivings, but I turned the beast on his back and broke the under-shell with a hatchet. Soon I had a large piece of meat, shell still attached, and suggested that she cook it with a little salt.

"First let me cut away this disgusting green fat," said my wife with a little shudder.

"No, leave it!" I exclaimed. "Gourmets pay handsomely to get it. If there is really too much, save some as lard and give the rest to the dogs."

"Look at that shell!" cried Fritz. "I could install it by the stream as a basin, always full of clear water. How about that?"

"An excellent idea," I replied, "if we can find enough clay to make a firm foundation under it."

Jack chimed in. "I have a big lump of clay over there, under that root."

"Well done, my lad! When did you find it?"

"He found a bed of clay near the river this morning," said his mother, "and came home a complete mess. I spent an hour cleaning him and his clothes up!"

"Well, Mother, I found the clay by slipping and falling in it."

"Probably, considering how you were covered in it," answered his mother. "This morning, however, you made it sound like you had gone hunting for the clay on purpose," she added.

"When you finish discussing this," said Ernest, "I'd like to show you some roots I found today. They're drying out now, and they look like radishes, but the plant was almost a bush. Our old sow was devouring them, but I haven't yet dared taste them myself."

"You did wisely, my boy. Pigs can eat almost anything. Let me see those roots." I examined them carefully. "Ernest! This is brilliant! If these are manioc roots, as I believe they are, then we will never starve here. In the West Indies, they press all the poisonous juice out of these, then bake cassava bread from them. I think I know a way to do that."

There was still enough daylight to make another sledge-trip, and I took the three older boys, leaving Franz to help his mother with dinner. As we went along, Fritz said, "Father, I've been thinking about this turtle. Isn't this shell too valuable to use as a simple water trough? At home people pay much for turtle-shell ornaments."

"You're thinking of a different species of sea turtle," I explained. "The kind you caught is only good for eating." His concept of value would change as time unfolded, but this process couldn't be hurried.

On our next trip, we loaded the sledge with chests, cartwheels, and the grinding mill. Adding a number of smaller items, we hurried back to Falconhurst. My wife welcomed us with joy and firm orders: "You have been working too hard, so

no more work today. Now come and see, because
I have something special for you!" She showed us
a small barrel, half buried, well sheltered with
leaves and branches. "You might wonder where
this came from," she continued. "Well, I found it
by myself on the beach, and I suspected it was
wine, so I brought it up here to be ready for you.
The boys are anxious to know what sort of wine
it is."

I was too, so I opened the vent hole and
inserted a straw. "This is dry Canary wine, some
of the finest I've ever had," I announced. My
wife clapped her hands with joy at her find. The
boys pressed around with straws, asking to taste
it. I could hardly deny them, after expressing
such enjoyment myself, but they must also have a
lesson. I let each have a brief taste—but only that.
"Never drink too much of it," I cautioned them
and was pleased that none got too greedy for it.

The turtle made a delicious dinner, and we
each had a bit more wine. Afterward we hauled
up the new mattresses and closed this highly pro-
ductive day in refreshing sleep.

Early the next morning, I got up alone to check
on the safety of our boat and raft. All the animals
were handy except the one I wanted: the donkey.
I couldn't use the cow because she hadn't been
milked, so I went hunting for him and found him
nearby. At first he didn't want to come, but he

soon realized he would have no peace until I got my way, and we headed down to the beach.

The boat and raft were safe. I collected a light load and then hurried to Falconhurst and breakfast. As I approached the tree, however, I heard nothing. No one was up! The sledge's clatter woke my wife, though, and when she looked outside, she was mortified. "We've overslept!" she exclaimed. "Get up, all of you! It must be these mattresses; they're too comfortable."

The boys came tumbling down the ladder with much stretching and yawning, Ernest last as usual. "Come on! This won't do!" I scolded. "Maybe we should go back to the hammocks!" Privately, however, I felt there was another reason for their sluggishness, and resolved to be very careful with the wine in the future. "Prayers and breakfast," I went on, "then off to work. We need all that cargo landed in time to get the boat out with the next tide."

When breakfast was over, we went to the beach and unloaded all the cargo. Fritz and I boarded the boat and sent Jack and Ernest home with the sledge, but Jack looked deeply disappointed. "Jack, you can come too!" I called out, and the boy splashed out and heaved himself into a tub.

I had meant to sail our rig around to the harbor in Safety Bay, but the beautiful day tempted me to visit the wreck. This took longer than I expected, so we had to satisfy ourselves with a small load. Jack came rattling and clanging up from the hold with a wheelbarrow, immensely pleased with himself.

Fritz had even better news: he had found a boat! It was in crates ready for assembly, complete with rigging, fittings, and a couple of small brass cannon. I was delighted, but there was not time now to assemble it for sea. We did take a copper kettle, iron plates, tobacco graters, two grindstones, a small barrel of gunpowder, a box of flints, and two more wheelbarrows besides Jack's. After this, we had just enough time to have lunch and sail for shore.

Along the beach, a number of little figures stood gazing at us. They looked like children in formal black and white clothing. Except for reaching toward us now and then, they stood very still.

"What are those, Father?" cried Jack. "Are they little people?"

"No, my son. They're penguins," I explained. "You may remember that Ernest knocked a penguin down just after we landed. They're excellent swimmers, but can't fly or run, so they're helpless on land."

As soon as we reached shallow water, Jack sprang ashore and began swinging his stick. Half a dozen were soon down, and the rest dove into the water. I regretted Jack's actions, for we had far better food than these oily, fishy-tasting birds.

To my relief, some of them were only stunned and had begun to get up. These penguins we caught, tied together with long grass, and loaded into the wheelbarrows along with the dead ones and whatever goods we could fit. We set off for Falconhurst at a good pace.

The unusual noise of our approach brought the dogs, barking furiously. When they saw us, they bounded forward to give Jack a rowdy welcome. This dumped over both the wheelbarrow and Jack, much to his irritation and our amusement.

Once we got the dogs off Jack and the wheelbarrow righted, Ernest, Franz, and my wife were very curious about our cargo. While I spoke with my wife, I sent Fritz and Ernest to catch some geese and ducks and tie a penguin to each, in hopes that we might tame them. "While you were gone, we gathered some potatoes and manioc root," she said.

"Ah, Father, wait until mother and I get you some corn and melons and pumpkins and cucumbers!" said Franz.

"You little chatterbox!" she cried. "I wanted to surprise your father with those when they grew up, but you told my secret."

"Secret or no," I answered, "I'm delighted to hear it. But where in the world did you get the seeds?"

"Out of my magic bag, of course!" she replied. "And every time I dig up potatoes, I plant some seeds, as well as more potatoes."

"Well done! What a wise, hardworking wife God has given me!" I exclaimed.

"But why the tobacco graters?" she continued. "I don't like that at all. You aren't going to make snuff, are you? We should concentrate on food, not bad habits."

"Rest easy, dear. I will not introduce a filthy habit into our family. I brought the graters to help us make fresh bread."

"How in the world do you plan to do that without an oven? You're teasing me."

"We can't bake loaves," I said, "but once we grind up and press the manioc, I can bake flat cakes on these iron plates. You could help by making me a nice strong canvas bag."

She went to work on this, but she also first put a pot of potatoes on to boil. Apparently she had less than complete confidence in my plan.

Spreading a large sailcloth on the ground, I summoned my boys to work. Each took a grater and a supply of well-washed manioc root. When all were seated round the cloth, I began to grind a root. The rest followed my example, with much laughter at each other's efforts. No one was tempted to taste the flour, which looked like wet sawdust.

"In much of the New World," I explained, "people like cassava bread. Some European settlers even prefer it to wheat bread. There are

three species of manioc, two of which are poisonous if eaten raw. The scrapings must be pressed,
but when that is done, they make good flour."

"Why press them, Father?" asked Ernest.

"To remove the poisonous sap," I replied.
"Even so, we will let the chickens and Knips try
them first."

Our roots were soon ground to damp powder. My wife had finished the bag, so I filled this
with our powder and tried to squeeze it. Nothing
came out. We would need mechanical aid, so I
laid a pair of heavy beams on the ground, then
put boards across and laid the bag on them. Next
the boys helped me put more boards on top.
"Now," I said, "we need the heaviest weights we
have." Working together, we piled an anvil, some
lead, and a number of iron bars on top. Under
this enormous pressure, the sap began to seep
from the flour onto the ground.

My wife came over to watch. "Will this flour
keep, or will we have to spend all day tomorrow
baking?" she asked in skeptical tones.

"Once it's dry, and kept in barrels, it will
keep a long time," I said. "But it won't need to.
We'll use a lot of it; you'll see."

"Can we start, Father?" asked Fritz. "There's
no more poison coming out."

"Certainly," I said, "but we will begin with
just one cake and feed it to the monkey and the
hens. If that works, we'll set up a bakehouse."

We took the weights off, and I took out a couple of handfuls of flour, then stirred up the remainder so that we could press it some more. When we got the press working again, I took an iron plate and put it over the fire. Mixing the flour with water and a little salt, I kneaded it into a thick cake and put it on the plate. When it baked yellowish-brown, I turned it over.

The finished cake smelled delicious, and the boys rounded up two hens and Knips, who gobbled up their cake without hesitation. "If it's poisonous, what will happen to them?" Fritz asked. "Will they suffer?"

"I hope not, but I don't know. We can only hope we have squeezed it all out. But now," I continued, "dinner is ready. We know for sure that roast penguin and potatoes won't hurt us." Leaving the hens to peck at the remaining crumbs, we assembled for dinner. The potatoes were excellent; the penguin was tough and fishy, but less unpleasant than I expected. Filled with anticipation, we climbed up to say our prayers and get some sleep.

The next morning, everyone was very concerned about Knips and the hens, so Jack hurried down the ladder to check on them. He soon returned with the good news that all three were in perfect health. My wife milked the cow while the rest of us built a large fire. We kneaded the flour into cakes and put them on to bake. To imagine our anticipation, one need only look back at what we had eaten so far: various types of strange meat, whatever we could gather, and hard biscuits. Real, soft bread seemed like a dream.

There were mistakes, of course; some bread was burnt, some undercooked. But we soon had a pile of tempting cakes. We had a royal breakfast of cakes and fresh milk, in the highest of spirits at our success. When I went to feed the crumbs to the birds, I saw that the captive penguins were not struggling to escape, so I let them loose to wander as they wished.

Our rewards seemed to grow every day, provided we kept our hands at work—and our minds.

CHAPTER 8

The Pinnace

With our food situation improved, I began to consider what else we might get from the wreck. The boat was the most tempting, but my wife was very much against the idea. "Your being away all day is bad enough," she said. "But you'll all end up staying overnight on that wreck, and I'll be worried sick."

"Suppose I promise not to sleep on the wreck?" I offered. "I'm only trying to make our lives easier, including yours. There are items aboard that will be lost forever when the wreck breaks up."

"Which would probably happen when you were asleep on it. Very well, my husband: I'll accept your promise, but in God's name be careful."

Neither of us was entirely satisfied. But it was the best compromise I was likely to get, so I smiled and agreed. The boys were looking forward to the adventure and began packing in the highest of spirits.

We had an easy hike to Safety Bay. After feeding the geese and ducks in the swamp, we put on our swimming-belts and boarded the tub boat. With the raft in tow, we caught the current for the wreck.

Once aboard the vessel, I directed my sons to hunt and load useful items while I studied the crated boat. It was a typical small craft, called a "pinnace" by sailors, and would be very difficult to salvage. The crates and large parts were in good condition, but were stowed at the far end of the hold in a very narrow space. I was not sure we had the combined strength to move the heavier parts to a better work area. On top of that, we knew very little about boat building.

On the other hand, every part was marked with numbers to aid in assembly. That would compensate for our inexperience. I considered the matter while listening to the sounds of my sons rummaging about. I realized the greatest problem was having enough room to assemble the boat. I made my decision. "Room!" I cried. "That's what we need, my boys—room to work!"

They gathered round, radiating confidence. I was not as confident as they were but pushed on, saying, "Get axes, all of you, and let's break this compartment down."

After a day of chopping and hacking, we had

made little progress. This would take many days of work; the pinnace lay like a fossil embedded in a rock. We set sail for Tentholm tired and disappointed.

To our great surprise and pleasure, my wife and little Franz awaited us at Tentholm. "I decided to move here while you're working on the wreck. You won't have to walk so far, and I won't have to lose sight of you!" she said.

"You are a good, sensible, and kind wife," I exclaimed. "We will work even harder, so you can return to your dear Falconhurst as soon as possible."

"Come and see, Mother!" cried Fritz. The boys showed her two small barrels of butter, three of flour, bags of corn and rice, and many other supplies we had brought back. I saw from her delighted expression that our disagreement was mended.

For some days, we followed a routine. We started early each morning. After loading the boat and raft, we got to work on the pinnace. Once we had the area cleared around it, we began assembling it in place. At dusk we sailed for shore. At length our pinnace was complete— yet imprisoned behind massive wooden walls. Timbers built to survive deadly storms were surely too strong for us. I couldn't think of any way to free it, but we were so close! I was beginning to despair when I got an idea.

"Put some rollers under the pinnace, boys, then make a small fire to heat up the tar and finish caulking it. Be careful." In the meantime, and without explanation, I got a large cast-iron tub and filled it with gunpowder. I secured a block of oak to the top, then drilled a hole. With their help I placed the tub with the top against the timbers on the seaward side, then secured it with heavy chains. If I had planned correctly, my device would blow a big hole without damaging the pinnace.

My boys were just finishing up the caulking. I told them, "Enough for today. I'll put out the fire while you board the boat." I put out the fire. Then I lit a slow-burning fuse attached to the tub and hurried to join my sons in the boat. We sailed for Tentholm, my heart pounding the entire way.

Once ashore, we began unloading the supplies and beaching the raft. No one noticed my anxiety as I listened for the result of my work.

It came a few seconds later with a tremendous flash and *blam!* There was a fireball, then a great cloud of smoke, but no visible change in the wreck. My family turned first to look at the wreck, then to me, terror in their eyes. I said nothing. "Perhaps," said my wife, straining for calm, "you left something burning near the powder magazine."

"Probably so," I said quietly. "If I failed to put it out, it's my fault. I'd better investigate. Will anyone come?" The boys needed no urging and jumped into the boat. I told my wife not to worry, then jumped in and piloted us out to the wreck.

On the shore side of the wreck, where we usually boarded, there was no change. We rowed around and were treated to a marvelous sight: the side was blown completely open to daylight, with the water covered with floating wreckage. Better still, the little boat looked uninjured. The boys eyed the damage in glum confusion. I shouted in delight, "Hurrah! She's ours! Now we can sail the pinnace free!"

At first my boys looked at me as though I were mad. Then they guessed my secret. "You planned it all!" "What a clever father!" "That machine was a bomb!" They followed me eagerly through the gaping hole in the side, and to my great satisfaction the pinnace was untouched. My device had directed most of the blast away from it. As we marveled, I explained the engineering method by which I had aimed the explosion.

We rigged levers, pulleys, and a rope to the pinnace. With everything arranged, all hands hauled, and the lovely vessel slipped gently into the water. She floated without a single leak. Our painful, backbreaking toil had paid off.

We stayed just long enough to tie up our prize to the most sheltered part of the wreck, then sailed the tub boat back to Tentholm. We explained to my wife that one side of the ship was blown out, but that a few more days of work would gain us the rest of its useful treasures. We spent those days completing the pinnace's rigging, mounting her two little brass cannon, and getting her ready for sea. My boys acted as though we now had our own navy; they kept talking about pirates attacking, brave defenses, and final defeat of the invaders. "I'm sure you would win brilliant victories," I said, chuckling at their bravado, "but I'll thank God if your fighting skills and courage are never put to such a test."

Soon we had the pinnace ready for sea. The boys had kept the secret; my wife had no idea. We prepared to tow the raft and tub boat behind the pinnace. I took the helm and Fritz handled the sail. Ernest and Jack each manned a gun. As we entered the bay, I said, "Boys, you've done very well. Prepare to fire a salute!"

"Load guns!" commanded Fritz. The two younger boys rammed powder and shot into the weapons. *"Fire!"* Jack and Ernest yanked lanyards, both guns boomed, and the sound echoed across the bay and off the cliffs. We added our own shouts of triumph.

My wife and Franz disappeared from sight for a moment, then hurried to the landing place. We brought the pinnace as close as we could to shore, enjoying the astonishment on the shore party's faces. Fritz disembarked to help his mother aboard.

What a state she was in! "You dear, awful, wonderful people . . . do I scold you or praise you?" she exclaimed. "You scared me to death! First I see a beautiful little ship sailing in, with no idea who it might be...then it opens fire! If I hadn't heard you shouting, I'd have run off in the woods with Franz." She paused for breath. "But did you really do all this yourselves? This is charming! I would enjoy sailing in this myself."

"It was in the hold, dismantled. We put it together," I said, eyeing my three older sons with great pride.

"Wonderful! I'm proud of you all," she said. "Now come see how little Franz and I have spent our time."

We followed her up the river toward the waterfall. There we found a neat little garden. "We don't scare people by shooting off cannons to announce our work, but we do our best just the same. Those are lettuce, cabbages, beans, and peas. Think what delicious dinners we will have!"

"My dear wife!" I exclaimed. "You and Franz have done wonders! Was the work hard?"

"The ground is soft here," she replied. "I have planted potatoes and manioc; there is room for sugar canes and the fruit trees. I want you to find a way to irrigate them, maybe with hollow bamboos. I will plant melons as well. It's too hot for some of these vegetables, so I planted corn around them to give them shade. Do you think that'll work?"

"It's a great idea. I think we all deserve a nice dinner and rest," I said.

We spent the rest of the evening in happy discussion of our many new projects. "I like the pinnace," Jack said, "but I like it twice as much because Mother is pleased."

"Life is like that, my son," I explained. "Doing something for yourself can never bring as much happiness as a kindness done for someone else." Fritz smiled, and I rejoiced to see him grow in wisdom.

The next morning, my wife said, "Today, dear husband, we should return to Falconhurst and take care of the fruit trees. I have put water and earth on their roots, but could not get them planted, and they will wither. Can you resist the call of the sea today?"

"For a day, I certainly can," I smiled. "As soon as the pinnace is unloaded, I will go to Falconhurst and do as you ask." Glad for the change of a day on shore, the boys and I got to work, sheltering the new supplies in the tent and making sure the pinnace was securely anchored. We loaded up the sledge with supplies for Falconhurst set forth.

After the merciless heat of Tentholm and the wreck, the shade of Falconhurst was a cool delight. We had spent several Sundays on the coast, and it was now the Day of Rest once again. We observed it with hearty devotion and praise, but I did little preaching. Instead, I gave a Bible reading and a few simple instructions, and my wife led us in hymns. Then the boys were set at liberty.

In the evening, I said to my sons. "I want all of you to practice running, leaping, wrestling, and climbing. These will make you strong, active men."

The next day, the boys were eager to obey me; they competed in running, jumping, and lifting. I gave a new order: "Work on your archery, my boys, while I make you something." While they shot, I took a long cord and two large, round bullets. The soft lead was easy to drill, so I attached a bullet to each end of the cord.

When they saw what I had done, they stopped shooting and bombarded me with questions. "This is a bola," I said. "In Central and South America, many people hunt with these. Their bolas are much larger, and they use rocks in place of lead. A mounted hunter can either swing it like a club or throw it to entangle the legs of larger prey. A skilled man can bring down a horse in full gallop."

They were delighted. "Father, that's great!" "Will you try it now?" "There's the donkey, Father! Let's catch him!"

"He wouldn't like that, and he might panic and break a leg," I said with a smile. "I'd better practice on something else." Ernest pointed to a thin stump; I nodded and motioned everyone to stand clear. My first throw wrapped the lead weights around the target in a way that left no doubt, and every boy immediately wanted a bola for himself. Soon they were all practicing with their bolas. All did well, but Fritz seemed to do best.

That night the weather began to change. Early next morning I could feel the wind picking up, and from our high perch I could see the seas roughening. How fortunate that our new pinnace was safely moored in the harbor, that we need not sail for the next few days, and that we had gotten so many supplies while we could!

In the morning, as we prepared to plant the fruit trees, I said, "If we get done with the orchard today, what do you all say to a trip to Calabash Wood for utensils tomorrow?"

Everyone liked the idea, so we began work with great vigor. The walnut, cherry, and chestnut trees we arranged in parallel rows so as to form a shady avenue from Falconhurst to Familybridge. Between the rows of trees we cleared a road. We planted the vines around the arched roots of our great mangrove. We put the remaining trees in suitable spots, some near Falconhurst and others near Tentholm.

By early evening we had finished. All set to work preparing for tomorrow's trip, for even my wife and Franz were coming. It would be a grand family outing.

We arose at sunrise. I harnessed the sledge to the donkey, then mounted Franz on his back. Turk was out front, in his fine armor. Next came the three older boys with guns and game-bags. I led the donkey, and my wife walked beside me. Juno followed us, not too pleased, for Knips insisted on a ride.

After an easy trip through Flamingo Marsh, the beautiful country beyond unfolded before us. My wife and two of the boys marveled for they were seeing it for the first time. Suddenly Fritz and Jack turned aside into the bush. There was loud barking, then a gunshot, and a large bird fell heavily to the ground just after taking off. Rather than give up, it sprang to its feet and took off at great speed. The chase was on.

Fritz and Turk pursued, followed by Juno, who turned so quickly that Knips lost his perch. When they had the bird at bay, it tried to defend itself by kicking with its powerful legs. By the time I arrived, Juno had the bird by a wing and was struggling against it. I threw a cloth over its head and got it tied up. It was a large, magnificent bustard. We brought it back to our party in triumph.

"Ha!" exclaimed Jack. "It's the one we missed that day, Mother, remember? Got you this time, old fellow!"

"I think this is a hen bustard, the mother bird," said Ernest.

"Poor thing!" said my wife sympathetically. "Her chicks will be left unprotected and miserable. Shouldn't we let her go?"

"My dear, kindhearted wife," I answered, "that was weeks ago! By now those little birds are all grown up, and I suspect Mrs. Bustard has forgotten them. Besides, she's badly wounded. We should try to cure her. If we can, she will be a valuable addition to our flock." We resumed our march, and soon arrived at the Monkey Grove, where Fritz had adopted Knips—or rather, Knips adopted him.

While Fritz amused us all with his lively description of the event, Ernest was standing under a coconut palm. As he admired the cluster of nuts high above, he sighed, "I wish one would fall down!" A huge nut came plumping down at his feet. He sprang aside in alarm and down came another.

"Why, this is just like the fairy tale of the wishing cap!" cried Ernest. "My wish is granted!"

"I suspect that the fairy is trying to chase us away, not give us gifts," I said. "I'll bet there's a grouchy ape up there." We examined the nuts and found them unripe, so they couldn't have fallen by accident. Anxious to find out the reason, we all gathered round the tree and gazed up.

"I see it!" shouted Fritz. "It's flat, as big as a plate with horrid claws, and it's coming down!"

Little Franz slipped behind his mother. Ernest looked around to find a retreat route. Jack raised the butt of his gun. The creature's descent was slow enough for us to identify it as a large land crab. When it came in Jack's reach, he swung at it but only managed to knock it off the tree trunk. The crab lunged at Jack; he dodged, then took off running with the crab in hot pursuit.

Our roar of laughter soon shamed Jack into turning around. He took off his jacket. Then he charged the creature, wrapped his coat around it, and began to pound it with his fists.

After I stopped laughing I ran over and struck the jacket several times with the flat side of my hatchet. The movement stopped. We pulled out the dead land crab.

"What an ugly rascal!" cried Jack. "If he hadn't been so hideous, I wouldn't have been so rough. I wasn't afraid. What is it?"

"There are many kinds of land crabs," I said. "I think this is a coconut crab, for it climbs these trees to get at the nuts. You were smart to wrap it up, Jack, because some large crabs are swift runners and fight fiercely. Let's take it, as well as the coconuts, and be on our way."

We soon reached Calabash Wood and got busy cutting, carving and hollowing dishes, bowls, cups, jars, and platters.

After some time, Fritz and Jack began to make a fireplace, hoping to cook the crab in a hollow gourd. Their mother attended to the hungry animals, releasing the donkey to graze and giving the poor hungry monkey some coconut milk. The wounded bustard was suffering, so she doctored its injury and tied it to a tree so it could move about a little.

The cooking operations halted with the realization that we were out of water. The boys proposed to find a spring. This seemed a safe place to leave my wife and Franz alone for a time, so I agreed.

Ernest took the lead. Not far from Calabash

Wood, he turned around in terror and shouted, "A huge wild boar! Father, come quickly!"

Sure enough, I heard a loud snorting and puffing as some large animal scrambled through the thick brush. "After him, lads! Call the dogs! Get ready to fire!" I ordered.

We pressed on to the spot where Ernest had seen the animal. The ground was dug up, and some potatoes lay about; we had disturbed the boar's lunch. Ernest and Jack were more interested in gathering the potatoes than chasing the quarry, so Fritz and I gave chase with the dogs out front.

Soon from up ahead we heard barking, snarling, and grunting. When we reached the scene, each mastiff had hold of a large pig ear. Oddly, instead of preparing for a last stand, the pig seemed to ask us for salvation. It was no wild boar, but our runaway sow!

Initial anger gave way to a gale of laughter at the absurd situation. We called off the dogs to free the old lady from her predicament.

Our laughter brought Ernest and Jack. "Much use you two would have been, if we needed help," cried Fritz.

"Ah, well," answered Jack, "we kind of suspected it was the old sow. And just look at these fine potatoes!" There was much good-natured kidding all around.

Ernest soon interrupted us. "See these fruits

she's eating," he said, pointing to apple-like fruits on the surrounding bushes and the ground near them. The sow was gorging herself on them.

"What if they're poison?" asked Fritz.

I examined one. "They're probably safe," I said, "but we'll know for sure if Knips eats them. But let's press on."

Jack took the lead, heading for a high rock protruding from the thickets. Soon he cried out, "Father! A crocodile!"

I chuckled. "Nonsense, boy! Crocodiles live in water, not dry forests!" When I caught up with him, I saw that he wasn't far mistaken. Perched on a low branch was a great iguana, one of the largest of all lizards, fast asleep.

"Don't worry, Jack," I explained. "It's harmless even when awake. But I've read that its flesh is tasty, so let's take it." At this point Fritz arrived and raised his gun, but I pushed it gently down. "You'd probably only wound it, and then it would escape," I said.

I took some cord and made a noose, then attached it to a strong stick. Then I took a light branch in the other hand. I crept slowly toward the sleeping creature, whistling a little tune. The iguana woke up and seemed to listen, craning its head to guess where the music came from. Once in arm's reach, I kept whistling and began to pet and tickle him with the branch. When the creature seemed lulled, I put the noose over its head and pulled. My goal was to knock it on the head with my hatchet, but the heavily armored creature was too quick for me and lashed out with its tail. Jack had come too close, and the impact knocked him over.

At the same time the iguana revealed a row of sharp teeth. The boys were frightened and wanted to beat him with sticks. "No," I said. "Fritz, hit him on the head with the flat of my hatchet." He did so, and we had our prize. The boys were impressed with my strategy, for they had never heard of such a method.

Fritz picked the iguana up and grunted. "It's very heavy, Father," he said.

"Even so," I said, "we don't kill things and leave them lay. It was my idea to kill it, so I'll carry it." With considerable effort I put the iguana over my shoulders, and we set forth to rejoin the others.

As we neared the Calabash Wood, we could hear mother and child calling out for us. We had been away a long time. We shouted joyously in reply, and they were relieved to see us—though not so relieved at the look of the creature on my shoulders.

By this time, we were all quite hungry. Since we had found no water to use for cooking the crab, we canceled our cooking plans and instead ate what we'd brought from Falconhurst. As we ate, we shared our adventures.

By the time we finished, it was getting late, so we decided to leave the sledge. We could return for it tomorrow. We put the iguana and the bustard on the donkey; tired little Franz would have to walk. Our road home lay through a majestic oak forest laden with hundreds of acorns, and we slowed to gather some.

We arrived safely at Falconhurst just before nightfall, exhausted and hungry. We dined on broiled iguana with potatoes and roast acorns— an odd feast, but no odder than our situation. It had been quite an exciting day!

CHAPTER 9

A Growing Menagerie

*T*he next day Fritz and I went alone to get our sledge back from Calabash Wood, and with it all the utensils we'd made. As part of this trip, I wanted to explore the chain of cliffs and rocky hills that cut our coastal plain off from whatever lay beyond them. I wanted to know if there was a passage through this barrier. If there were, we would someday be able to explore the unknown region beyond. If not, we were hemmed in by the cliffs on one side and the ocean on the other.

The sledge was quite safe where we had left it. I was pleased that we had made good time. This meant we could search for a way through the cliffs and hills—the key to discovering what lay inland. We advanced through meadows of manioc and potatoes and many unknown plants. The view all around us was open and pleasant.

We came upon some bushes with small, waxy

white berries. "Fritz, I think these are wax myrtles. If so, we might be able to melt the wax out of the berries to make candles." The wax wouldn't be perfect, but it would burn cleanly and smell pleasant. We filled a large canvas bag with berries, then pressed on.

Very soon we met with another natural curiosity: a large cluster of birds' nests in a tree, so close together they were like one huge nest. In and out of holes darted hundreds of grosbeaks: medium-sized birds, brown, chattery, easy to identify from their distinctive, short, thick beaks. A few beautiful little parrots also flew in and out.

Fritz wished to try to catch a young bird. I agreed, for he was an excellent climber. I also felt that a pet bird would help him learn to be more humane, for captive birds will not stand any rough treatment at all. The birds evidently did not agree on the value of his idea, for every time he put his hand into a hole he pulled it back with a sharp beak-nip. Finally he reached in and caught the shrieking bird. He slipped it into his pocket and buttoned the flap. He climbed down as fast as he could to escape the dozens of birds diving on him, pecking and shrieking.

When he reached ground, the protest ended and he examined his capture, a bright green parrot. "I want to tame him and teach him to talk, Father," he said.

"All right, Son, but for now best keep him in

your pocket. You already learned how sharp that beak is."

We continued on our way until we reached a grove of tall, broad-leafed trees bearing figlike fruit. We tried this, but found it sour and bitter. As Fritz spat his out, he saw some gummy resin seeping from the bark. "Remember how we collected sap from cherry trees back home, Father, and molded it into shapes?" asked he, scraping some off. He tried to knead it, but it sprang back to its original size. He tried to stretch it; same result. "Look, Father!" he exclaimed. "Could this be India rubber?"

"Let me see! That would be valuable indeed . . . and I think you're exactly right!"

"How could we use it, Father?" he asked. "I've only seen it used to erase pencil marks."

"We would need to tap the trees with a machete. When the rubber is fresh, it will flow thickly. It can be molded into different shapes. Once it hardens, it keeps that shape. Wouldn't it be nice to have rubber boots and shoes?" I asked.

"Yes!" he exclaimed as we continued on. Soon we reached the coconut wood, with the bay beyond leading to Cape Disappointment. Among the coconuts were a few smaller palms, one of which was broken by wind. Its inner core was a soft, creamy pith full of fat worms. I knew of one such tree: the sago palm, which is often infested with the sago beetle. These were the larvae of the beetles. "In the West Indies these are considered a delicacy. Shall we try some?"

"Eat worms? If you say so, Father," answered Fritz uncertainly. I made a roasting spit and impaled half a dozen, then salted them, and built a little fire. We also put some potatoes on to cook. Soon a rich fat began to drip from the worms, and they smelled so good that it was easy to forget what they were. When the potatoes were done, I boldly put a worm on one, then took a bite and swallowed. It was delicious. Fritz did the same. The larvae made a fine addition to our plain meal.

When we got moving again, we found our way blocked by a dense thicket. We turned aside and headed for the canebrake near Cape Disappointment. We had not been able to explore as much new ground as I had hoped; and we had found no passage through the cliffs. But we did cut a fine bunch of sugar canes. In time we reached the sledge in Calabash Wood, where we transferred all loads to the sledge and hitched it to our patient donkey.

We had no further adventures on the way back to Falconhurst and its joyful welcome. We shared our discoveries over a fine dinner. The boys were interested in the parakeet, but they were especially eager to make candles. With dinner done, we climbed up to our tree house and pulled in the ladder.

The next day, all the boys bounced out of bed talking of nothing but candles. This kept on through breakfast, and I couldn't bear to dampen their enthusiasm. "So be it," I said, though in private I was unsure of success. Keeping my doubts to myself, I had the boys put a pot of berries on the fire. A green, sweet-smelling wax began to separate from the berry juice, so we ladled it off into a separate pot next to the fire.

When we had enough, we mixed some lard into the hot wax. My wife had prepared some wicks of thick string, which we dipped one after another into the wax to make two candles per wick. Fritz hung them on a bush to cool, and we repeated the operation until we had a number of candles about thumb-thickness. That evening we sat up by candlelight for three full hours after sunset, enjoying the novelty of Falconhurst bathed in brilliant light after dark.

We were all delighted with the success. "Your cleverness makes me wonder," said my wife, "if you could find a way to make butter. Every day I have to throw away a lot of good cream. Can you come up with a plan?"

"I think maybe I can," I replied after a little pondering, "though I can't take credit for the method; that comes from the people of southern Africa. Jack, bring me one of our gourd bottles." He did. I filled it partway with cream and then corked the hole tightly. "Now, get a sail, and you four roll the gourd around for half an hour or so while I build us a cart." They obeyed, and half an hour later I looked up from my work and told them to take the gourd to their mother.

My good wife's eyes were delighted to see a large lump of fresh butter. "How will you get it all out?" asked Jack.

"Heat the gourd in hot water and melt it, of course," said Ernest. In the meantime, Fritz and I finished the cart, which turned out to be a clumsy vehicle but strong enough for our needs. At harvest time it would be of immense value.

My thoughts now went to making Tentholm more secure. I wanted to fortify it with a thick hedge that would stop any wild animal and even discourage potential human attackers. We began to spend our days transplanting thorny bushes and small trees. When that was done, I turned to the soft spot in Tentholm's defenses: Family-bridge. We brought two cannon from the wreck and mounted them on small hills nearby. With them we might hold off any enemy—animal or human.

This took six weeks of hard work, with each Sunday's rest a welcome opportunity to thank God for our continued health and safety. I could see the boys growing stronger, and I kept encouraging them to run, leap, climb, and swim. Unfortunately, what built their muscles destroyed their clothes. They looked like beggars, and all my wife's patching could only delay the inevitable. Soon they would have nothing to wear.

It was time to visit the wreck, both to get more clothing and to see how long the ship would last. Three of the boys and I went off in the pinnace, towing the tub boat and raft.

Not much had changed aboard the old ship. "Clean her out, boys," I cried. "Get everything of value!"

Soon there was a great heap of valuables on deck: sailors' chests, bales of cloth and linen, a couple of small guns, ammunition, tables, benches, window shutters, bolts and locks, barrels of pitch. Several trips later nothing was left. "One more trip," I said to my wife before we started again, "and it'll be the last of the old ship. Time to blow her up."

"Good riddance," she said. "Then you can never visit her again." Elizabeth was smiling, but a part of her tone was not. As we caught the outbound current, I thought to myself that I'd been very slow to realize how much she hated our salvage trips. I resolved to be a more perceptive husband.

I had left two barrels of powder aboard the wreck. We placed these, lit a slow fuse, and returned to shore to have dinner outside the tent. Shortly after dark, a vivid pillar of fire rose from the black waters followed a fraction of a second later by a sullen *boom!* Our good old ship was no more. Though we knew it was for the best, we were all a bit sad.

What we found the next morning chased away all sadness. The shore was lined with a rich supply of planks, beams, and boards. As we collected these, no small task, my wife came over to announce that two ducks and a goose had each raised families among the reeds by the river. Soon they all appeared, waddling past with the tiny ones trailing, happy as could be. Ernest said, "We'll be able to have duck and green peas for dinner some day soon, just like back home!" He spoke for us all.

The sight of these birds reminded me of our others at Falconhurst. "I had better check on our other flock," I said, and we all went together. On the way I noticed that several of our young trees were considerably bent by the wind. "Tomorrow we'll get bamboos to make supports for them," I announced. "We'll have to go toward Cape Disappointment."

As only Fritz and I had seen that country, everyone else wanted to come. The next morning we hitched the cart to the cow and donkey, and we loaded it with all the necessaries for a long expedition: tent, food, ammunition, tools, and utensils. It was a lovely morning to show my family the grosbeak nest-cluster and the wax myrtles.

When we had gathered a couple sacks of berries, we stored them in the bushes, marking the spot to pick them up on our return.

"Now for the rubber trees, for waterproof boots," I said, looking at Ernest. We arrived, and I showed everyone how to tap the trees and collect the thick sap. This done, we moved through the palm grove and reached a delightful plain: sugar canes on one side, bamboos and palms on the other, the shining sea ahead of us.

"How beautiful!" exclaimed Jack. "Let's move here!"

"We would enjoy it very much," I replied, "until a big tiger came out of those woods and pounced on us at night. No, thank you. I much prefer our nest in the tree, or our strong position at Tentholm. For now, though, we camp here. Boys, pitch the tent."

While they obeyed, I unyoked our animals and built a fire. My wife started dinner while the rest of us split up to cut bamboos and collect sugar cane. When we finished, dinner wasn't quite ready, and the boys were hungry, so they decided to get some coconuts. This time they got no help from either monkeys or land crabs. The boys gazed longingly up into the trees.

"We can climb," said Fritz. Jack and he each rushed at one of the smooth, slippery trunks, but neither got even a quarter of the way up before slipping to the ground.

"Here, you young athletes," cried I, holding up some sharkskin leggings I had made earlier. These I tied onto their calves, then put a short loop of rope around each boy and his tree. With the rough sharkskin for traction, and the ropes to help them hold their positions, both boys quickly reached the treetops. My wife and I watched while they climbed tree after tree, throwing down the best coconuts. Ernest lounged on the grass, gazing up at the palms.

When they returned, they needled Ernest about being lazy. He sprang up. "Here, I'll provide you something," he said, putting on a pair of leggings. "Now please give me a coconut shell," he added. I did so, and he pocketed it and ran to a tree. With surprising agility, he soon reached the top. As he did, Fritz and Jack burst into a roar of laughter. Ernest had climbed a tree that had no coconuts.

Their brother drew his knife and sliced off the leafy crest. As it fell, I glanced up at him, surprised at such a display of temper. He smiled down and shouted merrily, "Jack, pick that palm cabbage up and take it to Father. It's only half of my contribution, but it's worth all your coconuts put together." He made no move to descend. I saw him doing something else with his knife, but could not tell what.

He was right. The rare palm cabbage is highly prized in South America for the flavor and nutrition of its leaves. "Bravo!" I cried. "You've made your point. Now come down and we'll thank you. What are you waiting for?"

"The second half of my contribution," he replied. "I hope it will be as popular as the first." He stayed in the tree for a short time, then slipped down and presented his mother with the coconut shell. "Here, Mother," he said, "will you please try my wine?" The shell was filled with a clear, rosy beverage, bright and sparkling.

My wife tasted it. "Excellent," she exclaimed. "To your health, my dear boy!" We all had a taste, and Ernest got hearty thanks all around.

Dinner was ready at dusk. While we ate, the donkey set up a loud braying, then pricked up his ears and galloped off into the bamboos for no apparent reason. We gave chase and sent the dogs, but they returned without him. It soon grew too dark to continue the pursuit. What an unpleasant end to our day! Perhaps the near approach of some fierce beast had set off his instincts. I didn't speculate aloud, but I made a very large fire and had my sons sleep with loaded weapons by their sides.

We awoke early to greet a bright morning. I rose and looked out, thinking that perhaps our poor donkey might have been attracted by the fire-light. But there was no sign of him. We could not afford to lose him, and I determined to track him down if possible. After a quick breakfast, I left my older sons to guard their mother and little brother, and told Jack to get ready for the march. We took to the trail with the dogs out front.

For an hour or more we followed the donkey's hoof prints, often losing and rediscovering the trail. When we came to a great mish-mash of hoof prints, I nearly despaired. It seemed he had joined a herd of some larger animals, and we might never see him again.

Jack urged me to continue the search. "If we get up a hill," he explained, "we may spot the herd. Let's go on, Father."

"Very well, Son," I consented. "We must find him." At length we reached the edge of a wide plain, with a herd of grazing animals in the distance. Perhaps the donkey had joined them. I decided we should detour through a bamboo marsh, to get as close as possible without stampeding the animals.

The bamboos were huge, many over thirty feet tall and a foot thick at the base. As we passed through them, I told Jack about the giant bamboos of South America, which the Indians use intact as masts for canoes or cut up to make small barrels. "Maybe we should take one home," he suggested.

When we reached the grassy meadow, we found ourselves face to face with a herd of buffalo. They looked up at us in curiosity, but didn't move. Jack would have fired, but I stopped him. "Back to the swamp," I said, "and hold back the dogs!"

We began to retreat, but before we were back in cover the dogs joined us. In spite of our shouts and efforts at restraint, they dashed forward and seized a big bull buffalo-calf. The whole herd began to bellow and paw the ground, and then a huge bull led the charge. With no time to take cover, I drew a pistol and fired point-blank at the leader. He fell dead at my feet, and the rest halted. Those nearby snuffed the air, then turned tail and galloped across the plain.

The dogs were still tussling with the calf, but could not bring the husky young buffalo down. I could think of no way to help them without shooting it, and I preferred not to do that, for a tame buffalo calf might grow up into a fine pack animal.

I was about to reload my pistol when clever little Jack came up with a plan. He had brought his bola and some rope. Coming very near the struggle, he threw the bola and made a square hit on the calf's hind legs. His target went down struggling. While I called off the dogs, Jack tied his rope around the legs for a more secure capture. We tied the end to a strong bamboo, and the animal was at our mercy. It was a fine, unhurt calf about the size of Turk.

"Now what do we do with him?" asked Jack,

watching the poor beast panting on the ground.

"I'll show you," I said. "First help me tie his forelegs." With the young bull immobile, I had Jack hold his head while I carefully pierced his nose-cartilage. I felt badly at this but had no other option. I was pleased when the small flow of blood quickly slowed to a trickle. I then passed a strong cord through the hole and tied it into a short loop. We freed the young bull and let him up. He was subdued and followed us with no resistance.

I now turned to the dead buffalo. I had slain him in self-defense, but disliked leaving him behind. I had no time to skin him, nor could Jack and I carry all the meat. Our new, untrained captive might not be so calm with part of one of his former herdmates loaded on his back, so I contented myself with cutting off the tongue and a couple of steaks. I packed these in salt, then let the dogs have the rest. They fell upon it greedily, and we had a restful meal in the shade after our hard work.

It was time to turn back for camp. On our way through the tall bamboos, we cut down one of the shorter ones. The thicker sections would make fine containers, while those near the top could be used as candlemolds. The buffalo's manner was passive enough that I thought we might get him to drag the bamboo and carry some of our burdens. This worked, and we pressed on, for Jack was eager to show off his capture.

As we crossed a rocky stream, Juno dashed ahead toward a small cave. She was about to run in when a huge, snarling jackal sprang out. Turk immediately joined her in the assault. The jackal fought back with great ferocity, but against the two dogs together its struggle was doomed.

I examined the jackal: a female. "Jack, I'm guessing that her pups are close by, perhaps just inside that little cave."

"I should climb in and get them!" suggested my son.

"Be careful," I cautioned. "If the male jackal is in there, we could be in big trouble."

We peered into the darkness until Jack was certain it contained only a litter of little yellow jackal pups. He then crept in, followed closely by the dogs, and presently emerged carrying a handsome yellow puppy about the size of a small cat. "This was the only survivor," he explained. "Turk and Juno got to them first." I wasn't very sorry, because if Jack had saved them all, he would probably have wanted to raise them all. One jackal, along with our young bull, was quite enough to add to our menagerie.

By the time we reached camp, and our family's anxious welcome, it had gotten quite late. The children were delighted at the new animals, though they were all sorry we had lost our poor donkey. Jack was the center of attention, and told the story of our captures with such exaggerated boasting that I felt I must step in and give a more factual account. By the time I finished, dinner was ready. Jack and I enjoyed hearing about the camp party's work of the day.

Ernest had discovered a sago palm that we could use to make starch. That would be handy for our cooking and our clothmaking. With much hard work he had cut the tree down. Franz and his mother had collected a fine heap of firewood. Fritz had hunted a good bag of game. While they had all been busy, a troop of apes had apparently ransacked the camp: the food was eaten or thrown about, the milk drunk or spilled, boxes opened, pots and pans dumped over. Everyone had gotten to work immediately putting camp back in order. "You all did wonderfully," I said. "Neither Jack or I would have known if you hadn't told us."

After camp had been put back in order, Fritz had gone down to the shore. Wandering among the rocks at Cape Disappointment, he had found a young eaglet, identified by Ernest as a Malabar eagle. He had put a hood over the bird's head to keep it calm. "Maybe you could take up falconry, Fritz," I suggested. "If you train him well, he may learn to hunt for us." Everyone was delighted, but it was time for a word of warning. "Boys, listen to me. You are collecting a lot of pets. It is not your mother's job to take care of them; each of you must care for his own animals. If I find one neglected—beast or bird—I will free it on the spot. Remember that!"

My wife looked greatly relieved, and the boys promised to obey. Before we retired for the night I smoked the buffalo-meat by throwing a lot of green wood onto the fire. When it was thoroughly dry, we secured all the animals, Jack took his little pet in his arms, and we lay down for rest.

At daybreak we made ready to return to Falconhurst. We loaded everything on the cart. As the sun cleared the horizon, we set out.

I thought it unfair to the cow to make her haul so much, and with some persuasion managed to get the young buffalo in harness. His strength moved the cart along easily, but we had to take the clearest possible route and could not visit the wax myrtle and rubber trees. I sent Ernest and Jack aside to bring back the sacks we'd left.

They had not been gone long when I was alarmed by a terrible animal noise accompanied by the furious barking of the dogs and shouts from Jack and Ernest. My first thought was that some wild beast had attacked, and I ran to the rescue.

I arrived to quite a scene. My boys were

dancing and shouting around a grassy glade, and I too was delighted when I saw why: there lay our old sow with a promising litter of piglets. At first she had squealed and snorted defiance but was now giving comfortable grunts of recognition. I went back to the cart to get biscuits and potatoes for the happy mother while Ernest and Jack collected the rubber and candleberries. The sow declined to come, so we returned to Falconhurst without her.

The animals were delighted at our return. They looked less eager to see the new pets, especially the eaglet—a predator of the first rank. Fritz, determined to control his pet, chained him by the leg to a tree root and removed the hood. That was a mistake. The bird's savage nature returned with his sight, and he took off the full length of his chain. Before anyone could stop him, he seized the unfortunate parrot and tore it apart. Fritz's anger rose, and he was about to kill the eaglet.

"Stop," Ernest said, "don't kill the poor creature. He's just being an eagle. Give him to me, and I'll tame him."

Fritz hesitated, then calmed down. "No, no," he said, "I don't want really to kill him, but I can't give him up. If you can teach me how to tame him, I will give you Knips."

"Very well," replied Ernest. "If my plan works, I accept. Take a pipe and tobacco, and blow the smoke around his head. It will make him sleepy, and he won't give you any more trouble."

Fritz looked ready to ridicule this plan, but Ernest rarely suggested anything without a good reason. I loaned him a pipe, and he was soon inexpertly puffing away near the struggling eaglet. As each cloud circled round the eagle's head he became quieter, and soon he sat still.

"Excellent!" cried Fritz as he hooded the bird. "Ernest, Knips is yours."

CHAPTER 10

Changing Seasons

The next morning the boys and I got to work in the orchard. Some young trees were leaning badly and some were blown completely down. We drove a bamboo into the soil on either side of each tree. Then we lashed the tree to the bamboo poles with strong fibers. We were just in time to save many of the trees.

While we worked, Franz asked, "Papa, are these wild or tame trees?"

"Oh, these are wild trees, ferocious trees," laughed Jack, "that's why we have to tie them up. When they're tame, we'll put rings through their noses, like the buffalo, and they'll trot after us and give us fruit wherever we go."

"That's not true," replied Franz gravely, as he handed me some lashing fibers, "but there *are* wild and tame trees. Wild ones grow in the woods and tame ones in the garden, like the pears and peaches at home. Which are these, Papa?"

"They aren't wild," I replied. "These trees have been grafted." Franz looked puzzled. "Grafting is when you make a twig from one tree grow on another. The resulting branch will produce the fruit of its original tree."

"But where," asked Ernest, "did the twigs of good fruit come from?"

"From foreign countries," I replied. "In warm climates, the best fruit trees grow naturally. Not a single fruit tree is native to Switzerland: they were all imported, then grafted onto native trees that could handle the cold."

"Do you think all these trees will grow?" asked Fritz, as we worked our way toward Tentholm.

"I have no doubt," I replied. "We have pines, olives, figs, peaches, apricots, plums, and pears. These all come from countries with gentle climates and will do well here."

We talked and worked until every tree was strengthened. With immense appetites, we returned to Falconhurst. We ate the corned beef and palm cabbage so hungrily that I think we alarmed Elizabeth a bit. As we rested, we spoke of new projects.

"I wish," said my wife, "we had a better way to climb our tree. The ladder is the only thing about it I don't like. Could you make a flight of steps?"

I carefully thought this over, then said, "It would be impossible to make stairs outside. If the trunk is hollow, as I've often suspected, we could build them inside. Didn't someone say they saw bees coming from a hole in our tree?"

"Oh, yes," said little Franz, "I went to see. One stung me in the face, and I almost cried, but I didn't."

"Brave little boy," I said. "If the trunk is hollow enough to hold a swarm of bees, perhaps it's hollow most of its length."

Jack, practical as usual, sprang to his feet to investigate. Soon all four boys were climbing about, peeking into the hole, and tapping the wood to see how far down it was hollow. They had forgotten the bees who came out in a furious, stinging swarm. My sons retreated with yells of pain.

Once we drove off the angry bees, my wife and I began to tend the stings. Jack had the most; his face was grossly swollen. The others were hurting, but less so. It took about an hour's application of cold earth to relieve everyone's pain.

When they felt better, they wanted an organized assault on the bees—but I had other plans. I began by modifying a large calabash gourd in hopes the bees would occupy it as a new hive. By nightfall, the bees had calmed down and returned to their hive in the tree trunk. Once they were settled, Fritz helped me stop up every hole in the tree with wet clay. Then we went to bed.

Very early the next morning I took a hollow bamboo and pushed it through the clay, keeping it covered until I had lit a pipeful of tobacco. I blew all the smoke down the hole, fast as I could. When I finished I covered the hole while Fritz refilled the pipe. I could feel the cane vibrating as the bees buzzed in great confusion, then blew in the second pipeful. Soon the buzzing died down to a murmur; the bees were calm.

"Now then, Fritz," I said, "quick get a hammer and chisel and stand here beside me. Ernest, bring me a small barrel." They complied, and Fritz and I began to cut a small door beside the hole, leaving it attached by a small bit of wood rather than knocking it out. After blowing in one final cloud of smoke, I had Fritz give one more stroke with the chisel, and the door came loose. Carefully but rapidly we removed the insects, clinging in clusters to the inside, and placed them in their new hive. I then took every bit of wax and honey from their storehouse and put it in the barrel. To keep the bees from returning, I nailed a board over the hole and stood clear.

When the bees woke up, they left their new hive and headed for their old home. Unable to enter, they flew back and forth between tree and hive in much confusion. At length, they surrendered and began to make the new hive into a home. By evening they were quiet enough that we dared open the barrel. We poured off the honey, storing it in jars and pots, then threw the rest into a pot of water over a slow fire. When it softened, we put it into a clean canvas bag and pressed out the remaining honey. What remained in the bag was beeswax—excellent for candles.

The next day we began the long, hard job of step building. We had salvaged a door from the captain's cabin, hinges intact, which we placed against the tree to draw its outline. After much chiseling and chopping, we were ready to hang the door. Clearing the rotten wood from the middle took days. When we could stand inside the tree trunk and look upward at a circle of blue sky, it was time to build steps.

With much effort, we brought one of the ship's spare masts. It wouldn't fit through the door due to the angle, so we harnessed the buffalo. Jack and Fritz climbed high into the tree, set up the pulley, and ran a rope through. With the buffalo's help, we swayed the mast high into the tree and lowered it into the hollowed-out trunk. We planted it at the base like an immense fence-post, then began to cut notches in it and the side of the trunk. Into each notch we nailed a carefully cut board. Step by step, our spiral stairway took shape.

As we built upward, we cut windows in the trunk to let in light and air. On each side we built a handrail, to make the stairs easier and safer. A month later we were very proud of our work, even before we basked in my wife's delighted gratitude.

During this time, of course, we did our other work. We had animals to care for, including many newborns: the goats, sheep, and Juno had all borne young. The lambs and kids had to be kept from straying, but we were less strict with the puppies. The children wanted to keep them all, of course, but I couldn't agree to more than two. The rest soon vanished without a trace. "To console Juno," Jack said, "I'll give her Fangs," for so my son had named his pet. I suspected he really wanted to save himself work, but in any case, to Jack's great satisfaction she readily adopted the little jackal.

The other pets also did well. The buffalo gave us some trouble at first, but I soon trained him to do the donkey's work. The boys wanted to ride him, but this would take patience. In place of a bit and reins, I slipped a bar through the now-healed hole in his nose. "When he gets used to it, you can steer him, provided you're gentle," I told the boys. "If you're rough, it will hurt him. That would be very wrong and extremely dangerous." To accustom the buffalo to a rider, I sat Knips on his back and got him to hold the bar. Fritz went first, and when he mastered buffalo riding he taught his brothers.

Fritz also trained and cared for his eagle, hunting small birds each day to feed him. The eagle learned to pounce on living prey. My clever son taught the bird voice commands and whistles, and soon the eagle was allowed to bring down small birds in flight. We didn't want a tragedy, so we kept him well away from the domesticated birds.

Ernest decided to train Knips—and none too soon, for the monkey was rapidly growing up. With Jack's help Ernest wove a little basket with straps, slinging it on the monkey's back. Taking a pack on his own back, Ernest then took Knips climbing coconut and fruit trees, showing his imitative pet how to put the produce in the basket. This worked, though Knips also stuffed himself at every opportunity. Ernest wisely did not try to discourage this. I was pleased to see him treat his pet so fairly and sensibly.

Jack had a harder time with Fangs. Nothing could persuade the jackal not to eat his kills at once. By the time poor Jack arrived, little usually remained but a tattered skin. Here Jack's stubborn streak showed as a virtue. He vowed to succeed at training his pet, and armed with that determination, I felt he would succeed.

I turned shoemaker, for I had promised myself a pair of waterproof boots. I filled a pair of

socks with sand, then coated them with a thin layer of clay. When this hardened, I brushed on layer after layer of raw rubber, heat-curing it between applications. When I felt they were thick enough, I nailed some buffalo-hide to the soles, and brushed rubber over it. After some final heat curing, I broke out the clay and sand, leaving a pair of comfortable, durable, waterproof boots. Orders poured in from all sides, and soon everyone had a pair.

Next, I decided to address Falconhurst's water problem. With no nearby spring, the boys had to haul water from the stream every day. If we could pipe it in, it would save them a lot of hard work. We began by building a dam far enough upstream that the water would flow downhill to Falconhurst. Joining bamboos with nails and rubber, we ran a pipe to the turtle-shell basin, where the extra water flowed off through Fritz's harpoon hole. We celebrated this great convenience by washing a whole sack of potatoes in the basin, much to everyone's satisfaction.

Such tasks gave us recreation and variety during the long, difficult job of stair building. We had no time to loaf, and we were near each other and our animals. I remember the time most fondly.

One morning, as we were completing our spiral staircase, a terrific noise from the forest alarmed us. It sounded like the roaring or bellowing of a wild beast. "We'll see what's making this sound," I said. "Into the tree house, everyone. Load the guns, boys, while I secure the door." I armed the dogs with their collars and sent them out to protect the other animals. Then I closed the door and joined my family. Every eye was on watch, guns ready.

The sound drew nearer. Then all was still. We

saw nothing. After some time, I decided to investigate. Fritz and I descended the stairs, slipped out the door, and crept in the direction we had last heard the sound.

Not far into the woods, we heard it again very close by. Fritz raised his gun but lowered it immediately in a hearty fit of laughter.

Now there was no mistaking the *hee-haw, hee-haw, hee-haw* resounding through the forest. It was our donkey, merrily braying at full throat—and with company. His companion was another donkey, but slimmer and more graceful looking. "Fritz," I whispered, "hurry back to Falconhurst and bring me a rope—quietly now!"

Fritz had the foresight to bring oats and salt along with the rope. "Well done," I said, as we tied one end of the rope to a tree. We made a running noose at the other end, then silently watched the animals browse for a time. When they moved closer, Fritz rose, the noose in one hand and the oats and salt in the other. He kept his movements slow and smooth.

Our donkey advanced toward the treat and was soon munching contentedly. The wild donkey hung back at first. But when her companion came to no harm, she too approached. She sniffed and prepared to take some of the tempting food.

Suddenly Fritz slipped the noose over her neck. She leaped backward in alarm. The noose drew tight; she fell kicking to the ground. I hurried to loosen the rope and replace it with a halter, then left her to calm down.

Everyone hastened out to examine the beautiful animal, who got up kicking and snorting, giving us all fiery glances. I explained, "This is an onager, a type of wild donkey. She may be hard to tame, but what a prize if we could!"

The onager eventually wore herself out and stood quivering. I approached, and she allowed me to lead her to the roots of our tree, which served as our stables. There I tied her up close to the donkey, which my alert Fritz had already secured without resistance.

The next morning the onager proved as wild as ever. Kindness did nothing to tame her proud spirit, nor did hunger. Even with her feet shackled, she would not let me on her back. It was time for a last resort. "American Indians do this," I told my family. "It seems harsh, but it works." I stood near the onager until the right moment, then leaped on her back and took her long ear in my mouth, biting it.

The result was amazing. She stopped bucking and plunging. From that moment we were her masters. The children all rode her, and she carried them with quiet obedience. I was very proud. Here was an animal that naturalists said could not be tamed, yet thanks to the wisdom of the American Indian, I watched my youngest son lead her about the camp. Fritz named her Lightfoot, much to everyone's approval.

Our chickens, my wife's pride and delight, had increased to forty. "Don't forget, my husband, that all our animals will need shelter when the rains come," she reminded me.

"Indeed," I replied. "We will start immediately." My sons and I first went to collect a great deal of bamboo. The arching roots of our tree provided an excellent framework, and over them we laid carefully cut bamboos as close together as possible, with nails and vines to secure them. When the area beneath the tree was completely roofed, we covered the entire structure with moss and clay, then coated it with tar. When the tar hardened, we had a fine balcony, so I built a light rail around it. We then divided the area below the tree into compartments: stables, chicken coop, fodder storage, kitchen, pantry, and dining room.

Our winter quarters would need a large food supply. Day after day we worked, bringing in all the provisions we could gather. As we were returning one day with a load of potatoes, I decided we should get a supply of acorns. I kept a large canvas bag and sent Jack and Franz home. Fritz rode the onager; Knips rode Ernest. Our party detoured toward the Acorn Wood, as we had named it.

We reached the spot, tied Lightfoot to a tree, and began filling up the sack. As we did, Knips dove into the bushes. Soon we heard strange noises, and Ernest followed to see what was the matter.

"Come help me!" he shouted. "I've got a couple of ruffed grouse and a nestful of eggs. Quick!"

We hurried to the spot to find Ernest in a predicament. In each hand he held a fluttering, screaming bird, while he tried with his foot to keep greedy Knips from stealing all the eggs. We caught Knips and rewarded him with an egg, then tied the birds' legs and put the rest of the eggs in Ernest's hat. The nest was made of tall reeds, which grew thickly here, so we cut some for Franz to play at swords with. When we had enough acorns, I put some dry moss on the eggs to keep them warm and set our course for home.

At Falconhurst, I handed over the grouse family to my wife. She managed them so gently that the hen grouse returned to her eggs. In a few days, much to our delight, we had fifteen beautiful little grouse chicks.

Franz was greatly pleased with the "swords" his brothers had brought him. But with no one his size to practice his valor against, he quickly tired of slashing at the air. Instead he split the reeds and wove them into a riding whip for Fritz. "I don't mind," I told Fritz, "because I know you will use your brother's present with great care."

"You have my promise, Father," he said. "Franz, thank you very much. This is perfect."

Franz's creativity now had me wondering how else we might use these reeds. They had long, silky fibers; what were they? I thought and thought, then it hit me: this must be New Zealand flax. My wife was overjoyed. "Perfect!" she exclaimed. "Now no one will dress in rags. Just make me a spindle, and you'll soon have shirts and socks and pants! Quick, Fritz, and bring your mother more leaves!"

Fritz and Ernest mounted up and rode out. Soon the onager and buffalo were galloping home again, each laden with a great bundle of flax. The boys dismounted and unloaded the reeds at their mother's feet.

"Now you'll see," she exclaimed, "that I can match your inventions. With a little work I can turn these into cloth and then make you any piece of clothing you want!"

We decided that Flamingo Marsh would be the best spot for retting the flax. As we set out the next morning, I explained the process to the boys. "'Retting' means to soak the flax in water," I told them. "This destroys the connecting membrane while leaving the strong fibers. We'll let it soak for two weeks, and then dry it in the sun." Two weeks later, we had a supply of flax at Falconhurst.

In the meantime, I made Elizabeth the spindle she wanted, and we kept laying in supplies. We brought cart after cart of manioc, potatoes, coconuts, acorns, sugar canes, and more. The grumbling skies and sharp rainsqualls provided all the incentive we needed.

We had just completed planting the grain and housing the animals when down came the rain.

This was not the rain of Switzerland, cool and refreshing and lasting an hour or a day. This was week after week of constant tropical downpour. Our tree house became uninhabitable, so we retreated to the trunk, bringing any furniture that would not withstand the damp. It was very crowded under the tree roots, what with animals and supplies and beds and goods everywhere, but we had much time to shift our belongings for greater efficiency. This gave us enough room to work and sleep. In time we got used to the noise and smell of the stables. When we had to light a fire, it was hard to get the smoke out, but after some time we barely noticed it.

To ease the crowding, in daytime we turned most of the animals out, bringing them back every night. Fritz and I were invariably soaked to the skin. Fearing for our health, my wife attached hoods to two shirts, then took two pair of pants and hung them all up. She brushed a layer of rubber onto each to make us waterproof suits. We returned from our next night's work mostly dry and very happy. "They worked perfectly!" Fritz said. "Father, with respect, mother is as good an inventor as you!"

"I agree, and I'm delighted about it," I said as I embraced my glowing wife.

The days began to drag. We spent our mornings tending the animals. The boys amused themselves with their pets and helped me make clothmaking tools for their mother. In the evening, I kept a journal while my wife spun and sewed. Ernest made sketches of birds, animals, and plants he had met in the past months. Fritz and Jack taught little Franz to read.

Week after week rolled by, and still we were virtual prisoners. The rain simply did not stop. Despite all our best efforts, it was a scene of constant gloom.

CHAPTER 11

Our Estates

At length the winds grew quiet. Brilliant sun-
light shot through the clouds. The rain died
away. Spring had come!

It was like being liberated from jail. Everyone
rushed outdoors to bask in the beauty. We were
overjoyed to find our plantations thriving with
young plants and to listen to the song of equally
delighted birds. What a wonderful time!

With freedom came work, of course. Our
tree house was battered. The roof was torn and
the house full of leaves. It took several days to
repair. My wife asked for more tools to help her
spin flax, and these I made. I feared the worst for
Tentholm and with good reason. The tent was
blown down and torn, the supplies were soaked,
and two kegs of gunpowder were ruined. What
we might yet preserve we spread in the sun to
dry. The pinnace was safe, but our faithful

tub boat was shattered. "Fritz," I said, "we absolutely must find better winter quarters before the next rainy season."

"Could we hollow a cave out of the rock?" he asked.

I thought a minute before I replied. "It would be a difficult task, but I believe we must." After we had Falconhurst back in order, I took the three older boys and a cartload of tools to Tentholm. I chalked out the shape of an entrance in the cliffside, positioned my crowbar, and gave it the first stroke.

Six days of rock chips and sore hands later, our hole in the stone would barely have sheltered Knips, but we didn't despair. Soon we reached softer rock, and the easier going boosted our morale.

On the tenth day, Jack was pounding a crowbar when he shouted, "It's gone, Father! Fritz, my crowbar went through the mountain!"

"Then run around and get it," laughed Fritz. "Maybe it landed in Europe. You mustn't lose a good crowbar."

"No, really," insisted Jack. "I heard it crash down inside. Come see!"

We sprang to his side, and I thrust the handle of my hammer into the hole. I hit nothing. Fritz handed me a long pole, and this too probed only air. We had apparently broken through a thin wall to a great cavern. Shouting with joy, the boys renewed the assault.

Soon the hole was large enough for us to enter. I stepped near the opening to look in, but after a moment I felt faint. I staggered back, warning my sons to keep clear. When I got enough fresh air to recover, I explained. "Some caves have poisonous air. If the bad air seeps in constantly, the cave is useless, but sometimes it just needs venting. Ernest, light a torch." He did so. I carried it in, watching closely for signs of change in its burning. When I was near the hole, it began to flicker and fade. I handed the torch to Ernest. "Now, my young scientist, hold your torch here. If it goes out, we'll hurry out. Until then, the rest of us will work at a safe distance, in hopes of venting all the bad air."

Working by Ernest's light, we held long crowbars against the rock and pounded. The opening soon grew large enough to enter, but I ordered restraint. "We'll take a break, then put it to the test. Keep a torch going, Ernest." It was hard to rest in our excited state, but better safe than sorry.

After half an hour of relaxed conversation, it was time to experiment. Fritz bundled up some dry grass. I then lit it and carried it in. My sons followed in high anticipation.

I held the bundle near the opening. It burned normally. I threw it as far inside as I could, and much to my satisfaction, it lay burning on the floor. The fact that it didn't fall into some deep crevice was also good news. Now we knew the cave had breathable air and a solid floor.

While Fritz and I enlarged the opening, Jack jumped on his buffalo and rode for Falconhurst to share the news. We soon heard hooves and wheels on the bridge. Jack had hitched up the cart, bringing his mother, Franz, and all the candles he could find.

We lit candles, shouldered our guns, and entered. I went first, probing ahead with a pole. We marched silently into a scene of grandeur.

Jack's crowbar lay in a glittering crystal grotto so beautiful that even the dogs seemed awestruck. The cave was much larger than we had thought, with great crystalline pillars rising from the floor like mighty trees. Golden light reflected from the crystal-studded walls. Stalactites hung like icicles, sparkling in all the colors of the rainbow, sometimes meeting their stalagmite cousins that grew up from the floor.

The floor of this magnificent palace was hard, dry sand. This was another bit of good news, for the whole idea of moving into a cave was to stay dry. It was littered with fallen crystals, and out of curiosity, I picked one up to taste it. Just as I'd suspected: rock salt! Our cave had an endless supply of the purest salt. But this also brought risk: what if crystals tended to fall without warning? This could be very dangerous. "Stay out from under those," I told my family, "until I investigate." I took a torch and bent to have a closer look. The crystals seemed recently fallen, probably because of our constant battering. "Let's be sure," I said. "Fritz, Jack, Ernest, stand with me at the opening; Elizabeth, please stay behind us with Franz, and both of you cover your ears."

When everyone was in position, I commanded my sons to form line and aim into the cave. "On my order . . . *fire!*" Four weapons roared as one, and we watched to see if the concussion brought anything down. Nothing! Our marvelous cave was safe!

We returned to Falconhurst full of plans and ideas. The tree house that had once felt so safe now seemed frail and vulnerable. We decided to live there in summer and transform the cave into our winter dwelling and fortress.

To admit light and air, we chiseled through the thinnest places in the cave wall, fitting windows we'd salvaged from the wreck. We enlarged the doorway enough to hang the door from Falconhurst, leaving the latter's entryway boarded up and concealed behind a large piece of bark. The cave itself we divided into four parts: entryway, kitchen/workshop, stables, and deepest in the cave, our storehouse and powder magazine. One winter of choking on smoke was quite enough, so we built a proper fireplace and chimney. Our stables were better, and we made sure our workshop had room for many winter projects. When most of the work was done, we named it Rock House.

The long stay at Tentholm taught us more about its advantages. Lobsters, crabs, and mussels abounded. Turtles often came to lay delicious eggs in the sand, sometimes in great numbers. In such cases, we caught some and turned them on their backs long enough to pierce small holes in the edges of their shells. We then leashed them near the water on long ropes, ensuring a steady supply of fresh turtle for dinner. Turtles, however, were just the beginning of Tentholm's surprises.

One sunny morning, on the way back from Falconhurst, the sea began to look strange. The waters appeared to heave and boil, the surface peppered with fire-like flashes in the sun. Over this area of water screamed hundreds of diving, darting birds. The flashing mass rolled shoreward with the birds in pursuit.

"This must be a herring bank," I said. In reply to the inevitable torrent of questions, I explained: "Herring sometimes swim in great masses many feet deep. Flocks of hungry birds and schools of predatory fish converge to feast. The bank makes for shore, seeking the shallows where sharks and dolphins can't follow. When they arrive, the herring meet their deadliest enemy: fishermen. Though millions are caught this way each year, the survivors lay enough eggs to replenish the numbers."

My sons took the hint. Soon Jack and Fritz stood in the water with baskets, throwing the fish ashore to Ernest. As quickly as possible we cleaned, salted, and stored them. We kept on until we had many barrels of preserved fish, carefully closed and stored deep in our cave. What a divine gift!

The Lord's generosity had only begun. The next day, a great number of seals appeared to feast upon the remains of our cleaning. I doubted we could eat seal meat, but their skins and fat would be of great use, so we hunted almost two dozen of these. The oil would be good for tanning, soap making, and burning in lamps. The skins would provide fine harnesses and clothing.

These jobs interfered with our cave work for some time. I was eager to get back to it, for winter would not wait for us to finish. I had noticed some gypsum at the base of the salt crystals in places; perhaps I could make plaster. I heated some pieces until they were reduced to a smooth white powder, which I mixed with water and used to seal some of the herring barrels. "Why haven't you sealed them all, Father?" asked Ernest.

"I'll show you, son," I replied. "Fritz, let's build a small hut outside." We constructed this from reeds and branches, then strung our herring on lines across the roof. On the floor we lit a low, smoky fire of driftwood, brush, and moss, keeping it smoldering for several days. When I felt the fish were well smoked, we packed them away.

About a month after the herring bank episode, we had other visitors from the sea. Jack was the first to notice. "Fritz! Father! The water's full of young whales!" he called. He was not quite correct, but the reality was even better: the bay swarmed with great sturgeon, salmon, and trout, all headed for Jackal River to spawn. "Now these are proper fish!" cheered Jack. "How can we preserve them?"

"If you can figure out a way to catch them, I'll find a way to preserve them," I said with a smile.

"Watch me, Father," said Jack as he ran for Rock House. I was still weighing the merits of smoking and salting when my boy came back with a bow, an arrow, and a ball of heavy twine. At the arrowhead he had fastened a barbed spike, then tied the twine to the feathered end. He advanced to the river's edge, aimed, and shot. To my surprise, his shot struck a big salmon in the side.

"Help, Father!" cried Jack as the great fish darted off with great strength. "He'll pull me in!"

I ran to help him haul in the monster. The salmon thrashed mightily, but could not drag us in or break the twine. When his struggles weakened, we drew the exhausted fish ashore. Fritz and Ernest rushed off to gather their own weapons, and soon we were all in or near the water: Fritz with a harpoon, Ernest with a rod and line, myself with a pitchfork. Soon we had a fine pile of big fish.

Eventually Fritz harpooned a great sturgeon eight feet long but couldn't get him ashore. We all went to his assistance, but even struggling together we were losing the battle.

"The buffalo!" exclaimed my wife, and off went Jack for Storm, as he had named his favorite mount. When my lively son harnessed Storm to the harpoon rope, the sturgeon's moments were numbered; it soon lay panting on the sand. Next came cleaning and preserving. Some we salted, some we smoked like the herring, some we packed in oil. From the sturgeon eggs I decided to make caviar, the Russian delicacy. I washed them in vinegar, pressed out all the moisture, and stowed the result in small barrels in our storehouse.

The egg-bladders would make excellent isinglass when boiled and strained, which could be used to replace our limited supply of window glass. This experiment worked well, and while the resulting sheet of poured glass cooled on a flat rock, I took care to preserve the air bladders. I wasn't sure what use we would find for them, but my intention was to waste nothing.

An advantage of the local climate was that the kitchen garden flourished year-round with little effort. We had a constant supply of peas, beans, wheat, barley, rye, Indian corn, cucumbers, melons, and all sorts of other vegetables. I grew optimistic about the corn experiment we'd done at Falconhurst, and one morning we went to visit.

As we passed by the potato field, we found it covered with barley, wheat, rye, and peas. "Where'd all this come from?" I asked my wife in amazement.

"From the earth," she replied, laughing, "where Franz and I planted the seeds I brought from the wreck. You and the boys had already plowed up the ground; all we had to do was scatter the seeds."

When we got back to the cornfield near Falconhurst we discovered that the crop had flourished—and that it was already appreciated. As we approached, a tremendous variety of feathered thieves fled the scene. Fritz sent his eagle after some ruffed grouse. His noble bird made a clean capture, and Fritz was close by to save the grouse and hood his eagle.

Jack set Fangs loose among some quail that dared linger. To my surprise the jackal brought his master about a dozen. "You certainly kept your promise, Jack! Well done, both of you!" I said.

As we returned to Falconhurst, I brought up a new topic. "What if we had a small farm near here, to pasture some of the animals?" All agreed that we had too many to feed by ourselves. The next day we loaded the cart with a dozen chickens, four young pigs, two sheep and goats of each gender, and a pair of grouse. We hitched up the buffalo, cow, and donkey. Fritz led the way on Lightfoot, and we cut a new trail through the woods and tall grasses toward Cape Disappointment.

This difficult march led to a large plain with many curious little bushes. Their branches, and the ground around them, were covered with pure white flakes. "Snow!" exclaimed Franz.

I was not surprised Franz mistook the flakes for snow, but Fritz spoke first. "Perhaps these are dwarf cotton trees." Closer inspection showed he was correct; the flakes were pods of soft, fine fiber. My wife was not satisfied until we had three large sacks of it. We climbed a forested hill to a glorious view of luxuriant grass stretching down the hillside, dotted here and there with shady trees. A sparkling brook gushed down nearby into the rich green forest.

"What better place for a new farm?" I asked. "Pasture, water, shade, and shelter, all here!" We made camp, and my wife prepared dinner while Fritz and I looked for a good site for a shed. When we found four trees in a roughly rectangular shape, we began to make our plans and then headed back to camp to have dinner.

The next morning we got to work. I cut deep, square grooves in the trunks about ten feet above ground and again ten feet higher for a second floor. Into these grooves I inserted beams from the wreck, to form a framework for the building. I then built a roof of thin strips of wood, shingling it with bark and acacia thorns. While picking up the scraps to burn, I noticed a peculiar smell. I took a closer look. Some of the bark was American fir. "From the fir," I said to the boys, "we can get turpentine and tar. From tar and oil, we can make pitch to caulk the pinnace."

It took us several days to build the farmhouse. We wove strong vines to form walls up to about six feet high. The rest we made of thin strips spaced to let in air and light. We divided the house into three parts: stalls for the animals, perches for the birds, and a sleeping area with a rough table and benches for ourselves. We kept the animals well fed, so that they would like the spot and stay near.

I could see that we would exhaust our provisions before finishing our work, so I sent Jack and Fritz for fresh supplies. In their absence, Ernest and I went exploring.

Passing over a brook that flowed toward the wall of rocks, we skirted a large marsh leading to a lake. Much to my delight, the swamp was full of wild rice. As I waded in to see if it was ripe, a number of ruffed grouse took off. Ernest and I fired, bringing down two, and Fangs retrieved them for us.

As we advanced, Knips skipped from Juno's

back and began to eat something. This was always good news; this time it was strawberries. After picking as many as we could conveniently carry, we headed for the lake.

It was beautiful, calm, and blue, populated by many splendid black swans. What a joy to watch the graceful birds fishing, paddling, and chasing one another over the glassy surface. I couldn't bear to disturb their happy existence, but Juno had no such scruples and plunged into the water. She dragged out a very odd creature: like a small otter, but with a broad flat duck-like bill. We hurried up to get a good look before Juno devoured it. "Any idea what it could be, Ernest?"

He thought for a moment. "I think it's a platypus," he said. "I'll take it home and stuff it. My brothers will be amused."

Shortly after our return to the farm, Fritz and Jack showed up with the supplies. The platypus got the expected chuckle from them. That evening we named the farm Woodlands. Leaving plenty of provisions for the animals, we headed home without them—a decision that proved a mistake.

On the way back, we were passing through a forest when a shower of pinecones came raining down. A large troop of apes apparently didn't care for trespassers. We fired a couple of shots to scare them off, and Fritz picked up some of the missiles to show me.

"Gather some of these cones, boys," I said.

"The kernel in the middle tastes like almonds, and we can press them for oil." This done, we headed toward a nearby hill that promised a fine view all around. We were not disappointed. How rich and beautiful this land was! I decided we should also build a settlement here. With our recent experience at Woodlands, this construction went quickly. A few days later we had another new residence, which Ernest named Prospect Hill.

Near this new residence, I thought I'd seen some birch-like trees. I knew that American Indians built canoes from large pieces of birch bark, so I took Jack to look for some. We were very lucky to find two magnificent, straight, tall trees, either birches or something very similar. I chose the one whose branches began at the higher point, then sent Jack to bring back his brothers and the rope ladder. We slung the ladder over a stout branch and I sent Fritz up the tree. "Watch what I do, Fritz, and make a similar cut," I called to him. At the foot of the tree, I made a circular cut in the bark; he did likewise. We then made a cut the length of the tree and began the slow, careful task of peeling off the bark in one piece. The result was a moist, flexible piece of material, light enough for us to drag back to camp.

"We can't delay," I said. "We have to work while it's soft and pliable." I cut a triangular piece from each end of the bark roll, drew the ends together into points, and secured them with pegs and glue. This gave a boat-shape. But it was too flat in the middle, so we ran ropes around it to pinch its middle until it dried. Next we cut some naturally curved pieces of wood to use for the canoe's ribs. We cut and fit these into our craft while it dried in the sun.

At dawn the next day, we loaded the canoe and made for Falconhurst. Getting the sledge through the woods and the swamp was difficult. For part of the trip, we made our way along the foot of the cliffs that separated us from whatever lay inland. At one point, there was a narrow opening in the cliff. A small stream rushed through this gorge. This passage to the unknown territory inland seemed a serious threat to our security. We decided to stop here in order to build an earthen wall to close off the gorge. To further discourage wild beasts from coming through, we planted the mound with every thorny bush we could find. For our convenience, we left a small, winding path through the barrier. This we disguised with piles of branches and thorns.

This exhausting labor took two whole days, and we were glad to rest at Falconhurst before continuing on to Tentholm. A day's rest later, we went back to work on the canoe. We fitted a mast, hung sails, and made paddles. I worried about its balance until I remembered the large, airtight air bladders from our fishing spree. I helped my sons tar these well with pitch, and we attached them securely along the sides of the boat, making it less likely to capsize or sink.

An American Indian could doubtless have pointed out many flaws in our technique, but we were proud nonetheless, as with everything we had achieved.

CHAPTER 12

Anniversary

*B*ack in the rainy season, our cow had given birth to a bull-calf. Long before spring came, I pierced his nose and inserted a ring, so we could more easily manage him. At that point a question arose: who should be his master, and how should the young bull be trained?

As the family discussed the matter, I said, "People of southern Africa train bulls to guard their valuable herds and even do battle with other tribes."

"That would be fine," said my wife, "if we were in southern Africa. But we are not, and I don't want a mean bull around."

I knew that tone. "All right," I said, "who will train this calf?"

To my surprise, no one volunteered. Ernest preferred training Knips; Jack was busy with Storm the buffalo and Fangs the jackal. Fritz was content with his onager, Lightfoot. Their mother took care of the old gray donkey, whom she had named Grizzle. I didn't have time. Only Franz was available. "What do you say, my boy?" I asked him.

"Oh yes, Father!" he replied. "Do you think I'll be able to ride him when he grows up?"

I smiled. "He's yours, Franz. Make him as tame as you can, but remember he will grow up much faster than you. What will you name him?"

Franz listened for a moment, then said, "He makes a low muttering noise. How about Grumble?"

"Very good!" I exclaimed.

Franz leaped for joy. "Grumble! It's a lot better than your buffalo's name, Jack!"

"It isn't even close," argued Jack. "Imagine mother saying: 'Here comes Franz on Grumble, but Jack riding on Storm.'" Franz's older brothers reassured him that Grumble fit perfectly. Next, they proposed to name Juno's puppies Bruno and Fawn. This animal-management business was a helpful distraction from the boredom of our long confinement.

We spent two months improving Rock House. We built partition walls and animal stalls. After leveling the floors with clay, we paved them with a mix of gravel and melted gypsum. Finding this a bit too hard, I made a rug for our living room from a large sail, some glue, and a lot of sheep's wool and goat hair.

One morning, as I was making lists of summer and winter projects, I got to wondering how long we'd been here. I consulted my almanac and realized that tomorrow would be the first anniversary of our safe landing! My heart swelled with gratitude to God for our escape, our health, and our comfort and prosperity. I began planning a festival, but kept this to myself. I started the day's work in a typical fashion by telling the boys to spend the day cleaning up Rock House. This was such a normal order it aroused no suspicion.

At dinner I made the announcement. "Tomorrow is a very important day. It is the first anniversary of our safe landing here. In honor of God's mercy, let us celebrate it as Thanksgiving Day."

Everyone was surprised. My wife questioned my reckoning, but the records in my almanac convinced her. "Well, my husband," she said, "unless your bookseller has mailed you a new almanac for next year, we'll have to devise our own calendar."

As I laughed, Ernest suggested, "We should cut notches in a long stick, one notch per day."

"That's fine if you know how many days are in a year," I said.

"The year contains 365 days, 5 hours, 48 minutes, and 45 seconds," he answered promptly.

"Perfect!" I said, smiling, "but what will you do with those spare hours, minutes, and seconds in a year or two?"

"Add them together every four years," said Ernest, "to make an extra day in February, and call that 'leap year.'"

"Well done, Professor! As Official Astronomer, you're now in charge of all clocks, watches, and calendars." Everyone laughed except Ernest, who nodded agreement. Before they went to sleep, I could hear my boys whispering among themselves about "father's festivities," for I had given no details. I didn't suspect that the little rogues might plan their own surprise.

I awoke at daybreak the next morning to the thunder of cannon. At first, I thought I'd dreamed it, but my wife's fright proved that it was real. I turned to wake Fritz up, but his hammock was empty, as was Jack's.

I was dressing in haste and confusion when I heard shouting outside: "Hurray! How's that for a Thanksgiving Day salute?" Jack and Fritz rushed in, but when they saw our alarm, Fritz hurried to apologize. We forgave them—I had to admit it was a resounding way to begin a new holiday!

After breakfast we spent the beautiful morning relaxing and talking. I wanted my sons to remain thankful for their deliverance, and we shared our recollections of the fateful day. I read aloud passages from my journal, as well as many beautiful Psalms. Each thanked God in his or her own words.

After lunch, I revealed the next phase of the festivities. "It's time for the athletic competition. Your mother and I will be the audience and the judges."

"Father, what a great idea!" "Will we have races?" "And will there be prizes, Father?"

"The judges offer prizes for competition in every sort of exercise," I replied. "Shooting, running, riding, leaping, climbing, and swimming. Let's see your skill!"

I had planned the next moment with care. "Trumpeters, announce the start of the competition!" The ducks and geese were resting nearby in the shade, clearly not caught up in the festive spirit. I ran into their midst, flapping my arms and making a commotion. Startled, they all flew up in great haste with much quacking and honking. My sons laughed uproariously as they bustled about to prepare.

"What's first, Father?" asked Fritz.

"First we'll have marksmanship," I replied, "then the rest later, when it cools down. Here's your first target," I added, producing a board in the rough size and shape of a kangaroo. Jack insisted on adding ears and a long leather strap for a tail. I set it up in a kangaroo's typical

posture, walked off the firing distance, and told each competitor to fire twice. Fritz hit the kangaroo's head both times; Ernest hit the body once. By sheer luck and much to our amusement, Jack shot the ears clean away from the head.

Next I had them shoot at the "kangaroo" with pistols. Fritz won this too. I then had the competitors load with birdshot, and I threw a little board high in the air for each boy. In this, to my surprise, Ernest equaled Fritz. Jack's flying board escaped all injury, and we jokingly drowned out his excuses. Archery came next; I wanted my sons to practice hard at this, for one day we would run out of ammunition. In this my elder sons both did well, as did little Franz.

After a rest, I announced a race. "Fritz, Ernest, and Jack must run to Falconhurst," I announced. "I left a hammer on the table in my sleeping room. Whoever brings it back is the winner. Get ready…get set…*go!*" All three took off. Fritz and Jack took a quick lead over Ernest, who kept up a calm, steady pace.

Long before we expected to see them back, a tremendous noise came from the bridge area. Jack thundered in on Storm, with the onager and donkey braying along behind.

"What sort of foot race do you call this, Jack?" I asked with a laugh.

He reined up Storm, leaped off, and saluted playfully. "When I saw that I didn't have a chance, I gave up on the prize and rode back, so I could be in time to see the others puffing in. Lightfoot and old Grizzle invited themselves." Ernest returned next, holding up the hammer in proof of victory. Fritz puffed in a couple of minutes later, congratulated Ernest, and laughed at Jack's notion.

"Now let's see how well you climb," I said. Jack climbed the highest palms with wondrous agility. When he put on the sharkskin leggings, he played around like a monkey, peeping around the trunks and grinning at us. Fritz and Ernest climbed well, but could not begin to match their lively young brother.

The next competition was riding, and Fritz and Jack proved equal at managing their steeds. Just when I thought the event was over, little Franz appeared from the stable leading Grumble the bull-calf, now partly grown. He had attached a bridle to the nose ring and had even made a kangaroo-hide saddle.

The child marched up, saluted us with confidence and exclaimed, "Now, most learned judges, prepare to see something wonderful! The great bull-tamer, Milo of Crotona, asks the honor of performing for you."

I suppressed my laughter and gave Franz a solemn nod of encouragement. He took a riding crop in one hand, leading his calf with the other. On command, young Grumble walked, trotted, and galloped in a circle around his master. When Franz mounted up, Grumble proved a bit clumsy but very tame, rarely needing even a tap from the riding crop. We gave him a fine round of applause. "I'm twice as proud of you, Franz," said my wife, "because you treat him so gently. Your kindness has bred kindness."

As his mother went back to the cave to arrange the awards ceremony, I made a point not to notice little Franz's tears of pride and happiness—in part because I had to hold back my own.

The last sport was swimming. Fritz swam effortlessly and with great endurance. Ernest was too tired to do well; Jack's energetic haste soon exhausted him. Franz showed such great promise that I foresaw a day when he would surpass Fritz. I was immensely proud of all my sons.

It was getting late, so we went back to Rock House. The boys marched in, pretending to play various instruments in imitation of a band. My wife sat in a dignified position, the prizes at her side. All four halted before her, bowed respectfully, and waited.

She addressed the boys in order of age, adding a few words of encouragement for each. "Fritz, you swam and shot the best. Here are a double-barreled rifle and a hunting knife." His eyes lit up, and he thanked his mother.

"Ernest, you showed great stamina in the running. This handsome gold watch will help you keep track of time." Ernest admired it with quiet pride.

"Jack, you had no equal in climbing and riding. This riding-crop and these silver-plated spurs are your prize." Jack hurried to put on the spurs, then strutted about like a little rooster while everyone tried not to laugh.

"Franz, my little Milo of Crotona, you have taught Grumble gentle obedience at a young age, just as I hoped. This rhinoceros-hide whip is a man's tool, but you've shown that you're old enough to know when not to use it." Franz ran a hand over the smooth surface, beaming with joy.

When everyone thought the ceremony was over, I advanced with a gift for my wife: a beautiful box filled with every imaginable requirement for a lady's needlework. She embraced me with surprise and delight.

The boys wanted to waste some more ammunition to end the day, and I could hardly deny their high spirits after their fine showings. As the cannon blasts echoed away, we went to dinner, followed by worship and rest.

Soon after the great festival, I remembered the huge flocks of ortolans and wild pigeons we had caught feasting on Falconhurst's figs at about that time last year. The preserved birds had been a great winter food supply, and I felt we should catch and preserve more this year.

We set aside our construction work and hurried to Falconhurst. Just as I had suspected, the early arrivals were already gorging on figs. To spare ammunition, I decided to try a device of the Palm Islanders called birdlime—a very sticky mixture of raw rubber and oil, known to trap even larger birds. When I sent Fritz and Jack with containers made from gourds to get the rubber, I remembered something. "Elizabeth," I said, "we really should go to Calabash Wood and make more containers, but that will be a very long trip just for gourds."

"Don't forget about my plantation near the potato field," she reminded me.

"Yes!" I replied. "That's much closer." Jack and Fritz would be gone for awhile, so the rest of us went on our own expedition. The plantation was a great success, full of fine gourds and pumpkins. When we had a cartload of the best ones, we hurried home to start making basins, dishes, plates, flasks, and spoons of all sizes. The results reflected our growing skill.

When the riders returned with the rubber, they brought several novelties as well. Fritz had shot a crane. They had also taken time to collect aniseed, fir cones, candleberries, and a curious root they called "the monkey plant."

"And why do you call it that?" I asked.

"Well, Father," answered Fritz, "we came to a clearing near Woodlands, and saw a troop of monkeys tearing up and eating some sort of roots. The funniest part was when a monkey couldn't pull up the root; he would take the stem in his teeth and fling himself over backward, and up it would come! What a silly sight."

"We wanted to try them ourselves," added Jack, "so we turned the dogs loose. That cleared the apes out. The roots tasted good, so we brought some for you to try."

I went first. "This might be ginseng," I said. Everyone wanted to know more. "The Chinese prize the ginseng root very highly and use it in their medicines."

Then Fritz continued, "After this we went on to Woodlands. It was a mess! Everything smashed or torn, and covered with mud and dirt. The birds were terrified, the sheep and goats scattered. It looked like a hurricane had hit!"

"What?" I exclaimed. My wife looked very

worried. I knew what she was thinking. I would take no chances with my own family's safety. "Did you find the culprits?" I asked.

"It must have been the monkeys," said Jack. "When they were done messing up the yards and sheds, I suspect they slipped a young monkey through some small opening to unfasten the shutters—you know how clever they are. After that, they stormed into the cottage and tore everything up. They probably only left when the food ran out. Miserable creatures!"

"While we were standing there in shock," continued Fritz, "we heard a lot of bird noises overhead and looked up. A wedge-shaped formation of big birds was coming down to land in the lake. A closer look told us that they were cranes. They played in the water a while, then flew over to the rice fields and began to feast.

"We sneaked up, hoping to get off a shot, but they had posted lookouts! The whole flock took off before we could shoot, so I turned my eagle loose. He dove and caught a crane, and they fought fiercely on the way down. They landed close to us, and I was sad to see that the beautiful crane was already dead. Luckily the eagle was unhurt, so I gave him a small pigeon from my game bag.

"After this, we went back to Woodlands to get some fir cones for turpentine, then headed home."

Dinner was ready, and we found the new roots a tasty addition to stew. Even so, we would use the "monkey plant" with caution, like any plant thought to affect one's health. We saved some to plant in our kitchen garden.

As we prepared for sleep, I gave thanks for my sons' growing wisdom. They performed well as a team, and when alone, they showed initiative and sense. My final thoughts as I drifted off were of the resourceful, intelligent wife who had borne them. Though stranded in a remote land, I was as blessed as any man in the world.

CHAPTER 13

Unpleasant Tasks

*T*he next day I had the boys coat some large sticks with birdlime, then climb up and put them near the figs. The plan was a success, though I felt badly for the birds as they fell protesting to the ground. Encouraged by our success, I took boys and birdlime off to the acorn-wood, another location the birds favored. Before long we had a fine winter's supply of pigeons, ortolans, and other game birds.

At one point, Jack brought me a survivor— one of the European pigeons we'd released upon arrival. We cleaned it up and put it in a wicker coop, and I said, "Boys, if you get any more of these, save them. Now we can properly manage them."

It took us the entire next day to preserve and store the birds. Next we had to deal with the monkeys. If we could catch the vandals in the act, we might inflict such punishment that they would never return to Woodlands. I dreaded it, but I saw no other way.

My wife packed several days' provisions. I mixed a much stickier batch of birdlime than before and also loaded up some short posts, lots of rope, raw food, and a supply of coconut shells and gourds. The buffalo carried all this without complaint. I didn't want my wife and Franz to see this job, so I left Turk with them at Falconhurst.

As we neared Woodlands, I asked Fritz to select our campsite. He chose an excellent spot, hidden from the cottage by thick bushes and with room for a small tent. If Juno and Fangs got loose, it could ruin my plan. From this base, we advanced on our cottage. It was quiet and deserted. "Get to work," I ordered, "and be quick. We must be out of sight before they return."

We drove the stakes lightly into the ground all around the house, winding rope in and out of them in all directions. Nothing could pass through without touching something. We smeared every rope and stake with birdlime. We coated the outsides of the coconut shells and gourds with birdlime; then we filled them with rice and grain and set them out. I had the boys spread the remainder of the mixture on nearby tree-branches. Nothing interrupted us, and at nightfall we returned to camp to rest.

Very early in the morning we heard a commotion in the distance. We armed ourselves with strong clubs, leashed the dogs, and crept toward our trap. We halted in a well-hidden spot to watch and wait. The scene was one of the wildest I ever saw.

Soon we heard rustling, crackling, and creaking among the branches accompanied by the shrieks and chatters that confirmed our guess. From the forest sprang a disorderly rabble of monkeys, leaping and racing toward the house. Many hurried to feast while others scrambled onto the cottage roof, trying to break in.

In the process, most of them got the birdlime on themselves. Some sat down and tried to clean it off, which made it worse; others got hopelessly entangled in stakes and cords, or had a coconut shell or gourd stuck to their hands. Some tried to help each other and got stuck together.

The few who had escaped capture took to the trees, but most got stuck on the branches. When most of the monkeys were hopelessly stuck, I ordered the boys to let loose the dogs. They launched the assault as though exacting personal revenge, and I felt we must hasten the end. Clubs and fangs bashed and tore in a terrible scene.

When an awful silence reigned, we looked around with a shudder. At least forty apes lay mangled and dead. My sons, to their credit, looked as sad as I felt. I said only, "Sons, let's bury them, along with all this trapping stuff. God grant we never have to do the like again." This work helped take their minds off the massacre. After this we began to put our cottage back in order, then round up the sheep, goats, and chickens.

While we were resettling these, something fell heavily to the ground. We went to see and found three splendid birds, caught on some of the limed sticks we had placed loose in the branches. Two were Blue Molucca pigeons. The third had lovely green, bronze, and steel-blue plumage that looked like that of a Nicobar pigeon. "Boys, what if we could domesticate these at Rock House?" I asked.

"Do you think we'll catch more?" asked Fritz.

"Perhaps some will decide to join our colony on their own," I said with a smile.

Several days later, with everything at Woodlands back in order, we returned without further adventure to Falconhurst's happy welcome. Everyone liked my pigeon house proposal, and we had some other jobs to do at Rock House, so we arranged for a long stay.

My plan was to hollow out room in the cliff close to our cave. We would outfit this as a pigeon coop, with entry holes, partitions, and nesting places. I wanted the birds to have both light and room to move about. This took a few weeks of pounding and chiseling. We finished the pigeon house with a front door we could slide up and down. A window in the middle let us look inside and gave the birds light.

When the pigeon house was done, I sent the younger boys to gather shellfish and told Fritz to remain. After they were out of earshot, I said, "Now that we've built a nice home, let's see if the colonists will take up residence. Back home, as you know, not only do pigeon keepers have clever ways to keep their own birds safe, but they have a strange way of also ending up with other people's pigeons."

Fritz laughed. "So they do. What do we do next?"

"I'll show you. Bring me some aniseed, soft clay, and salt," I answered.

"Yes, Father."

"The mortar and some oil, too," I added. When my son returned, I ground up some aniseed in the mortar, then poured in oil to soak up the spicy aniseed aroma. We put the captured pigeons and the European ones in the little cave, then strained the crushed seeds from the scented oil with a cloth. This odor would cling for days to anything it touched.

I mixed the seed remnants with plenty of grain and slipped a bowl of this inside the sliding door. When the other boys came back, they peeked in to see all the pigeons happily pecking away at the food. I gave the birds three days to get used to their new home, and each morning I had Fritz pour fresh aniseed oil all around the entrance.

After breakfast on the third day, I summoned my family to the pigeon house. "What are you going to do, Father?" asked Ernest.

"I've briefed our new pigeons on their mission: to recruit others of their kind as colonists." I raised the slide with a flourish as I said, "Go now, and tell all your friends about the new colony!"

Out popped the beautiful birds, looking around in all directions. After a quick glance around the area, the three native pigeons flew away immediately. I worried that they might not return, but this I kept to myself. Only the European pigeons remained.

We saw nothing of the fugitives until the next day around noon. Most of us were working inside the cave, but Jack had gone outside to get something. He ran in, exclaiming, "He's back! He came back!"

"Who came back?" "What do you mean?" asked his brothers.

"The blue pigeon!"

"Nonsense," said Ernest. "You're playing a joke."

"It isn't nonsense," I said. "I expect the rest back soon."

veled at her nimble skill as she "played the loom," as they put it.

About this time, Lightfoot the onager had a beautiful little colt. From the first, he showed signs of a pleasant disposition—rare and helpful in a donkey. I named him Swift and planned to train him as my mount.

With the cavern's interior in good shape, we turned to the issue of fresh water. It was a great nuisance to haul water every day from Jackal River. I wanted an aqueduct in place before the rains came. We built one similar to that at Falconhurst using bamboo pipes sealed with rubber. These led to a large, partly-buried half-barrel. The result was helpful to all, but especially my practical Elizabeth, who said, "I like this better than if you'd built me a marble fountain decorated with mermaids and dolphins!"

It was time to store up food. We made many trips with cart, sledge, animals, sharkskin leggings, and garden implements to harvest our plantations and to forage for wild food. Load after load arrived at the cavern, and my wife was constantly making new bags.

We kept up until every barrel of every size was full. As we were finishing this work the weather grew unsettled and stormy, with heavy clouds on the horizon most of the time. The turbulent sea drove masses of water hissing and foaming against the cliffs. It was almost June.

Everyone ran out to the pigeon house. There stood the beautiful pigeon, but not alone. He had brought a mate! She seemed hesitant to enter, but he kept cooing and encouraging her, and finally the shy little lady hopped inside.

"Hurry up! Shut the door!" shouted the boys, rushing for the rope that lowered the panel.

"Quiet down, and leave that alone!" I said. "You'll frighten them. That's no way to treat colonists, as you ought to know. Besides, you'll lock out the others."

The next news came courtesy of Fritz's keen eyes when he called out, "Here they come!" To our delight, the second Blue Molucca pigeon arrived with his own mate. He had an easier time getting her to enter the little cave. The third and handsomest of the new pigeons had yet to appear.

Late in the day Franz and his mother went out to start dinner, but the child soon rushed back inside, exclaiming, "Come see! They're beautiful!"

We came out in a rush, and it was true: the Nicobar had brought a bride. All the pigeons seemed content. The Blue Moluccas had already begun building nests, and the Nicobars got to work. They were settling in happily with our European birds.

We worked without incident for some time after this. Eventually Jack got restless and decided to go off by himself. He loved to surprise us with new, interesting discoveries, and we liked this as well.

This time, true to form, he had something interesting: he returned with a great bundle of Spanish canes on his back. He was also a miserable-looking mess, covered from head to foot in mud and green slime. The canes were just as muddy, and he was missing a shoe. We would have laughed, but he looked ready to cry.

"Jack, what in the world happened to you? Where have you been?" I asked.

"In the swamp, Father," he answered, unloading the bundle with relief. "I went to get reeds to weave baskets and hen coops, and I saw some fine ones in the swamp. When I tried to get them, I slipped and sank in over my ankles. I tried to keep going, but I got stuck up to my knees in the mud! I screamed and shouted, but nobody came. It was terrible!

"At last who should appear but my faithful Fangs! He came close up to me, but all he could do was help me make noise. No help came, so I got to thinking. I cut down all the reeds I could reach and tied them in this bundle, which gave me a firm place to lean while I got out of the mud. It took a lot of working and kicking, but I eventually got on top of the bundle.

"There I sat, kind of floating on the bundle, while Fangs ran yelping back and forth between

me and the bank. He seemed to expect me to low him, which didn't make sense. Sudden thought of grabbing his tail, and he dragged pulled me. I crawled and waded, sometimes my bundle as a raft and other times draggi along with me, until we got back to solid gro I thought I'd never get out of that swamp a

"A fortunate escape indeed, my boy!" I "I thank God for it. Fangs is a hero, and showed great presence of mind. Now since liness and Godliness go together, please go your mother and clean off all that slimy m have the perfect use for your canes."

One of my wife's greatest talents was ing, and I wanted to build her a loom. I with two fine strong canes, which I split an tied together again so they would dry st and equal. I had my boys cut up smaller ca comb-teeth. My boys had not figured o plan and made great fun of "father's m toothpicks." I kept the project secret fro wife, and when the children asked what it be, I said mysteriously, "Think of it as a sort of instrument that your mother will how to play."

When the loom was done, we all ga around. Jack had brought the material, so him the honor of bringing his mother "My men!" she cried joyfully. "Wait until the things I can make us!" Soon my so

The rains could not be far off, which meant twelve weeks of bad weather.

We moved the cow, Grizzle, Lightfoot, and Storm into their cave stables. We brought the dogs inside. Knips, Fangs, and the eagle were sure to provide amusement during the long evenings. The boys would make regular trips to check on Falconhurst and bring back anything we needed.

Our minds turned to improving the cave. Its worst feature was lack of light, and after giving this some thought, I called for Jack. He was able to climb up a bamboo pole and attach a pulley to the ceiling. I then attached a large ship's oil-lantern to one end of the rope we ran through the pulley. Our dark cave was now pleasantly lit.

Each room needed improvements. Ernest and Franz built a library, making shelves and sorting the books salvaged from the ship. Jack and his mother improved the sitting room and kitchen while Fritz and I arranged the work-shops. The carpenter's bench, the turning lathe, and a large chest of tools were set in convenient places, and many tools and instruments hung on the walls. We had brought the pieces of a forge from the wreck, complete with fireplace, bellows, and anvil, and these we set up in an adjoining chamber.

Our work never ended, but I didn't mind. I kept coming up with new plans, because hard work in progress toward a good result is always a morale builder. Being comfortable was a full-time job but a very worthwhile one.

Education was another fine use of time. Ernest and Franz took custody of our fine library. We had volumes on travel, divinity, natural history, science, and history as well as novels in several languages. In addition to our native German, we all spoke passable French. Fritz and Ernest had begun to learn English in school. Elizabeth had learned Dutch from some family friends. We decided to broaden our knowledge of languages. We all planned to improve our French. The older boys were to study English and Dutch with their mother. Ernest wanted to improve his Latin, the language of many books on natural history and medicine. Jack announced that he meant to learn Spanish "because it sounded so majestic."

I myself was interested in Malay, widely spoken in the Eastern Seas; it might well be useful. Soon scraps and bits of each language were buzzing about our ears from morning to night. With constant practice we all learned quickly, and everyone learned a few words of each language under study.

Occasionally we amused ourselves by opening chests and packages previously untouched, bringing to light unexpected treasures: mirrors, a pair of marble-topped end tables, elegant writing tables, handsome chairs, lots of clocks, a music box, and more. We had grown used to primitive furnishings made from bamboos and ship's wreckage. Now our home began to feel like a palace. The children decided that Rock House was a dull name and asked to rename it.

"Have you a name in mind?" I asked them.

"We like 'Rockburg,' Father," answered Franz.

"Elizabeth?" I asked my wife, busily weaving on her loom.

"Rockburg it is," she said without interrupting her labor, and it was done.

This rainy season seemed to pass more swiftly, perhaps because we knew its approximate duration. I spent most of my time in study, but I took time for some carpentry. I made a yoke for the animals, a pair of wool carders, and a spinning wheel for my wife. The rainy season delivered a final blast of wild weather, as if to remind us of its power.

At last the uproar died away, and nature once again wore her peaceful, beautiful smile. Soon all traces of the floods and storms would disappear beneath the luxuriant tropical growth. How delightful to roam once more in the open air! We crossed Jackal River for a walk along the coast, and presently Fritz's sharp eyes spotted something on the small island near Flamingo Marsh. "It looks like an overturned boat," he said.

I looked with the telescope and agreed. "I

can't think of anything else it might be. Let's fix up the pinnace today, then go investigate tomorrow!" As expected, my sons loved the idea of beginning the warm season with an adventure. The next day we sailed for the steep, rocky islet.

As we drew near, we got a better look. The overturned boat was actually a huge, stranded whale. The sea was rough and we had to land on the sea side of the island, at some distance from the whale. The boys hurried toward the whale while I climbed to the island's highest point. After taking a moment to enjoy the view of the mainland, I joined my sons, who were only halfway to the whale. They had stopped to collect shells and coral branches that lay scattered about. "Father, just look at all these glorious shells and coral branches! Why are there so many?"

"Probably the storms tore them loose and scattered them," I replied. "Waves large enough to strand a whale could probably move anything in the sea."

"Yes, he's quite a brute!" cried Fritz as we drew near. "Much bigger than I thought. I can't figure out what use we can make of his carcass."

"We can get oil, I'm sure," said Ernest. "Gathering shells is a lot more fun than cutting up blubber, though."

"Then go ahead," I said. "This afternoon, when the sea is calmer, we'll come back with tools. We can't let this whale go to waste."

As the boys sweated and strained to row us back, Jack asked, "Is coral of any use?"

"It was once used in making medicines, but now most of it is made into jewelry. For now, though, let's put the pieces you collected in the library and begin a Museum of Natural History."

"Coral is almost a combination of animal, vegetable, and mineral, isn't it?" remarked Fritz. "It's hard like stone, makes branches like a shrub, and is built by tiny insects."

"Correct, Fritz." I engaged my sons in a discussion of how coral grows and is gathered, and we soon reached the landing place.

"We're here already!" exclaimed Jack. "That wasn't so hard."

When we reached Rockburg, my wife and Franz were delighted with the lovely shells and corals. "Would you like to go this afternoon, Franz?" she asked. Our youngest boy jumped for eager joy. I could not deny such enthusiasm so I agreed that Franz and my wife could come along.

After lunch we began to prepare. We wanted all the oil we could collect; our lantern used a lot of it. After three months cooped up in Rockburg, we had plenty of empty barrels, which we arranged to tow behind the pinnace. The boys packed knives, hatchets, and their climbing leggings, all in high anticipation.

The sea was calmer than it had been in the morning. We found it easy to land close to the whale. After securing the pinnace and barrels, we went for a closer inspection of our prize.

Its immensity startled my wife and Franz, for it was over sixty feet long and half that wide, weighing perhaps twenty-five tons. It was black, with the head comprising about a third of its bulk. The eyes were tiny. The jaws opened sixteen feet back from the snout, and their most curious part was the strainer-like whalebone all along them. Few Swiss had ever seen such a thing!

The tongue was remarkably large, soft, and full of oil. The throat was strangely tiny, barely two inches across. "What can he possibly eat?" wondered Fritz. "He can't possibly get a decent mouthful down that little gullet!"

"Perhaps Ernest can explain," I suggested.

"Whales are very interesting," he began. "They're not fish. They breathe air and must surface or they'll drown. They eat shrimp, small fish, lobsters, some shellfish, and other small sea-creatures. The whale swims through these with its mouth open until it has a mouthful, then closes his jaws and forces the water out through the strainer-like whalebone. See how his nostrils are on top of his head; he can breathe without showing much of his bulk. When he exhales, the mixture of water and air can go twenty feet high."

As he described each part, my family inspected it with great interest. "And now, boys," I said, "put on your leggings and climb up this slippery mountain of flesh. Let's get to work."

Fritz and Jack got on top of the whale and helped me cut my way to the whalebone, of which we took a good quantity. Ernest worked at the creature's side, cutting out slabs of blubber, which his mother and Franz put into barrels.

Soon the shrill screams of birds filled the air. They had come not to help but to steal. Sometimes they swiped food from beneath the very stroke of a knife or hatchet. While the birds seriously hindered our work, I couldn't blame them. They were no greater thieves than we. Blows meant to ward them off killed a few, and my wife confiscated these for the feathers.

Before we left, I stripped off a long piece of the inch-thick skin to use in leather craft, for I doubted we would find such thick leather on land. I also took part of the gums, which some travelers feel is a delicacy. The boys thought the tongue would be tasty, but I valued it mainly for its oil.

Towing all this heavy freight was hard work, but we motivated ourselves with the strong desire to get home and clean off the disgusting evidence of our day's work. Over dinner, I explained my next plan. "If you thought today was messy, wait for tomorrow, when we open up the carcass and take out the intestines to use as oil containers."

"Franz and I will pass, thank you," said my wife, and I agreed. The next day we got a very early start on this all-day job. Only when we were sure we could get nothing else of use did we abandon the remainder to the birds. We headed home with a full load. I was very satisfied with my sons, who had not complained at all.

On the way back, the boys wondered how I had thought up this use for the intestines. "In some countries," I explained, "there's no wood for barrels nor hemp for ropes. By now, you all know that necessity breeds invention. Greenlanders, Eskimos, and other similar peoples have come up with useful substitutes. The whale's intestines make good containers, and the tendons and nerves can be used as ropes."

Everyone was glad to land and clean up. After a refreshing bath, clean clothes, and dinner, we were all cheered up, and we rested up for the next phase.

CHAPTER 14

A Casualty

"Now to finish this dirty job," I cried merrily as we got busy the next morning. We had many tubs of blubber to boil, dipping off the oil and storing it in the whale intestine containers. It took all our combined effort to store these in the cellar, as my sons called our roughest storeroom. It was a great relief to finish this smelly task. I think Elizabeth hated it most, but she showed her usual tact and good temper. In her words, "If you built an outpost on that island where you found the whale, you could leave animals there. It would also be a fine place to boil whale blubber."

The boys loved the idea and wanted to begin right away. "After today's work, you want to build right next to a rotting whale carcass?" I said with a smile.

"Birds and insects will help us clean that up," said Ernest. "Let's wait." His brothers agreed, and we put off the outpost on Whale Island for a while. We put our energy into repairing the damage the storms of the rainy season had done to our farms.

A few weeks later, after much hard work, I felt it was time for my family to have an outing. One evening at dinner I proposed, "It is time to begin our outpost at Whale Island. Let's take the pinnace and go to Prospect Hill tomorrow by way of Cape Disappointment. We can have our lunch there and gather sugar cane shoots which we can plant on Whale Island." All agreed enthusiastically, and we spent the evening preparing for an all-day trip.

After breakfast the next morning we set out across the bay. The weather was calm, and everyone enjoyed the beautiful coastal scenery. We moored the pinnace near Prospect Hill and walked through the woods to our little farm, collecting some coconuts and young shrubs to begin our plantation on Whale Island.

I heard the rooster's crow before we came in sight of the cottage, and I felt a sudden rush of homesickness. At home, this sound would have announced our approach to a friend's home. It would have meant warm welcomes, comfortable seats, something to drink, and good company. Here, except for the animals, there was utter solitude. I loved my family, but I missed other people.

No sooner had my animals reminded me of my loneliness than they distracted me from it. The original sheep, goats, and chickens had forgotten us; their young had never seen a human. They all reacted by crowing, bleating, and scattering in every direction, as though we were wolves. It took some time and all our combined efforts to get them all rounded up and the goats milked.

My sons had persuaded their mother to cook a piece of whale tongue to bring along. What a surprise they got at lunchtime! One by one, they tried it and proclaimed it horrid. My foresighted wife had brought along pickled herring as well, and the boys clamored for this to kill the taste. They gave the supposed delicacy to Fangs, a far less picky diner. The fresh, delicious coconuts and goats' milk soon put everyone in a better mood.

After lunch Fritz and I gathered some sugar cane shoots to plant on Whale Island. Once we were back in the pinnace, I would have liked to explore beyond Cape Disappointment, but the cape ended in a long sandbank dotted with reefs and breakers well out to sea. I couldn't risk the pinnace, much less my loved ones, so we caught a light breeze for Whale Island.

At first the boys helped plant sugar cane, but they soon tired of this and wandered off in search of shells and coral, leaving their mother and me to finish the work. They had worked hard enough lately that I didn't mind. Presently Jack came back, shouting: "Father! Mother! Come look! There's a huge skeleton—a mammoth, I think!"

"Why, Jack!" I replied, laughing, "have you already forgotten our whale? What else could it be?"

"It's not the whale, Father," he answered. "They're animal bones. The whale must have floated out to sea. This is much bigger—come see!"

As I was about to follow, Fritz's voice called from another direction, "Father! A great big turtle! Hurry—he's trying to get back to sea!" Jack's skeleton, whatever it was, would wait. I grabbed an oar and hurried over. It was indeed a huge turtle, eight feet long, scrambling quickly toward the water despite Ernest's grip on one of its hind legs. I sprang down the bank and levered the turtle onto its back with Fritz's help. He would keep while we investigated Jack's "mammoth skeleton."

There could be only one conclusion. "It's the whale, Jack," I said.

"It can't be! These aren't fish bones!" he protested.

"Then explain these human shoe prints just like ours," I suggested. "Where'd you get that notion about a mammoth?"

"From Ernest, Father. He told me there was

a monster's skeleton, so I ran to look closer. I saw no fish bones, so I didn't think of the whale. I guess he was joking."

"Whales aren't fish," I explained. "They nurse their young, like all mammals. Their hollow bones help them float, just as the hollow bones of birds enable them to fly. You can see God's wisdom in every living creature."

"And His generosity," added Fritz. "Surely we can get some use from these bones?"

"Let's leave them here to bleach for awhile. Maybe we can make furniture from them someday. Right now, let's bring the boat around and figure out how to handle the turtle."

It was obvious that the large reptile would have to swim. I tied one end of a long rope around his neck and forepaws, then tied a big empty barrel near this as a float. We fastened the other end to the pinnace's bow and heaved the turtle right side up. He made for the water and tried to dive, but the barrel prevented him. Then he began to swim hard for the open sea.

"Hurry! Everyone on board!" I ordered. We all hastened into the pinnace, and the helpful turtle began to tow us toward the mainland. I was ready to cut the line at any sign of danger, but I learned to steer him. If I splashed on one side of him with a boat hook, he swam the other way. "You're like Neptune in his cart, Father, pulled by dolphins!" Jack exclaimed.

"Let's hope I'm not a pagan god," I laughed as we landed safely near Rockburg. Putting the turtle to death wasn't a very kind reward for its hard work, and I made sure it was done with one clean stroke. The immense shell would make a fine water trough, and we saved and salted the meat. The expedition had been a great success.

I wanted to increase our farmland before the next rainy season, but I found it very difficult to train our animals to the yoke, so I gave up for the moment. Instead, I applied myself to improving my wife's loom, in which Ernest had noted some minor flaws. Fortunately, in my youth I had spent many hours in the workshops of weavers and other artisans, and Ernest and I tinkered with the loom until we got it right.

While Elizabeth took advantage of the modified loom, I set the rest of us to harnessmaking. We had plenty of leather and wood and moss, so I had all my sons make saddles, stirrups, bridles, yokes, and collars for each mount. These proved most helpful, and it was good that each boy prepare his own animal's equipment.

Before long, the herring bank returned, followed by many other fish and seals. The work was far easier this time: the boys were a year older, and all knew what to expect. After we had laid in a large supply, the boys wanted to go on a hunting trip, but I felt basketmaking was more important.

Our sacks were beginning to wear out, and we needed ways to carry crops and fruit. When we had a fine supply of baskets, I had my sons make a very large one with openings for a strong stick. With one person on each end, we could carry a great deal.

My sons got an idea. Hoisting little Franz into the basket, they carried the delighted child around for a while. Then Fritz suggested, "Father, couldn't we make something like this for mother? She would be a lot more comfortable. The cart jolts her around a lot."

His brothers cheered the idea, but Elizabeth was skeptical. "I'd be sitting in the middle, just peeking out over the edge now and then," she objected. "I'd feel isolated."

"We would make a comfortable chair on a litter," I reassured her. "But how would we carry it? You boys would get tired of it, and what if you stumbled?"

"The bull and the buffalo!" cried Jack. "Let's try them!" The boys ran off, and in a short time the basket hung securely between Storm and Grumble. Fritz and Jack sprang into their saddles, and Ernest very gingerly climbed into the "cradle," as Franz called it. They set out at a sober pace. The animals were cooperative, if a bit surprised.

"Mother, this is fun," cried Ernest as they passed us. "It rocks gently. Quicker, Fritz!" The riders spurred their animals into a trot, which pleased Ernest equally—until I saw Jack and Fritz exchange looks and crack riding crops. Their mounts took off at full gallop, jolting the basket around fearfully. Ernest began to protest. "Slow down! This is too fast! Stop this thing! Let me off!" His brothers, in no hurry to heed his protests, did a full lap around the level ground near Rockburg. They finally pulled up in front of us like performers awaiting applause.

Elizabeth and I couldn't help laughing, but Ernest wasn't amused. "I asked you to stop!" he complained. "I felt like the rocks we put inside a calabash!"

"You asked us to speed up, and we did," Fritz said hotly. "Stop crying about it."

"What was the matter?" asked Jack, not kindly. "Was the Professor scared?"

I could see tempers rising on all sides and felt bound to step in. "All of you be quiet," I said in tones of command. "See how easily a joke can go too far. In case any of you have somehow forgotten, you're stuck here with no one to depend on but your family. You can't afford to quarrel—we all need each other."

Fritz looked uncomfortable. "I'm sorry, Ernest," he said. "It was meant in fun."

"And I'm sorry for making fun of you, too," added Jack.

Ernest broke into a smile. "I forgive you both," he said. "To show it, I'll help you unharness the animals. Let's give them some salt and grain as a reward, and practice this litter carrying another day." So good fellowship was restored.

Not long after that, I was working on a basket with my wife and Fritz on the porch. Fritz suddenly got up and took a few steps toward Jackal River, looked, then exclaimed, "Father, I see something very strange coming toward the bridge. First it seems to be coiled up on the ground, then it rises up, then sinks, and the coils move again. What could it be?"

Alarmed, Elizabeth hastened to herd the younger boys into Rockburg. I told them to close the entrances and stand watch with loaded guns at the upper windows. I was glad we had made these windows, for they made the cave a strong fighting position. Fritz remained with me while I examined the object with my spyglass.

"It's a huge snake, just as I suspected!" I exclaimed. "It's coming, and it's sure to cross the bridge. This will be very dangerous!"

"Can't we attack it, Father?" exclaimed the brave boy.

"With great care," I answered. "They're very hard to kill, very strong, and most dangerous when wounded and angry. Thank God we're at Rockburg, where we can retreat to safety and watch for a chance to destroy it. Go inside and supervise the defense. I'll join you after I get a sense of the monster's movements."

Fritz left me unwillingly, while I continued to watch the immense snake. It was already too close to Family-bridge for anyone to block its path by lifting the span, and it could easily break Rockburg's windows if it wanted to enter. From time to time its head reared up to fifteen or twenty feet high, as if hunting. When it crossed the bridge, I withdrew to Rockburg and joined the garrison, much to everyone's relief. After we had barricaded the lower windows we took up positions at the higher ones; even my wife pointed a weapon.

The snake soon approached Rockburg's front door. It hesitated, sticking out its long tongue as if trying to puzzle out an unfamiliar smell. Unable to resist, Jack fired a shot into the monster, followed immediately by Franz, Ernest, and Elizabeth. The barrage seemed only to startle the snake, so Fritz and I fired with steadier aim but equal lack of effect. The great snake hurried along into the reedy marsh to our left, then out of view.

It felt as if a weight had been lifted from our hearts—at least for the moment. "That was a boa constrictor, at least thirty feet long—large even for its kind," I explained. "It crushes its prey in its coils, then swallows it whole. Neither a boy nor an adult would be a difficult meal for it. No one is to go outside for any reason without my express permission."

We spent three full days in suspense, not daring to go more than a few hundred steps from the door. The boa showed no sign of returning. "Maybe it's gone someplace else after we scared it?" suggested Franz.

"I doubt it," answered my wife. "See how odd and restless the geese and ducks are acting? I suspect he's still in their swamp." Eventually they grew so disturbed they took flight for Shark Island. What would we do? We didn't have the force to defeat it, but we couldn't exist this way forever. In the end we were delivered from it not by bravery and cleverness but by sheer stupidity.

We didn't yet have a large supply of animal fodder. Late in the third day, we ran out of hay. I planned to send Fritz on a mission to herd the animals to the grazing area across the river. He would ride Lightfoot, keep the animals fastened together until they crossed, then disable the bridge.

The next morning, as we were tying the animals into a line, my wife opened the door. Old Grizzle, frolicsome after his long rest and regular feeding, broke away. After some awkward capering, he took off at a joyful gallop.

He was headed straight for the marsh.

We all called his name, but in vain. Fritz would have rushed after him, but I held him back. We could only watch in horror as the snake rose from its lair, glanced around, opened its dark deadly jaws, and darted forth a greedy forked tongue.

Only then did Grizzle realize his peril, and he splayed his legs and began the most piteous, anguished bray ever to echo from a cliffside. Swift and straight as a fencer's thrust, the boa was upon him.

The great snake wound all around Grizzle, cunningly avoiding the donkey's agonized kicks. To my family's urgent appeals to shoot it, I could only tell the sad truth. "It's impossible, I'm afraid. Our old friend is lost to us. However, when the boa is full, its turn may come."

"Surely it isn't going to swallow Grizzle whole, Father?" exclaimed Jack. "That's awful!"

"That's all it can do," I explained. "Snakes can't chew. They have no teeth. It's horrible, but no worse than lions and tigers tearing up their prey in a bloody mess."

"But," said Franz, "how can the snake separate the flesh from the bones without teeth? And is it poisonous?"

"Not poisonous," I said, "just strong and fierce. It can digest bones, skin, hair, and all after it has crushed them."

"It seems impossible," exclaimed Fritz. "I can't imagine Grizzle fitting into that mouth."

"The boa will crush him first," I explained. "Elizabeth, this might be a good time for you and Franz to find something to do inside." They needed no persuasion and hastened into the cave. The rest of us bided our time in fearful fascination as the boa worked over his prey, a process that took from seven in the morning to noon. Finally the boa lay stiff and distorted along the edge of the marsh.

"Now or never!" I commanded. "Be brave, but be sensible! Follow me!" I led my sons from Rockburg with a new exhilaration I had never known before, approaching the snake with leveled gun and rapid steps. Fritz followed me closely; Jack followed more timidly. Ernest hesitated, then stayed put.

The monster's body was motionless, which made its fiery eyes and the slow twitches of its tail more fearful by contrast. Fritz and I advanced to point-blank range. When I halted, so did he. We raised our guns.

My son and I fired together, and both bullets entered the skull. The light went out of the monster's eye, and the snake's body thrashed and writhed. Advancing carefully, we fired our pistols directly into its head.

A convulsive quiver ran through the mighty frame, and the boa constrictor lay dead.

As we raised a cry of victory, Jack made his move for glory. He ran close to the creature and fired a pistol into its side. The immense tail jerked and bowled the boy over. Unhurt, Jack got to his feet. "I finished it off!" he cheered.

My wife approached, holding Franz tightly by the hand. "I hope those were the sounds of victory," she said.

"They were. Let's thank God we succeeded," I said meaningfully, looking around. Fritz knelt, followed by the rest, and I led my family in prayer.

Afterward, Jack asked, "What do we do with him now?"

"Stuff him and put him in the museum," said Fritz. We agreed to this plan.

My wife went to make lunch while we rested in the shade near the snake. It was pleasant to be outdoors, and we couldn't leave the snake's carcass unless we wanted it damaged by birds of prey. We discussed snakes, snake poison, and the snake charmers of India.

"What should we do in case of snake bite?" asked Fritz.

"It varies depending on the snake," I answered, "and we probably don't have any of the remedies here, so be careful not to get bitten. But Ernest," I added, "how shall we remember our poor friend the donkey? He deserves better burial, for he was faithful if unwise."

Ernest thought a moment. "Let's bury him near here, not in the swamp of course, and place a board as his tombstone. We can burn his name onto the board, and—" Here he stopped to think a bit longer. "—Yes! The words: 'Here lies our faithful donkey Grizzle, whose tragic death saved our lives.'"

"Very good, Ernest! Perfect epitaph!" I said, and the others agreed. Fritz brought a scrap of lumber. Ernest heated a poker originally meant for a colonial fireplace and marked the board with the words.

After lunch, we got to work on the snake. First we recovered the mangled remains of Grizzle, whom we buried in a quiet ceremony. Then we yoked Storm and Grumble to drag the boa's corpse near Rockburg. Skinning, stuffing, and sewing took three days. We coiled it around a pole in the museum, arranging the head with jaws wide open, and making realistic-looking replacement eyes and a long tongue. Our taxidermy was skillful enough that our dogs growled each time they passed the monster. They must have wondered at our sense in keeping such a pet.

CHAPTER 15

We Explore Inland

*T*he danger had passed, but my concern hadn't. What if another huge snake showed up? I saw a need for two expeditions: a sweep of the swamp and woods for snakes, and a visit to the gap in the rocks we thought we had fortified so well.

Ernest and Jack showed no enthusiasm. "I get chills every time I think of that snake's tail," Jack explained.

"That's why you have to come," I said. "You must face what you fear, and the sooner the better. Plus, we need your eyes and gun."

Bearing in mind Jack's story of getting stuck in the swamp, we used boards and wicker bundles to help us through. We found the snake's lair in the swamp but no sign of other snakes. Going a little further onto firmer ground, we noticed clear water flowing from a cave in the rock wall.

"Get some torches going," I told my sons. When we had light, I peered inside.

The cave was very large, pillared with stalactites, and its floor was covered with fine white dust. I knelt and rubbed a bit through my fingers. It was fuller's earth, which could substitute for soap. "Your mother will be very happy. We're almost out of soap in camp," I explained.

Fritz followed the streamlet back into the cave. Soon I heard him calling back to us, "It gets wider! Father, come look at this!"

"Jack, Ernest, stay here," I ordered and strode forward to join Fritz.

"Look at the walls!" said Fritz when I arrived. The torchlight reflected lovely colors from a crystalline roof onto the sides of the passage. "It's another salt cave!"

"But the water leaves no track through the crystals," I replied. "Taste it; it's not salty. I think this is a cave of pure rock crystal!" I fired a shot to see if anything fell from the roof. Nothing did.

"Then we've found a great treasure!" he exclaimed.

"If we had anyone to trade it with," I said. "Without that it's not very useful."

"I'll break some off anyway," said Fritz. He cracked off a piece with the butt of his gun, then another, until he found a piece that pleased him. Fritz fired a farewell shot just to hear the echoes, and out we went.

Back at the entrance, poor Jack was sobbing. He threw himself into my arms. "What's the matter?" I asked, anxiously.

"I thought you were lost! I heard loud noises, like rocks shattering down, and I thought you and Fritz were buried in a rock fall! It was horrible!"

I explained the noises and comforted him. "Where's Ernest?" I asked him.

"Over in the reeds. He probably didn't hear the shots, but I heard him shoot something."

I found Ernest busily weaving an ingenious basket, shaped like a funnel, to catch fish. "Also, Father, I shot a big snake," said he. "It's over there, about four feet long."

"A snake?" I said, hurrying that direction in alarm. This soon turned to relief when I saw the carcass. "Son, this is an eel, not a snake. It'll make an excellent dinner."

We made our way back to Rockburg on the firmer ground near the cliffs. When we arrived, my wife was washing clothes at the fountain. It was a good time to show her the fuller's earth. "Yes, this will work!" she said, testing a bit. "Otherwise, we would have had to start boiling our own soap soon." Over our dinner of boiled eel, we told the full story of our day. All agreed that we must continue to search for snakes in the woods of our territory between the cliffs and the sea. We began to prepare for a trip beyond Jackal River, as far as the Gap. The trip might take several weeks so we decided we should all go.

The next morning we got moving early. Jack and Franz yoked the cart to Storm and Grumble, helped their mother in, then saddled and mounted their steeds. Franz's great success with Grumble never ceased to amaze me. Fritz led on Lightfoot. Ernest and I walked. All five dogs—Turk, Juno, Bruno, Fawn, and Fangs the jackal—flanked the party.

On the way to Woodlands, we saw furrows in the soil where the boa had pushed off or glided through. Our path led through the beautiful clearing of Falconhurst, where we checked on the chickens, sheep, and goats before moving on. Night was falling as we reached Woodlands, which was in good order. There were no signs of great boas or mischievous apes or any other unpleasant surprise.

Over breakfast in the morning, I said, "First we'll gather cotton for new pillows and cushions. In the afternoon, Franz and I are going exploring."

My youngest began to leap for delight, then seemed to remember that men didn't do so, and made a great effort to contain himself. Fritz smiled knowingly and gave his brother a light slap on the back. "Take good care of father, Franz," he said. "He has a way of finding strange things. You won't forget what I taught you about gun safety, right?"

"I promise," said Franz solemnly.

When we had enough cotton, I summoned my youngest son in the same no-nonsense way I would use with his brothers. "Franz, get your gun. Round up Fangs and Bruno, and let's get moving." Beaming with pride and excitement, Franz collected our escorts and came to my side. All exchanged farewells, and we were on our way.

We moved slowly through the reedy thickets on the left bank of the lake, sometimes having to detour far from the water. The dogs scared up ducks, snipe, and herons, but Franz couldn't get a good shot. He grew impatient. "Father, I could probably hit one of those swans," he said.

"No, Fr—" A harsh, slow booming noise interrupted me, and I paused to listen.

"Father, could that be our young onager Swift?" my son asked.

"No," I said, listening attentively. "It sounds like the call of a bittern, a water bird much like a heron."

"Can I shoot it? But how can a bird make that sort of noise? It sounds like an ox or something."

"Every bird is designed differently. Some believe that the bittern makes this odd booming noise by sticking his long bill into boggy ground."

"A rare bird for my first trophy, Father! May I?" I nodded. We sent the dogs into the woods and stood ready.

All at once there was a great rustling in the thicket. Franz fired, and I heard his happy voice calling out, "I've hit him! I've hit him!"

"What have you hit?" I shouted.

"A wild pig," he said.

I soon joined my boy, who was very excited over his quarry. It was much like a pig, but not quite, for it was yellowish-gray and had no tail. It looked like a very large guinea pig. "Franz, I think this is a capybara. They normally live in South America," I said.

"Hurray! I discovered a new creature!" he said. "But how can I carry it?"

"Think."

After a few seconds Franz said, "We should clean it here, to make it lighter." We cut it open and cleaned it, and he put it in his game bag. Even so, after a while it began to slow him down. "Father, this is heavy. Do you think Bruno would let me strap it onto his back?"

"Try it and see!" I answered. Bruno proved cooperative, and we soon reached Woodlands, where Ernest was surrounded by a lot of large, rat-like carcasses. "I thought you and your mother were going rice gathering, not rat hunting!"

"We did," answered Ernest. "While we were in the swamp, Knips jumped away to a sort of long mound and pounced on something. It tried to duck into a hole, but Knips got it by the tail. When I got there, I saw that it was a big rat, so I killed it with a stick.

"I decided to break open the mound. It turned out to be a big rats' nest. About a dozen came out, and I killed some, but the rest swam away. I saw similar ones close by, so I put my game bag across an entrance and hammered on the roof. A whole bunch of rats sprang out, and I caught some in the bag. I started clubbing the rest, but they fought back! What a mess! They were also trying to bite Knips, and he got a lot more bites than he gave.

"I was about to yell for help when Juno came dashing in. She made short work of them. Mother helped me collect these. Their skins at least might be useful."

I asked Ernest to show me the scene. To my surprise, it was much like a beaver dam, though somewhat smaller and less complete. "These are muskrats, also called beaver rats," I said. "Notice their webbed feet and flat tails. Let's skin them to make hats."

We went back to the house and met Fritz and Jack returning from their own excursion. "No snakes of any size, Father," reported Jack. He had about a dozen eggs, and Fritz had shot a couple of grouse. We sat down to supper, Franz eager to try his capybara. Even he made a face at the peculiar flavor.

Presently Jack remembered something and ran for his game bag. He came back with several pale green apples for our inspection.

"What are those? Are they good?" I asked.

"I hope so," said Jack, "but Fritz and I thought we should let Professor Knips sample them first."

I took one and cut it in two. While I examined one half, Knips sneaked up, grabbed a half, and began to munch with lively satisfaction. The boys hurried to follow suit, and I had some difficulty securing a couple for Elizabeth and myself. They tasted delicious, much like the cinnamon apple of the Antilles. "Excellent discovery, Son," I complimented Jack. "Now let's get ready for bed, so we can get an early start tomorrow."

In the morning we quickly ate breakfast and got going. I remembered us building a tree branch shelter between the canebrake and the Gap and told Fritz to lead us there. The shelter had held up well so we made it our campsite. Fritz, Jack, Franz, and I went snake hunting, and while we found no snakes, a trip through a sugar canebrake had its own delicious rewards.

The loud barking of dogs and a great rustling soon disturbed our refreshment. We couldn't see very far in the canebrake, so I led us to the open ground, where we readied our weapons and waited.

In a few minutes, a herd of small gray pig-like creatures trotted out of the thicket. My trusty double barrel accounted for two, and Fritz and

Jack got several. The others followed their leader at a steady pace, barely stepping around their comrades' bodies. They looked like peccaries, a breed of wild pigs, which meant we must act quickly. "They have scent glands that must be removed immediately, or it'll taint the meat," I told them, taking out my knife. "Watch how I do this, then get to work." Their swift action gave me hope that this large supply of meat would not be ruined.

At this point we heard shots coming from camp. "Jack, find out what that was all about, then bring back the cart while we clean these."

When he came back, he brought Ernest, who explained: "This same peccary troop came near camp. Juno and I got three."

"Good job, Son," I said. "Fritz, show him what to do. We'll have to smoke this fine supply of hams." As we loaded the peccaries onto the cart, the boys struck up a song of triumph. They had done well, and they knew it.

After dinner we started the smoking process, singeing off the bristles and cutting out the meat. The dogs gorged on tremendous portions of rejected peccary. While I salted the meat, the boys built a smoking shed and gathered green wood. This work continued into the next day, broken up only by Fritz's experiment at cooking a peccary in a ground oven.

The following day we took a trip to Prospect Hill only to find that the apes had ravaged it as well. Animals and birds were scattered, and the cottage was a disaster. Setting things right would have to wait for another day, for we needed to press on to the Gap. We closed the smoking shed up very tightly, leaving the peccary meat hanging inside, and began our next march in the usual formation.

In a few hours we reached the bounds of our coastal territory, halting at a little wood just downhill of the Gap. To the right of the woods and behind it rose frowning mountain cliffs. The river that rushed through the Gap flowed to the left of the woods and on toward the sea. I felt this would be a good camping spot. Once we were satisfied there were no dangerous animals nearby, I ordered a general rest until evening. Tomorrow we would explore inland.

In the morning, my brave wife agreed to stay behind with Franz and Juno. The three older boys and all the other dogs went with me, as did Knips. The way through the narrow, barricaded portion of the pass was much easier than it should have been because our barrier was mostly broken down. This was apparently the result of storm damage and flash flooding. We also saw signs that the great snake and the peccary herd had entered our territory through this narrow gorge. "Shall we fortify it again, Father?" asked Fritz.

"I believe we must try," I replied. "Not

today, but soon. We'll have to make the defenses twice as strong." With that we passed into the interior. Before us lay a great plain leading to green hills and wooded valleys, with a range of tall peaks in the distance. We halted to fill our water flasks at the stream, which we named East River. It was good that we did for the soil grew drier and drier as we headed inland.

"We've crossed into Arabia," groaned Ernest.

"Or the Sahara Desert," sighed Jack.

"It must be Hell," said Fritz. "I expect to see demons any moment."

"That's not funny," I scolded. "Don't be so easily discouraged. Who knows what lies ahead in those lovely mountains? I expect to find water, fresh grass, trees, and a pleasant campsite." Despite my cheery optimism, by the time we found a clump of spiny euphorbia trees, we were all grateful for some shade. I remembered from my studies that these trees exuded a poisonous sap. I cut some notches in the bark high off the ground.

As we broke out our traveling rations, Knips began to snuff about in his ridiculous way, then gave a shriek of pleasure and set off at full speed toward a valley we had passed. The dogs followed, and we decided to let the little rogue have his way while we ate lunch.

When our hunger was satisfied, Fritz looked out over the plain for a moment, then exclaimed, "Do I see a party of horsemen riding toward us?"

"Take the spyglass and give us a better description. We'll be on guard."

He did so. "I can't quite tell," he said. "It could be wild cattle, loaded carts, or almost anything else. Here, have a look," he added as he passed the glass to Jack. He and Ernest looked in turn and agreed—they seemed to be men on horseback.

This could be very serious. I took the glass and looked for a few moments. "Those are ostriches! We should try to catch one—the feathers alone would be worth it!"

"If we caught one alive, Father, could we ride him?" asked Jack.

"Worth a try," was my answer. "Fritz, Jack, bring back the dogs. Let's hide in the shrubs and see how close they come."

The boys were gone for some time, for they found Knips and the dogs at a pool of water along a mountain stream, and sensibly took time to fill their flasks before returning. When we were all together again, we leashed the dogs and waited.

The ostriches came on, making no great haste, and I saw that there were only five. "Four females and a male, to judge by the contrasting plumage," I observed. "I don't see a way to catch them, except perhaps by sending Fritz's eagle. Even then we'll have to let them get as near as possible."

"How do people catch ostriches?" asked Fritz.

"Sometimes on horseback. But ostriches can often outrun horses so the rider must tire the ostrich out and then attack. Sometimes a hunter will wrap himself in an ostrich skin, putting his arm up the neck to imitate the bird's feeding movements. This enables him to get very close. But it takes a lot of courage, because ostriches can kick hard enough to maim a man. But get ready—they're almost here!"

As they neared, the stately birds sensed our presence and halted with uneasy steps. When nothing happened, they came closer to investigate us. The dogs broke loose and rushed the ostrich flock, which fled with the speed of the wind. In a few moments they would have been beyond our reach, but Fritz unhooded his eagle. Singling out the male bird, the eagle dove with great precision and pierced the skull to bring the magnificent creature down. Before we could reach the spot, the dogs had joined the eagle in a feast, splattering the splendid plumes with gore.

Fritz spoke for all as he collected the beautiful feathers. "What a pity we couldn't capture him alive! He could probably have carried two of us at once!"

"How do ostriches survive in the desert?" asked Ernest.

"On melons, wild grasses, dates, and grain," I said.

"Interesting. What sound do they make?"

"It's a deep hollow rumbling sound, so much like the roar of a lion—wait! Why's Jack waving his cap like that? I wonder what he's found?"

Jack ran a little way toward us, shouting, "A huge nest of ostrich eggs, Father! Come quickly!" We all hurried to see. In a slight hollow lay over twenty eggs, each as large as a baby's head. The boys wanted to bring them all.

"They're heavier than you think," I said. "Two will be enough. Let's cover the rest, and put up a landmark so we can check on them again if we pass by."

True to my warning, Jack and Ernest found their fragile burdens awkward, even when slung in handkerchiefs. Remembering the clever device of Dutch milkmaids, I cut a strong, long stick and slung a handkerchief at each end. From there, Jack carried the eggs much more easily.

We presently reached a marshy little watering hole. The soft ground was full of animal tracks—buffalo, antelope, and perhaps onager, but no trace of snakes. We sat down to rest and eat.

Our journey soon led to a charming valley dotted with graceful trees, which we named Green Valley. What a joy after our hot, dry march! We could see herds of antelope or buffalo feeding in the distance, but the dogs ranged far ahead and stampeded these out of the valley. Soon we came to open ground. I told Ernest to run ahead with Turk and look for signs of any other herds. They raced off and we lost sight of them for a few minutes. Suddenly we heard a cry of terror, then a series of violent barks and deep surly growls.

The rest of us rushed forward, meeting a white-faced Ernest. He ran to me, quivering in panic. "What is it?" I asked.

"A bear's coming!"

"Courage, my boy!" I urged. "Let's get ready for battle!" The dogs dashed bravely forward as we loaded our guns. We were not long in doubt for an enormous bear soon appeared with Turk snarling and barking at his advance.

Worse yet, along came a second.

With leveled guns, my brave Fritz and I advanced slowly to meet them. Jack was also ready to fire, but Ernest fled. We fired together, one at each bear, but the monsters were only wounded; one had a broken lower jaw, the other a wounded shoulder. This was very bad. One of the few things more dangerous than a healthy, angry bear is a wounded, infuriated bear. As our dogs kept the bears occupied, I gave a quick order: "Don't take any chance of hitting a dog. If you do, the bears will tear it apart. Fritz, load your pistol; we must get very close. Jack, cover us."

When the bears were fully distracted by the snapping, darting courage of our dogs, Fritz and I each advanced on a bear. As the bears began to react, we fired. I shot mine in the head, dead as he fell. Fritz's bear reared to spring on him, but a pistol bullet in its heart ended the battle.

"Thank Heaven!" I cried. "That was our narrowest escape yet!" The dogs continued to tear at the fallen enemies, as though distrusting the appearance of death. I drew my hunting knife and with two quick slashes made sure the creatures would never be a danger again.

Seeing all safe, Jack raised a shout of victory to summon poor Ernest back from hiding. My frightened young intellectual soon joined us in marveling at their mighty claws, their sharp teeth, their powerful shoulders, and the glossy white tips on the brown hair.

"Well, my lads," I said, "we haven't found any huge snakes, but we've gotten rid of another danger! One day they would have harmed us, unless I'm much mistaken. Now what?"

"Bearskin rugs!" said Fritz.

"It'll take a long time to skin them," I said. "Let's hide them, along with the eggs, and move camp here." We dragged the huge bodies into their den, blocking up the entry with every tree-branch we could find, and buried the eggs in a sandy hole.

By sunset we returned to camp, where my wife and Franz had prepared us a hearty meal and gathered plenty of brushwood for the watch fire. We gave a full account of our adventures, then listened as Elizabeth told what they had accomplished in our absence. She and Franz had scouted the area and discovered a bed of pure white clay, which she thought might be good for porcelain. She had made a drinking trough for the cattle from a split bamboo, then built a hearth of large stones and clay. After this she had cut us some strong canes for building material.

"Excellent work, dear!" I said. "Let's put some pieces of your clay near the fire tonight. In the morning, we'll see what we have." When this was done, we lay down for a well-earned rest.

I roused my little party at dawn. The clay had baked to a fine hard glaze, but the heat had melted it out of shape before it hardened. Given the fine quality of the clay, it would be well worth our time to solve this problem. After breakfast and devotions, we harnessed the cart for a move to the bears' den.

Fritz headed the party and, coming in sight of the cave, called out softly, "Hurry, and you'll see a whole crowd of wild turkeys. Apparently they've come for the bears' funeral, but there's a watcher out front, and he won't let them in for the viewing!"

Fritz's "watcher" was an immense condor, with a sort of comb on his head and loose fleshy skin hanging under his sharp beak. Part of the neck was bare, wrinkled, and purplish. His feet were armed with strong talons. This great bird guarded the entrance to the cave, occasionally going inside for a few minutes. When the others tried to follow, he hurried out and chased them back. "Fritz, those aren't turkeys—they're turkey vultures."

As we stopped to watch the scene, a mighty rush of wings overhead startled us. We looked up. Fritz fired and brought down an enormous bird. It was a second condor, perhaps the mate of the first. We had been holding back the dogs, but now Fritz and they rushed the cave, chasing away the vultures and the surviving condor. I entered the cave with caution, glad to see the bear carcasses mostly intact. A little later and the scavenging birds would have torn their fine skins to rags.

I measured the dead condor's wingspan—eleven feet at least! We all got to work on the long job of skinning and butchering the bears. The fallen monsters provided magnificent hams, and we planned to smoke the remainder of the meat before transporting it. The paws were a delicacy, and we got a tremendous supply of bear-grease, which Elizabeth began to melt and prepare for storage. The bones and remaining flesh we dragged far from the cave, a consolation prize for the birds. The turkey vultures worked so efficiently that the skulls were picked clean by the time we left, ready for us to carry home to our museum.

As my sons gathered brush, I examined the brush pile and spotted a vine bearing clusters of small berries like currants. Some seemed red and ripe; others looked green. The leaves smelled spicy. "Pepper plants!" I exclaimed. My boys hurried to collect all the berries.

"How do we prepare them?" asked Fritz.

"Leave that to me," said my wife. "They need to soak in salted water for a few days. The unripe ones will ripen if left out. After soaking, they'll turn white, and I'll dry them in the sun. We'll have enough pepper to last us a long time, and if you collect some of the young plants, we'll plant them at Rockburg." In the process, my sons found another type of plant with bean pods, and collected some to cultivate as well. We also prepared the condor for stuffing.

These were useful diversions during the long and rather dull process of smoking the bear meat, but I could see that the boys were getting bored. I could also see that, just as I had made Jack face his fears, I must now face one of mine.

If I wanted my sons to grow into men, I had to give them the opportunity.

CHAPTER 16

A Winged Steed

*T*he next morning, I had a proposal for my boys: "If you wish, you may go exploring without me."

"Hurray!" shouted Fritz and Jack. Ernest showed little interest, and since this was a pleasure trip, I wouldn't pressure him. Franz, however, was delighted to go. In high spirits they got their mounts ready and came to say goodbye.

This was an important moment. I had long realized that fate—or the will of God—could orphan my sons in an instant. In such a case they could only survive if they developed bold self-reliance, a quality Fritz constantly displayed. I gave orders. "Fritz, take care of your brothers. Jack and Franz, learn from Fritz, and obey him as your leader."

"We will, Father," my two younger sons replied. I was sure that Franz would, at least, and

"Well, perhaps we didn't ride quite that long, and our speed is only a guess. In any case, Fritz heard us, and he and Franz tied their legs."

"I am pleased at how well you three worked together," I said. Then, turning to Fritz, I continued, "I agree we should establish your rabbits on Whale Island. I've been thinking of fortifying it as a retreat in time of extreme danger. Having a constant food supply there would be a great benefit."

When we had taken care of the fawns, I tried to interest the boys in the talc I had discovered, but just then their mother called us to dinner. The bears' paws were delicious, despite their resemblance to giant human hands.

I was very satisfied with our work. The bear meat was smoked, the fat rendered, and we had a large supply of bamboos. I had another venture in mind and planned to wake the boys up at dawn.

After prayers and breakfast the next morning, I said, "Boys, let's go back to the euphorbia and collect the sap, then see if the ostrich hen came back to her eggs." Only Ernest showed little interest, and I excused him while the others ran to get ready. Fritz rode young Swift the mule. I rode Lightfoot; Jack and Franz took their usual steeds. We took Turk and Juno. Ernest stayed to help his mother and study.

could only hope that Jack would too. They were well armed, well mounted, and had a couple of good dogs. I could do only one more thing: wish them well.

"God bless you, my boys, and Godspeed!" As I watched them ride away, I felt a mix of pride and sadness. I took a moment to appreciate each boy in my mind, to value a moment that would soon be lost forever with his maturity. Each was a blessing.

Ernest decided to make the ostrich eggs into ornamental cups. I helped my wife smoke the bear meat and explored the cave. Its wall was made of a kind of talc, and I found some mica—a thin, clear mineral. I carefully broke away a large block of this, and was pleased to find that I could split it into clear transparent sheets. "Those will be fine window panes," said my wife. "We can never get enough replacements for glass."

Evening drew on. We sat talking around the fire, enjoying the savory aroma of bear paw stew, listening anxiously for the sound of returning explorers.

At last we heard the sound of hooves. It felt odd indeed going out to meet returning adventurers, and I got a glimpse of my wife's everyday experience. The little troop gave a ringing cheer as they saw us and leaped down from their saddles.

Franz and Jack had each a fawn antelope

slung on his back, so that the four bound little hooves stuck out under their chins. Fritz's game bag had bulges in every direction, some of them moving. "Nothing like real hunting, Father!" cried Jack. "Storm and Grumble giving chase on a grassy plain! That's how we managed to tire out the fawns."

"Yes, Father," said Franz, "and Fritz has two angora rabbits in his bag!"

"My brothers forget the main thing," said Fritz. "We have driven a little herd of antelope right through the Gap into our territory. We can hunt them when we like, or tame them."

"Most impressive!" I cried. "But the main thing is that God has brought you safely home. Now, let's hear the whole story!"

"We had a splendid ride down Green Valley and through the Gap," said Fritz. "On top of a grassy hill, we saw a herd of antelope grazing by the stream. We were about to gallop down for a shot at them, when I got the idea to try driving them all through the Gap. That would pen them in our domain, free yet within reach.

"We rode downhill, fanned out in a semi-circle, and drove them along the stream toward the Gap. As we came near the opening, I thought they might turn and bolt past us, but eventually one made the rush through the Gap. The rest followed to become New Switzerland's newest settlers."

"That's great, Son," I said, "but just return through the Gap when the

"We thought of that, Father," "We stretched a rope across the Gap feathers and rags all along it, so they make the antelope afraid to approach

"Well," I said, "the antelopes are New Switzerland, but your rabbits ar breed so rapidly your next trouble w rid of them."

"That's why I thought we mig on Whale Island," replied Fritz. " have plenty of food without bother get furs and rabbit stew. Did you k eagle caught these?"

"Now, Father," interrupted J Fritz starts to put you to sleep v descriptions, will you hear my story

"Certainly, Jack," I said. "Hov those fawns?"

"We ran them down. The dog while Fritz was hunting the rabb took off at about thirty miles an h I chased them for about a quarter outran the dogs. When we caught collapsed with fatigue. So we sho and—"

"Son, by your statement, Fritz a half miles away."

Our steeds carried us quickly down Green Valley. We retraced our steps to the slope where Fritz had spotted the ostriches a few days earlier. Jack and Franz were eager for a gallop, so I allowed this while Fritz and I visited the euphorbia trees. Some milky sap had leaked from the cuts I had made, and I scraped it off with a stick and stored it in a bamboo jar I'd brought.

As we rode after the boys, Fritz remarked, "I remember you telling me that sap was poisonous, Father. Why did you collect so much?"

"If the apes ever bother us again, I'll use it against them," I replied. "It can also be used to keep insects off a surface, but we must be careful—it's poisonous to touch as well as to swallow."

The two boys were still far ahead of us when four magnificent ostriches—a black-plumed rooster and three ash-gray hens—suddenly rose from a dip in the sand. Jack and Franz saw them, gave a shout, and skillfully maneuvered to drive them toward us. The birds ran at an amazing pace. They were within gunshot range before they spotted Fritz and me.

Fritz had made a binder for his eagle's beak, so that it could bring down an ostrich without killing the quarry. Now he fitted the binder and released the eagle, which soared high and then dove on the rooster's head. The huge bird slowed in fear and confusion. Jack was first to catch up and threw his lasso about the great body. We let the others escape while we surrounded the captive, whose violent kicks kept us at a safe distance.

I was beginning to doubt we could take him alive when I remembered that we had calmed the eagle by covering his eyes. I sneaked up behind the ostrich and flung my game bag over his head. The eagle dodged backward, just as I had expected. The huge bird stopped kicking.

"Do you know," I said to the boys, "how they tame a newly captured elephant in India?"

"Tie him between two tame elephants," said Fritz.

"Too bad we have no tame ostriches," remarked Jack. "Perhaps we could tie him between Storm and Grumble."

"Let's see your method," I said. Franz and Jack tied a broad sealskin strip around the base of the bird's neck, leaving slack so he could breathe, then roped each end of the sealskin to their mounts' saddles. Using a third rope, they hobbled his legs so he could trot but not gallop.

When they were mounted up, I removed Jack's lasso and unhooded the ostrich. He lay still for a few moments, then bounded up and tried to run. After the hobble brought him down, he got up and set off at a sharp trot. Jack and Franz let their steeds run with him, but not too fast. When they reached loose sand, Storm and Grumble slowed. At that point the ostrich seemed to realize the futility of his situation, and the boys led him back with merry shouts.

"Now march him home," I ordered, "while Fritz and I examine the nest." The eggs were quite warm; the mother must have just left. Leaving about half, I packed the rest of the eggs in a large bag. Before long we caught up with Jack and Franz and reached our tent without further incident.

Elizabeth was not pleased. "My dear husband," she exclaimed, "do you think we have so much food that you must scour the desert for great beasts to help us eat it? I wish you'd be content with the menagerie you've already collected, instead of bringing home one of every useless monster you find!"

"Useless!" exclaimed Jack. "Mother, if you'd seen him run, you wouldn't say that. He'll be our fastest mount. I'm going to make him a saddle and bridle and learn to ride him. As for his appetite, Father says he only wants a little fruit and grass, plus a few rocks to help his digestion."

"You're not the only one who captured the ostrich," protested Franz.

"He's right," Fritz chimed in. "What right do you have to claim him?"

"Come, come," I said, "I think that Jack has a very good right to the ostrich, seeing that he brought it to the ground. He's now responsible for it. If he can tame and ride it, it's his."

It was too late in the day to start for Rock-burg, so we fastened the ostrich between two trees and spent the evening getting ready.

At early dawn our caravan set out for home. The ostrich was still troublesome, so we had to march him between Storm and Grumble. The cow hauled the cart, with all our finds and my wife. I rode Lightfoot, and Fritz brought up the rear on Swift.

At the mouth of the Gap we halted to build a strong bamboo fence in place of the boys' rope. We also collected plenty of pipe clay, for winter was coming—a good time to try making some china. While we were picking up our peccary hams at the canebrake, my wife discovered some sweet-smelling vines that turned out to be vanilla plants. She collected some plants and seeds before we moved on to our night's rest at Woodlands.

Early the next morning we examined our farmyard, which was prospering nicely. The sight of our domestic animals made us long for Rockburg. The pigs, goats, and birds had all increased in number, and my wife wanted to take back two fine broods of chickens. The antelope herd had also taken up residence here. We saw them browsing in the woods. We made some repairs to the animals' stalls and our dwelling, and the next day we set out for the final short leg of our journey. What a relief to see our comfortable salt cave again!

While I directed the unloading and storage work, I spent as much time as possible with the ostrich, whom we fastened between two bamboo posts in front of our home. I thought we might hatch the eggs, so I wrapped these in cotton and put them near our cooking-stove. "Franz, Ernest, Jack, keep a small fire going in here at all times," I ordered.

Next morning Fritz and I sailed for Whale Island to release his angora rabbits, then to Shark Island to turn loose the young antelopes. We hurried back to get started curing the bearskins. After we landed, we caught up with Jack carrying a large eel. "How'd you catch him?" I asked as we fell into step.

"Last night Ernest put out a couple of fishing lines. One was gone, but this splendid fellow was caught on the other."

"Well, he'll make a delicious lunch," I replied, and it was true. After we'd eaten, we started some home improvement jobs. I planted vanilla, pepper, and other creeping plants around the bamboo pillars of our porch, for the pleasant smell and the eventual shade. I built a couple of new hencoops for the chickens from Woodlands.

Everyone voted that Ernest's smelly muskratskins must go outside. But even out of doors,

Jack made a great show of pretending to pass out every time he came near them. "That's funny," said Fritz once, "coming from someone I remember wearing a putrid-smelling jackal hide belt." We put the condor in the museum, to be stuffed during the rainy season. The clay, mica, and other minerals were stockpiled for later use.

All this took two days, at which time we needed to plant wheat, barley, and corn. The much more interesting work of taming the ostrich would have to wait. Even though the animals pulled the plow, we did the digging and hoeing. This was such exhausting work that we could do only two hours in the morning and two in the evening.

The ostrich proved very stubborn. None of our taming methods worked. In desperation I tried the smoke method, but the effect was alarming: the great bird sank to the ground unconscious. When he got up again, he paced up and down between the bamboo posts. He no longer tried to kick us, but he refused to eat for three days. I could see him weakening and feared for his life. "Elizabeth," I asked, "can you think of something?"

My wife went into Rockburg and returned a little later with balls of corn meal mixed with butter. She placed one in the bird's beak. He swallowed it and stretched out his long neck, looking for a second mouthful. A second, third, and fourth ball followed the first, and his strength soon returned. This kindness tamed him, and we found that he liked rice, guavas, wheat, and corn. Franz asked why he "washed them down" with small rocks. "All birds do that," I explained. "They can't chew. They use the stones to grind up their food."

After a month of careful training, our captive would trot, gallop, come when called, and eat from our hands. Very good—but how did one saddle and bridle a giant bird? He wasn't a horse; we couldn't put a bit in his beak. I turned over vague idea after vague idea, rejecting them all, until I remembered something. When we'd first caught him, sudden darkness had calmed him down. Perhaps light and dark could be used.

I made a leather hood reaching from neck to beak, cutting holes for the eyes and beak. Over the eyeholes I positioned square flaps, with whalebone springs to keep them closed. I connected the reins to these flaps, so that the rider could open either at will. When both blinkers were open, the ostrich would gallop straight ahead; close his right eye and he turned left, close his left and he turned right, shut both and he stood still.

In order to test my idea, the bird needed a rider. That would require a saddle. This proved challenging as well, but after several failures, I made one that satisfied me. It was peaked in front and back to help the boys stay on. I placed the odd-looking device on the ostrich's shoulders, as near the neck as possible, and secured it with strong straps in front of the wings and across the body.

Now came the problem of habit. On most mounts, one tightened the reins to halt them and slackened them to let the animal run. My rig required the rider to do just the opposite. The boys named our new mount Hurricane, and we all practiced riding him—he could even carry me, though I saw it was a strain. The bird's marvelous speed again raised the issue of ownership. After the boys bickered a while, I felt bound to interfere.

"Jack gets to keep Hurricane," I said, "because he's lighter than his older brothers, and Franz isn't yet strong enough to manage him at high speeds. But the ostrich will remain partly common property, in that everyone may practice riding him. In an emergency, anyone may ride him."

To add to our fine field of wheat, barley, and corn, we planted potatoes and cassava on the other side of Jackal River. We had not neglected the ostrich's eggs, and one day Fritz introduced me with great glee to three little ostriches. Sadly, the little creatures didn't live long. One died shortly after hatching, and the others tottered about on their oversized feet for a few days before also passing away.

We had salted and dried the bear hides, but they needed tanning. I used a mixture of honey and water on them. This made the skins flexible, with soft, glossy fur. We got a side benefit from this, for as I boiled the honey and water, I realized we might make a drink like English mead. I set some aside, then boiled it again with nutmeg and cinnamon. Everyone tried it in moderation and found it delicious, so my wife asked me to brew a larger supply.

With our winter stores well laid in, I now turned to minor details. The boys had been clamoring for hats, and I agreed to try making some from the muskrat skins. I treated them heavily to remove the smell, then trimmed off the fur and mixed it with raw rubber to make a sort of felt. This I molded and stretched until I had the shape of a hat. When this cured, I dyed it bright red. The next morning I presented my wife with a neat little red Swiss cap. She lined it with a little of our precious silk, then plumed it with an ostrich feather and put it on little Franz. We all said he cut a handsome figure, and everyone else wanted one. "Very well," I said, "if you get me the raw materials. Boys, make half a dozen rattraps, but be sure they will kill the muskrats at once, so they don't suffer."

While they got to work, I tried making some porcelain from the pipe clay and talc. My first results were not very good; some of my vessels were oddly shaped, and some cracked over the stove. Eventually I succeeded in making a set of white cups and saucers, a cream jug, a sugar bowl, and half a dozen small plates. Despite the awkward appearance of some of these, my family was most pleased. Filled with tea, cream, sugar, and fruit, they brightened up our dinner table.

As we used them for the first time, we heard the sound of thunder.

CHAPTER 17

Bounty and Peril

Great black clouds and terrific storms announced the arrival of winter. We left our spacious home only as needed. Though we had plenty to do, the time dragged. We went riding whenever the rain slackened. Despite my best efforts, morale was sagging. When someone would complain, Fritz and I would exchange glances, and I knew he understood.

Soon my eldest brought me a helpful idea. "Father, could we make some sort of light canoe, faster and more maneuverable than our other boats?"

Everyone liked this idea except Elizabeth. In her words, "We already have a pinnace and a canoe. Why do we need a third way to drown by accident?"

"I will make it very safe, dear," I told her. "The Greenlanders make a boat called the kayak, which is easy to right once capsized, yet hard to fall out of. Fritz, let's get to work. We must make it sturdy enough to ease your mother's fears."

We began with a whalebone skeleton, with split bamboos to strengthen the sides and a covered top. The rider was to sit in a square hole in the middle. It was the perfect winter project.

By the time we finished, the rains were gone. Our porch was beautiful and fragrant with the vines, and our croplands promised bountiful harvests. Thousands of happy birds soared over a land teeming with life.

Once we could move the kayak outside, we finished her by covering the sides and deck with sealskin. Then we caulked the seams with rubber. The boat was so light I could lift it with one hand. We voted Fritz her owner, but his mother set a condition. "We still have the swimming-belts. You will wear one in case that thing runs against a rock or something," she ordered.

His brothers laughed to see him in a swimming-belt for he had always been the best swimmer. Fritz wisely held his tongue and got into the kayak. With a few swift oar strokes he was headed toward Shark Island with us behind him in the pinnace.

At the island, we were glad to see our antelope thriving. They had grown much over the winter and had used the shelter we built them. And to my delight our palms and mangroves had sprouted nicely. The other seeds I had scattered were also doing well. We climbed up the rocks and made another good discovery—a bright sparkling spring, most welcome to the antelopes.

This good news made us curious to see if Whale Island was doing as well. There the news was mixed, for all the saplings except the coconut palms had taken rabbit damage. While we were glad the rabbits had flourished, we couldn't let them continue to ruin the young trees, so my sons and I enclosed them in thorny hedges.

It was impossible to forget the whale's skeleton, long since picked clean and bleached to perfect whiteness in the sun. I thought the vertebrae might be useful in making a crushing machine, so I separated ten or twelve and rolled them down to the pinnace. Since they would float, we tied them together to tow behind us.

The next morning, I wanted to find a suitable tree to provide building blocks for the crusher. When I went to our stables for a mount, only the bull and buffalo were there; the boys had gone off with their guns, mounts, and traps, so I'd have to go alone. I saddled Storm, collected Fawn and Bruno, and headed over Family-bridge.

The cassava field was a shambles, with many of the roots dug up and eaten by animals. Pig-tracks were everywhere, and I decided to trail the invaders. At the old potato field, I nearly lost the trail. As I tried to rediscover it, I heard a loud barking from Fawn and Bruno and ran to see.

They had our old sow at bay, complete with her family, all baring their teeth and grunting fiercely enough to keep both dogs—large mastiffs, and by no means timid—at a distance. I raised my gun and fired twice, bringing down two pigs and putting the rest to flight with the dogs after them.

I loaded the pigs on Storm, called off the dogs, and continued through the forest until I found a suitable tree, which I marked before heading home.

Having stayed behind, Ernest was available to help me butcher the young pigs, which I handed over to my wife for dinner. I hoped my other sons would be back in time to share in it.

Late in the evening we heard the unmistakable trampling sounds. Jack came thundering up on his ostrich with Fritz and Franz soon following, game bags full. They emptied them to reveal four birds, a kangaroo, at least twenty muskrats, a monkey, and two hares. Without explanation, Fritz also threw down a bundle of thistles.

The boys seemed almost wild with excitement at the success of their expedition. Jack exclaimed, "Father, you can't imagine how much fun it is to hunt on an ostrich. We flew so fast that I had to shut my eyes to keep out the dust. You must make me some sort of riding goggles, or I'm going to go blind."

"Indeed?" I replied, annoyed. "I must do no such thing."

"Why not?" he asked, surprised at my tone.

"First, because I'm your father, not your servant; and second, because you're perfectly capable of making your own. I congratulate you on your successful hunt, and I appreciate your hard work, but I wish you'd let me know before going off all day like this. It's inconsiderate to leave us here wondering and worrying, with no idea what you're up to. Now go take care of your animals, and then you can have dinner."

Over our delicious roast pork, washed down with moderate amounts of fragrant mead, Fritz began to describe the day's expedition. "We checked the traps near Woodlands and found the muskrats and a platypus. We spent the rest of the day hunting and fishing."

"I ran down the kangaroo," interrupted Jack. "No one else could keep up!"

"As I was about to say," continued Fritz, "we also gave some thought to the garden. I got some cinnamon plants and sweet apple cuttings. Father, I'd like you to have a look at my thistles. They look like a plant used to make wool." I did so, and he was right. They were fuller's thistles, very useful for brushing cloth. By this time it was late. After evening devotions we went to sleep.

After breakfast, I examined the boys' kills. It would take days of hard, messy work to skin them all, but I had a plan. The surgeon's chest from the wreck had included a large syringe, which I fitted with a couple of valves to create an air pump. I laid out the kangaroo, took this pump in hand, and said, "Let's get started."

My sons looked at me in amazement. "Skin a kangaroo by squirting it?" they asked, laughing. I hung the kangaroo by its hind legs from a tree branch, then made a small cut in the skin. Inserting the end of the syringe in this opening, I pumped with all my might. The kangaroo's hide bloated into a grotesque shape, and I kept working until I could force in no more air. With a bold cut down the belly and a few other quick slashes, the animal was cleanly skinned.

"What a splendid plan!" cried the boys. "But how can that work?"

"Simple," I replied. "By now you've cut up enough animals to realize that the skin is attached only by slender fibers. Forcing air inside stretches and breaks the fibers, and one can then easily remove the skin. The Greenlanders find this very efficient, but since most of their kills are made at sea, they get a second benefit: the inflated kill can be towed ashore." This method turned a long job into a couple of days' work.

I now summoned the boys to help me cut wood for my crusher, and we set forth with wood-cutting tools. At the marked tree, I sent Fritz and Jack up to cut off the high branches and run ropes through the top. Once that was done, Fritz and I attacked the trunk with a two-man saw, and when it was cut halfway through, we adjusted the ropes to guide its fall. After some more sawing, we gave a united pull on the ropes. The trunk cracked, swayed, and came crashing down.

After two days of limbing and sawing the tree into four-foot blocks, we carted home four large blocks and two small ones. With these and the whale vertebrae, my machine was complete. Unfortunately, this work had kept my eyes off our grain fields. One evening the birds declined their evening feed, and I recalled that they'd come from the direction of the grain field. I hurried off to see what damage they had done and found to my great joy that the grain was perfectly ripe.

"How will we get all this done?" asked my wife. "Harvesting, threshing, fishing, salting, pickling . . . and think of my potatoes and manioc roots! What will become of them? We need to harvest those as well, but we have no time."

"Don't worry, dear," I said. "There's no hurry about the manioc, and this fine, light soil makes potato digging much easier than in Switzerland. If we leave the younger plants in the ground, we won't need to plant more. We'll harvest Italian style, which will save time and trouble. Since we're getting two crops this year, we can afford to use this method."

Without further delay, I began leveling a large space of firm ground to act as a threshing floor. Then I covered it with a thick layer of wet clay. This we rolled, beat, and stomped until it was hard, flat, and dry. We then slung our largest wicker basket between Storm and Grumble, armed ourselves with reaping hooks, and went out to harvest. My instructions were: "Just grab the stalks where it's convenient, without bending over, and cut. If they're too short to reach standing up, leave them. Bundle up the stalks into sheaves, then throw them in the basket."

We saved a lot of work this way, much to my boys' satisfaction, but we left a field of tall, headless stubble. My wife was horrified at the untidy scene. "This is dreadful!" she cried. "You've left a lot of it growing on short stalks and wasted all that straw! I don't approve of your method at all."

"Fear not, my wife," I assured her. "The Italian method doesn't waste the straw; they pasture their cattle there and let them have whatever grain is left. They then let the grass grow up and mow it for winter fodder. And now we'll thresh it Italian style as well, which will also save us time and trouble."

The boys laid the sheaves in a large circle on the threshing floor, then mounted Storm, Grumble, Lightfoot, and Hurricane. They went round and round, with much joking and laughter, trampling the grain as dust and chaff flew in clouds around them. From time to time the animals took mouthfuls of the tempting food.

After threshing came winnowing: throwing the threshed grain high in the wind with shovels so that the useless husks blew away while the grain fell to the ground. Of course, the fallen grain was very attractive to our birds. My wife wanted to keep them away, but I thought they deserved a share of our bounty. "Let them enjoy themselves," I said. "What we'll lose in grain, we'll gain in chicken pie and roast goose."

Our harvest left our pantry full to bursting. In anticipation of a second harvest, we mowed the stubble to prepare the field. Flocks of quail and partridges came to pick at the scattered remnants. We only shot a few, but next year we planned to spread nets to catch larger numbers.

My wife was very satisfied to see the straw carried home and stacked. The cornhusks would make good mattress filler, and burning the stalks would yield alkali-rich ashes with many uses. I planted rye, barley, and oats, in hopes they would ripen before the rainy season.

Just as we finished our farming work, the herring bank showed up, but this year we pickled only two barrels. We were more aggressive with the seals that came next, for we needed a lot of sealskins. I had built a little compartment on the deck of the kayak to carry provisions and ammunition, and now I made it watertight. I also furnished the little craft's harpoons with seal-bladder floats so that the quarry couldn't dive away. Fritz could hardly wait to take his first solo trip.

At last I pronounced the kayak ready for use. Fritz put on his swimming belt without complaint, for his mother had not relented. We all went down to the beach to see him off, and I readied the pinnace. I doubted he would need rescuing, but it seemed to reassure Elizabeth.

The kayak floated lightly on the smooth greenish sea, and Fritz began to practice many nimble moves with his paddles. What a maneuverable craft! At last he deliberately capsized the kayak, bringing a shriek of terror from my wife until he bobbed back up to his brothers' cheers. If his intent was to prove the kayak safe, he succeeded. When Fritz recovered his balance, he paddled into the Jackal River current and was carried out to sea.

This was more than I'd bargained for. "Ernest, Jack, into the boat," I said sharply. "After him!" My wife urged us to hurry, and my sons did indeed row for all they were worth.

As we left the bay near the rocks that had wrecked our old ship, we strained our eyes for a glimpse of the runaway. After a time we saw a faint puff of smoke, then heard a pistol shot from beyond a rocky point of land. Jack fired an answering shot, and we steered toward the sound. Soon we heard Fritz's cheery hello as the kayak darted from beyond a ridge of rock. "Come to this beach," Fritz called. "I have something to show you." It was a young walrus, dead with harpoons in his neck and shoulder.

"Did you kill this creature, Fritz?" I exclaimed.

"Of course, Father! How can you doubt it, with my harpoons in him?"

"Point well taken," I admitted. "I was so worried about you that it affected my good sense. Good work. But you alarmed us very badly, especially your mother. You shouldn't have left the bay; she's worried half to death for you."

"I didn't mean to, Father, but the current caught me. Then I came on a walrus herd, and I really wanted to get one, so I kept chasing them even when I was out of the current. He took two harpoons and a pistol shot to kill."

"Fritz, that was risky," I said. "Walruses aren't normally aggressive, but a wounded one is. It can sink a strongly built whaleboat. I need hardly remind you how fragile your kayak is. That said, thank God for your safety, which I value above a thousand walruses! Now what's to be done with him? He's got to be fourteen feet long."

"I'm glad you followed me, Father," said Fritz, "but even together I don't think we can move him. But please let me take away the head with those impressive tusks! I'd like to mount it on the kayak's bow."

"Certainly we should take those beautiful ivory tusks," I replied. "But hurry. The air feels strange. I suspect a storm is brewing."

"Mounting the head on the kayak will look fearsome!" cried Jack.

"Not as fearsome as it'll smell when it starts to rot," added Ernest. "What a treat for the kayaker!"

"We'll prevent that," said Fritz. "By the time I finish soaking and drying it, it won't offend your delicate nose in the least."

"Father, aren't walruses Arctic animals?" asked Ernest.

"Mainly so," I replied, "though they're occasionally seen elsewhere. Perhaps this one wandered from the Antarctic." I gave a further description of walruses as I helped my sons remove some long strips of skin in addition to the head.

"This would be easier if the kayak carried a hunting knife and hatchet," commented Fritz. "A compass mounted in front of the rider would also help, if protected from salt water, and mother would approve."

"You're right, Son. When we get back, we'll make those improvements," I said, beginning to think of methods and materials. When the walrus parts were loaded onto the pinnace, I suggested, "Fritz, let's carry the kayak in the boat, so we can all arrive together."

"Father, I'd really like to return alone, as I came, and go out in front so mother can see me." I relented, for this was a good example of that bold independence I wished to encourage. Soon he was skimming the surface at a quick pace, far ahead of us. Black clouds gathered thick and fast around us, and by the time the storm came on, Fritz was out of sight.

The seas began to rise, and we buckled on the swimming belts and lashed ourselves to the boat so as not to be tossed overboard. I was anxious for Fritz, and I could only imagine how my wife and Franz felt, alone in the storm with no news of the rest of their family.

The horizon was dark and angry. Fearful gusts of wind lashed the ocean into foam. Torrents of rain slashed down while livid lightning blazed and crackled in the gloom. Both my boys faced the danger nobly, and I was pleased to see how well the pinnace weathered the squall.

What a relief when I saw the clouds begin to lighten! The storm cleared as quickly as it had come, but the heavy waves remained dangerous for some time. I never lost hope for ourselves, but I feared the very worst for Fritz. In my mind, I gave him up for lost—but I prayed with my whole agonized heart. Never had the words "Thy will be done" been so difficult to express even in silent prayer.

At last we rounded the point into Safety Bay.

I took the spyglass and strained to see. Soon I could make out two small figures—no, three! "Fritz is with them, boys! I see the kayak!" Tension flowed from all of us like water from a bottle, and I joined my boys in cheers of joy.

It was perhaps our happiest reunion yet, and my entire family knelt on the sand to give thanks for God's mercy, my wife's words spoken through tears of joy.

At Rockburg, we changed into dry clothes. As we had dinner, we told our stories of the walrus hunt and the storm. Fritz had arrived as the worst of the storm began to pass. "The kayak handled the seas very well, Father," he said. "Fine work!" Never had so much rested upon that workmanship, I reminded myself, and I knew that in the future I must do even better.

After dinner, the boys carried the walrus head to our workshop to begin the embalming process. It would surely be an imposing figure-head, provided it didn't unbalance the craft. And the hide strips promised to be valuable leather— but I was simply glad we hadn't paid a terrible price for them.

CHAPTER 18

Repairs and Fortifications

The storm had done a lot of damage to our crops, our bridge, and our water delivery system. As we began the extensive repairs, I wondered how we might storm-proof our facilities. We had enough clay to build aqueducts; perhaps those would hold up better. They would also allow us to irrigate the fields.

While reassembling some pipes one day, we found a lot of dark, aromatic, tasty-looking red berries. The boys tried them, but each spat his berry out in disgust. After Knips rejected them, I picked up a berry and smelled it. "Cloves!" I exclaimed. "Another find for our spice garden, boys!"

It was a good fishing season for salmon, sturgeon, and herring, followed by many days of hard farm work. I could see that my sons needed a break and was trying to decide between a cruise and a trip to the woods when Fritz offered an idea. "Father, we're almost out of bamboo. Shouldn't we get some? We could also use more clay from the Gap to strengthen the aqueducts."

"That sounds good, Fritz," I said. "Who wants to go?"

Everyone did but Ernest, who chose to stay and help his parents build a sugar mill. As they prepared to leave, I saw Jack quietly slip a basket of live pigeons under the packages in the cart.

We urged them to be careful, and Franz, Jack, and Fritz set forth in high spirits. Storm and Grumble pulled the cart, ridden by Fritz and Franz. Jack led on Hurricane the ostrich, whose name had by now been shortened to Hurry. Fawn and Bruno were at his heels. Ernest, Elizabeth, and I got to work on the sugar mill.

That evening we rested on the porch at Rockburg. "I wonder what they're up to," I said idly.

"Maybe they'll write to us," said Ernest, sounding sincere. Before I could ask the obvious question, a bird landed near the pigeon coop and went inside. It was too dusky for me to see whether it was an intruder or one of ours. Ernest volunteered to check.

He came back in a few minutes with a scrap of paper. "Father, Mother, here's the latest news, sent by carrier pigeon!"

"Well done, boys! What a fine idea!" I said. I took the note and read it aloud.

Dearest Parents and Ernest,

A brute of a hyena has killed a ram and two lambs. The dogs caught it, and Franz shot it. We've skinned it. We're all fine.

Love to all.
Fritz
Woodlands, the 15th

"A true hunter's letter!" I laughed. "But what exciting news! When do you expect the next mail delivery, Ernest?"

"I hope tomorrow night," he said.

Elizabeth sighed. "I'm not sure I like this. I'd rather wait and hear all about it when I have them home safe again." The winged letter carriers kept us informed from day to day of the boys' adventures. Here are the details:

At Woodlands, the boys had heard a very odd sound: laughter. The buffalo and bull grew uneasy, the dogs growled and drew close, and the ostrich bolted into the rice swamp with Jack. Fritz took charge: "Something's wrong. Franz, while I tie up the mounts, take the dogs and find out what's the matter."

Franz advanced calmly, his gun ready and a dog on each side. At an opening in the thicket, he saw the trouble. There was an enormous hyena, forty paces off, dancing and laughing around a freshly killed lamb. My boy waited patiently for the hyena to calm down and start eating, then fired both barrels into its chest and foreleg.

When Fritz arrived, the dogs were fighting it out with the hyena. My eldest stepped forward with a pistol, took careful aim, and finished the fight. Both boys gave a cheer to summon Jack, then hurried to tend injuries the dogs had received in the fight. The hyena was as large as a wild boar, with exceptionally strong jaws and sharp teeth. Without Franz's well-placed shots, both dogs might have died.

They spent the rest of the day skinning the hyena, then wrote the message previously described and sent it to Rockburg by pigeon before going to sleep.

The following day they started surveying swampy Wood Lake for shallow fording spots. Fritz launched the kayak while Franz and Jack walked the shore, and where they found firm footing, they planted tall bamboo markers. They also caught three young black swans and a heron, taken alive thanks to Fritz's eagle.

My sons were apparently keeping a poor watch. Suddenly there came a curious whistling sound and the very near tramp of a large, powerful animal. It bolted before they could get a good look at it, and I later surmised that it was a tapir. If so, it was just as well they didn't provoke it, for the gentle tapir can turn very fierce when threatened.

Fritz followed it for a time in his kayak, but the tapir was too nimble for him in the swamp. In the meantime, Franz and Jack returned to the farm by the rice fields, where they found a flock of cranes. This was the time to try out one of Franz's ideas: blunted arrows with loops attached and dipped in birdlime, fired with partial force. Their accurate bow shots captured half a dozen cranes.

The young hunters lived very comfortably on peccary ham, cassava bread, fruit, baked potatoes, and milk. After collecting a supply of rice and cotton, they went to Prospect Hill.

As Fritz told us later, "There were a lot of monkeys in the pines, chattering like demons and throwing pine cones at us. We shot a few to scare them away, but when we got to Prospect Hill we found that we owed them harsher punishment. The house was torn up and overrun, just the same as Woodlands last summer! It was so filthy it took us all day to clean up.

"I wasn't sure how to prevent this in the future, until I saw a bottle of the euphorbia sap in the tool chest. I could mix the poison with milk, millet, and anything else the monkeys might eat, and put it out in coconut shells high enough in the trees to keep the mix away from our animals.

"It was a lovely evening, with a beautiful moonrise and the sea murmuring in the distance. We were just remarking on the sights and sounds when a barrage of hideous noises broke the spell. It seemed as though every creature in the forest was in full cry. We heard the howls of jackals, answered by Fangs and then by Fawn and Bruno. From the direction of the river we heard sounds that might have been hippopotamus. We also heard some deep, majestic roars—perhaps lions or even elephants.

"We tried to sleep, but pretty soon we heard much nearer cries of apes in pain and panic. The dogs wouldn't be quiet. Between them and the apes, we couldn't sleep until dawn.

"When we finally got up, we went to see. Father, it was awful. There were dozens of monkeys and baboons, all dead, with their bodies and faces contorted in pain. I wished I hadn't found the poison. We were in a hurry to bury the dead bodies and the dangerous food. When that was done, we traveled on to the Gap."

That evening, a pigeon arrived at Rockburg with a note that ended like this:

"The barricade at the Gap is broken down. Everything is laid waste as far as the sugar canebrake. The hut is knocked to pieces; there are huge footprints in the field. We're unhurt and safe for the moment, but please come, Father. I don't think we're any match for this danger."

Despite the late hour, I saddled Swift and told Ernest to prepare the small cart. I would ride now, and he and his mother were to follow at daybreak with a week's camping supplies. The bright moonlight helped me find my way to the Gap, where my boys were surprised to see me so soon.

Early the following morning I inspected the footprints and ravages. It had to be an elephant, or elephants, for nothing else could have done such damage. The trampled canebrake was just the beginning. The barricade's thick posts had been snapped like toys. The nearby trees were stripped of leaves fifteen feet high and more. No single animal could have done all this; it must have been a herd. Their tracks told the story. They had bulled through the Gap, eaten the tenderest young sugar canes and anything else they wanted, then withdrawn. We were in no danger. We stayed up very late that night discussing ways to keep the elephants out.

My wife and Ernest arrived the next morning. Her joy knew no bounds: "Who cares about trampled crops and canebrakes. My sons are safe, that's all that matters!"

We settled in for a long stay and a lot of hard work at the Gap. Rather than live in a tent all month, Fritz suggested we construct a type of dwelling used in Siberia, a tree house built where four stout trees stood in a square. This proved safe and successful, for few dangers could reach us twenty feet above the ground, and the space below could shelter the animals. After that we lived in comfort while we remedied the weak spot in our defenses.

To liven up the days, my sons often roamed the woods in search of new discoveries. One day Fritz brought back a cluster of bananas from beyond the Gap as well as some cocoa beans, the source of chocolate. The bananas were awful, and the beans were so bitter it was hard to imagine making chocolate from them, but my wife was determined. "Please get some cocoa plants for the garden, Fritz," she asked. "Bananas too. I'm sure I can find a way to prepare both." The day before our return to Rockburg, Fritz built a raft of canes to haul his discoveries, then took the kayak up the nearby stream.

When he came back that evening, his brothers rushed to see what he had found. Fritz handed Jack a dripping wet bag, then joined Ernest in hauling the plants, branches, and fruit. I saw something moving in the bag, but Fritz didn't explain, and Jack ran behind a bush with it. I could just hear him exclaim, "What monsters! Makes my flesh crawl to look at them!" With that he hastily shut the bag and put it out of sight in the water.

Fritz's great prize was a beautiful water bird with rich purple, red, and green plumage. I recognized it as a Sultan fowl, a gentle bird that promised to make a fine pet. Fritz gave a stirring account of his trip.

"I went way upriver," he began, "and I saw and heard more types of parrots, peacocks, and other birds I didn't recognize. I saw the Sultan fowls in the Buffalo Swamp, and I wanted to catch one alive, so I set a wire snare. Further on I saw some dark masses moving very deliberately through a grove of mimosa trees. Guess what they were!"

"Your words suggest elephants," said Ernest.

"Right you are, Professor!" Fritz confirmed. "From fifteen to twenty elephants were eating leaves and bathing in the marsh. What a sight! The river was very broad at that point, and I felt safe from wild animals. A good thing, for I saw a few jaguars crouched on the banks. I considered taking a shot at one but decided that it would be smarter to retreat, so I stayed in midriver and headed downstream.

"I stopped to rest in a sheltered bay, and all of a sudden there was a violent bubbling commotion. For a moment I thought a hot spring was coming up, but instead, it was a hippopotamus! His head was gigantic—and what jaws! He let out a huge snort and charged toward me! I didn't wait around to see the rest of him, and I paddled downstream full speed until I reached the Gap."

This narrative thrilled us all and proved right my supposition about elephants. With jaguars, elephants, and hippopotami nearby, it would take much energy to defend this small, fertile territory that had become our home. Among the plants Fritz brought back was one with pretty white flowers and a strong, pleasant odor: the tea plant. This would be especially welcome in our garden. "And I'll be very glad to get home where I can plant them," added Elizabeth, a sentiment we all echoed.

"Father, I'd like to return to Rockburg by sea in the kayak," said Fritz.

"Around Cape Disappointment?" I asked, thinking aloud. After some hesitation, I gave permission. "Yes, Fritz, you may. I know you'll be very careful."

Our land journey was uneventful. Jack rode Hurry, of course, and at Family-bridge he rode ahead with the mysterious wet bag slung carefully at his side. The rest of us saw no more of him until we reached Rockburg, where we met him casually returning from the swamp. "That must be where he deposited his moist secret," said Franz.

We were all glad for the safety and comfort of Rockburg. There wasn't enough room for all our new birds, so we took most of the cranes to the islands. The black swans, the heron, two of the cranes, and the Sultan fowl were happy to move into the swamp. Their varied beauty enhanced the look of the neighborhood.

Fritz paddled in by early afternoon. After dinner, while we were on the porch listening to his tale, a hollow roaring noise sounded from the swamp. It was a little like the angry bellow of a bull. The dogs started barking, and I was about to investigate, but I noticed a look of quiet humor in Fritz's eye. He made no move to accompany Jack, who took off for the marsh. "Come back, you silly boy!" cried his mother. "You don't even have a pistol! Who knows what you might face?"

"Perhaps he won't need weapons," I said, meeting Fritz's eyes. "That could be a bittern's cry."

"Don't worry, Mother," reassured Fritz. "Jack's safe. I think he wanted to wait to show off his treasures, but the secret won't keep. Here he comes!"

Jack was lugging the "moist secret," which he set down before us: two immense bullfrogs. "They were to grow as big as rabbits before you saw them!" he exclaimed, puffing from the hurry. "What a shame! I never thought they would make so much noise. Father, Mother, meet Grace and Beauty." The frogs rolled clumsily on the ground, recovered their feet, and sat swelling and puffing with an air of insulted dignity.

"Ladies and gentlemen," continued Jack, "these are two very handsome young specimens of the famous African bullfrog. I had hoped to

wait until they were fully grown, so I could introduce them with proper ceremony, but their musical talents have given them away. With your kind
permission, I shall return them to the swamp."

Everyone applauded Jack's little speech,
commenting on the great size of the frogs. They
were green with yellow and reddish-brown mot-
tling, and we all voted them "handsome in their
own way." Nonetheless, no one minded when
Jack took them back to the swamp.

Shortly after our return to Rockburg, my
wife drew my attention to our neglect of dear old
Falconhurst, asking that I take some time to
restore and improve it. I was willing, and we soon
put it in good order. After this, I consented to a
plan Fritz had long advocated: to construct a
watchtower and mount a cannon on Shark

Island. This military engineering effort took us two months. After we hauled the cannon, we realized that we needed a means of signaling, so we added a flagpole. The guard at the tower could run up a white flag to signal the seaborne approach of something harmless. If the approaching object looked at all dangerous, he would hoist a red flag instead.

To celebrate the completion of this great work, we hoisted the white flag and fired a six-gun salute.

CHAPTER 19

Independence

"We spend our years as a tale that is told," said King David in the Bible. As I reviewed ten years of our lives in New Switzerland, described in my journal, those words came back to me. Though I felt sad to see time passing away, my sons past their boyhood, my wife and me growing older, I also could thank God. My sons were now healthy, self-reliant young men.

I need not detail every hunt, excursion, awkward invention, or new plant we discovered in those ten years. This is a family history, not an encyclopedia. Before I conclude my tale, however, I should tell how New Switzerland evolved under our management.

Rockburg and Falconhurst continued to be our winter and summer quarters. Rockburg became green and lush as the aqueduct fed our orchard, plantations, and decorative vines. We diverted water to transform the swamp to a lake, with plenty of marsh around the edges for the waterfowl. Black swans, white geese, and brightly colored ducks swam in harmony with Sultan fowls, red flamingoes, graceful herons, and blue-gray cranes. To Jack's delight, the giant frogs eventually grew as large as small rabbits.

The palms on Shark Island grew tall and graceful; the flagstaff and cannon guarded Safety Bay. The rabbits on Whale Island kept us well supplied with food and soft fur.

The farm at Woodlands flourished, as did our flocks and herds. We had all the food we could wish, even with four athletic, growing boys. My sons always loved to name animals. They had a beautiful creamy-white cow called Blanche and a bull with such a tremendous voice they named him Stentor. Two fast young onagers were named Arrow and Dart. Jack gave the name Coco to a descendant of his old favorite, Fangs. Ernest chose the name Flora for one of Fawn's puppies.

Elizabeth had a few slight fevers and the boys had a few accidents, but in general we enjoyed fine health. They were all handsome fellows. Fritz, now twenty-four, was of moderate height, uncommonly strong, active, and high-spirited. Ernest, two years younger, was tall, slight, calm, and studious. My brilliant second son had long overcome his youthful laziness and selfishness. At twenty, Jack looked like a lankier version of Fritz, with tremendous grace and agility; he was unquestionably the family joker. Franz, a lively, handsome youth of seventeen, was like a mixture of all his brothers. All were honorable, God-fearing young men, loyal and kind to their parents and each other.

I had always believed we would one day rejoin civilization, but the years that brought our sons to manhood carried their parents toward old age. I worried over my sons' fate when I was gone, but I shared such thoughts only with the Almighty Father, my eternal source of hope and strength.

As they matured, my sons increasingly went off without telling us, but their return always made me too happy to rebuke them. One evening at Rockburg, no one had seen Fritz all day and his kayak was gone. We figured he was still at sea, and I was anxious to have him back by nightfall. Ernest, Jack, and I went off to Shark Island to keep watch from the tower. Ernest raised the flag, Jack loaded the cannon, and we gazed across the water well into sunset.

Finally we could make out a small black speck in the distance. I trained the telescope and saw that it was our wanderer, sailing more slowly than usual. On my command, Jack fired the cannon to let him know we saw him, and we hurried back to welcome him at the harbor.

As he drew near, we could see that the kayak was heavily laden and towing a large sack. "Welcome, Fritz!" I cried. "Welcome back, wherever you come from and whatever you bring. You seem to have quite a cargo there!"

"Yes, and I found some things we will want to investigate," he answered. "Ernest, Jack, help me carry these things up, and I'll tell you all about it afterward." This done, we gathered on the porch to hear the story.

"I'm sorry for being inconsiderate, Father; I should have told you where I was going," he began. "Ever since I got the kayak, I've wanted to explore the coast past where I killed the walrus. I prepared beforehand so I could leave as soon as the weather was good. When the perfect morning came, I headed out to sea. As I passed the spot where our ship was wrecked, the water was very clear. I could see the guns and other ironwork on the sea bottom.

"Moving on, I passed among rugged cliffs and rock outcroppings full of sea birds. On the lower ridges I saw seals, sea bears, and walruses swimming and lazing around. After all the rocks and cliffs, I came to a high cape running far out to sea. In the side of this rocky wall was a magnificent archway, like the entrance to a vast vaulted cavern. I decided to paddle in.

"The walls were covered with little swallows and their nests built on curious little platforms.

These looked strange, more like sponges than birds' nests. I brought some of them home to show you."

"If we traded with the Chinese," I said, looking at the nests he produced, "we'd be wealthy. This bird is called the esculent swallow, and the nests are considered a great delicacy in China. Fresh ones are worth their weight in silver. Elizabeth, perhaps you might try cooking some?"

"I can't say I find them very appealing," she answered, "but I don't mind trying. I don't have much experience boiling birds' nests."

"I hope I don't get any feathers in my soup," laughed Jack.

"After getting the nests," continued Fritz, "I paddled on through. It was like a large tunnel, opening into a lonely bay with very calm waters—nearly landlocked. A river-mouth fed it and beyond was a thicket of cedars. Here, too, the water was wonderfully clear. I could look down and see clusters of oysters attached to the rocks and each other. These were bigger than our Safety Bay variety, so I fished some out and put them on the sand. I went back for another load, and when I returned, the shells were all wide open; must have been the sun. I wanted to try them and started poking around with my knife. In the process, I found these." Fritz took out a small box, containing a number of shiny, glassy balls colored nearly white.

"Pearls!" cheered his brothers.

"Treasure indeed!" I exclaimed. "Obviously, we have no way to spend them, but if we ever rejoin the civilized world, they'll be of great value. We should return for more the first chance we get."

"After I'd had some lunch," Fritz went on, "I kept going. The bag slowed me down somewhat, but I reached the other side of the bay. There I found a small channel dotted with rocks and sandbars leading to the open sea. Other than that, Pearl Bay—as I named it—is completely sheltered. The tide was stirring up the water, so I chose not to risk the exit. I explored to see if there was another vaulted archway I could paddle through.

"I didn't find one, but I did find thousands of sea birds—gulls, sea swallows, and huge albatrosses. I was evidently trespassing, because they started diving at me, screaming and wheeling over my head. Finally I lost patience and started swinging the boat hook. After I stunned one of the albatrosses, the rest left me alone. By this time the tide had calmed, so I made another try at the channel. Once in the open sea, I set my course for home. What a joy to see our flag flying and to hear your welcoming salute!"

We all praised his discoveries, and after evening devotions we went to bed.

The next morning, Fritz took me aside and confided something truly remarkable.

"Father, I left out a detail," he said. "Perhaps you wondered why I didn't bring the albatross back. When I pulled it into the kayak, I found a piece of rag tied around one of its legs. The bird surely hadn't tied it there, so I untied it for a closer look. I was stunned to see English words written on it: 'Save an unfortunate Englishwoman from the smoking rock!'

"For a moment I doubted my sanity—could there really be another human being in this lonely region? I recovered my senses when the bird started to stir. I tore off a strip of my handkerchief and wrote 'Don't worry—help is near!' on it. This I carefully tied around one leg, replacing the rag on the other. Then I did my best to revive the albatross. After a few moments, it drank a little water and flew away westward.

"Now, Father, I can only think about one thing: will this Englishwoman ever get my note? Will I ever be able to find and save her?"

"My dear son," I began, "you were wise to confide this only to me. Until we know more, we mustn't unsettle the others with it, for we can't know when or where the note was written. A castaway might have penned them on some distant shore and might since have perished alone. The only sort of 'smoking rock' I can imagine would be a volcano, and there are none here."

"I have more hope, Father," answered my son. "The rag didn't look so old. Perhaps smoke can rise from a rock without a volcano. I believe I can find and help this woman."

"Then let's come up with a sensible plan of action," I advised.

"I want to go looking for her in the kayak," he said.

"Ah," I replied, "but if you found her, where would you carry her? Your kayak only seats one."

My son thought for a moment. "I'll have to modify it to hold two," he said. I nodded. "I must devise a cover for the second opening, to maintain safety. I'll also have to be able to carry enough supplies for a long trip. What an annoying delay!"

"A good plan, Son. We'll work on it. For now, let's go back to the house and see what's happening."

We returned to find the boys busily opening the oysters, always excited whenever they found a pearl. "Father, can we establish a pearl fishery at Pearl Bay?" they asked. "We could build a hut. It would be great fun!"

"Good idea," I replied. "Start getting ready. You know what we need." Fritz smiled at me, for Pearl Bay would be a fine departure point for his search, and the general preparation would camouflage his work from curiosity.

As our departure day neared, I realized it was time for an important statement. I waited until everyone was present and then asked for quiet so that I could make an announcement.

"My dear wife, I've been thinking. Our oldest son is now mature enough to make his own decisions. Therefore, Fritz, from this day forward, you shall be the judge of when and where it's safe for you to go, without fear of alarming us if you stay away longer than we expect. I have complete confidence in your good judgment, and I know that you will never cause us needless anxiety." Though I had a hidden motive, all my words were sincere, and I was as proud as any father in history.

Fritz reached out to shake my hand, man to man, a grateful light in his eyes. His mother embraced him affectionately and said emotionally, "God bless and preserve you, my boy!"

I decided we needed some raking and scraping machines in order to collect oysters. This delay also gave Fritz plenty of time to modify his kayak. His brothers assumed that the second seat was for one of them, a notion he didn't refute. They spent the time making tools and packing supplies, patiently accepting the delay.

At last came the day. Franz stayed behind with his mother. We took some of the dogs aboard the pinnace. Fritz took his constant companion, the eagle Pounce. With Jack proudly in the kayak's second seat, he and Fritz led the way.

We passed safely along the familiar coastal sights until we rounded a long ridge of rock that jutted out from the coast. In the distance we saw the grand cliffs of a headland running far out to sea.

Soon we saw the majestic archway leading to Pearl Bay. The pillars, arches, and pinnacles of this noble entrance reminded me of a fine place of worship, and I proposed to name it Cape Cathedral. As we entered, a cloud of little swallows stirred from their nests. We took time for Fritz and Jack to climb the walls and collect a few empty nests, then resumed our voyage.

We emerged into the dazzling sunshine onto the calm expanse of Pearl Bay. When our eyes got used to the light, we saw that Fritz hadn't exaggerated its beauty. It was studded with romantic islets and surrounded by fertile meadows and shady groves. Fritz pointed out the oyster beds, and we spent some time cruising in search of a good campsite. This we found near the mouth of the stream he had described, so we landed and built a watch fire just in time to see a marvelous sunset.

I decided we should spend the night on the pinnace, anchored within gunshot of land. The dogs and Coco we left ashore. Whatever animals might live nearby, I doubted any of them would swim to attack us. If they did, I could expect a lively warning from our little ape Mercury, who had inherited Knips's role after the latter passed away.

Night passed with no trouble. We awoke at daybreak for a quick breakfast before going to work at the oyster beds. After several days of diligent effort, we had collected a boxful of pearls and built up an immense pile of shells on the beach. Each afternoon we went hunting. Between the hunts and the generous supply of oysters, we ate well.

On the last day of our fishery we started hunting earlier than usual, intending to explore the nearby woods. Ernest set off first with Flora, with Jack and Coco following. Fritz and I meant to follow when we finished loading up the last of our tools. Suddenly we heard a shot, a loud cry of pain or fear, and then another shot. The other two dogs rushed in that direction. Fritz released his eagle, seized his weapons, and darted after them.

Before I could reach the scene, I heard more shots and then a shout of victory. Before long I saw my sons returning through the trees. Jack hobbled along like a cripple, supported by his brothers, moaning and groaning. He felt his ribs gingerly, as if expecting to find them broken. "I'm pounded like a half-crushed peppercorn!" he lamented.

I examined him and found nothing worse than severe bruises. "Who or what beat him up?"

I asked.

"It was a huge wild boar," said Ernest, "with fierce eyes, monstrous tusks, and a snout as broad as my hand."

We took Jack down to the pinnace, bathed his bruises, and gave him a cool drink. He soon went to sleep, where I left him and returned to the shore.

"Now, Ernest," I said, "tell me more!"

"Flora and I were walking along," he replied, "when suddenly there was a nearby rustling and snorting. A great boar broke through the bushes, making for the outskirts of the wood. Flora gave chase and brought the boar to bay. Then up came Jack with Coco, and the gallant little jackal attacked the monster in the rear. The boar knocked Coco over and sent him sprawling and yelping. Jack lost his temper and fired, too quickly I'm afraid; he missed. He did get the boar's attention with his shot, and it took out after him. I shot the monster, but my bullet didn't seem to do much.

"Jack stumbled and fell over a tree root just as the boar caught up. 'Help! I'm going to die!' he shouted. Happily, all the other dogs showed up and tackled the boar. Otherwise I suspect Jack's prediction would've come true. Even so, he got mauled and trampled pretty badly. I was waiting for a chance to fire without risking hitting Jack when Pounce came diving in on the boar. At that point, Fritz came up and shot it dead with a pistol."

It was now late. We had dinner, then built up the watch fire and slept peacefully aboard the pinnace.

Early next morning we visited the field of battle. The wild boar proved much larger than I'd imagined, and I gave thanks again to God for the brave dogs that had saved my son. The boys began to butcher out the kill. We carried the mighty hams and monstrous head back to the beach with much effort and strain. As soon as the dogs were released, they rushed back to the woods to feast on the remains of the boar. "No one has more right, that's for sure," said Jack, still sore.

Fritz had hoped to begin his solitary expedition that day, but this work postponed the journey. Late that evening, we were getting ready to board the pinnace for sleep when a deep, fearfully blood-curdling sound echoed through the woods. We strained to listen, hoping it wouldn't be repeated, but the dread voice gave another roar—this time nearer. Worse yet, a second roar answered.

"We'd better find out who's giving this evening concert!" exclaimed Fritz, springing to his feet and grabbing his rifle. "Build up the fire, then get aboard the pinnace and load all the guns. I'm going off in the kayak to have a look."

Even as I found myself obeying his orders, I reflected briefly on my lack of hesitation. Fritz would always be my son, but he was now truly a man. Whatever became of Elizabeth and me, my sons would be just fine, I thought as I piled branches on the fire.

We kept watch from the pinnace, bristling with loaded guns. Soon our whole pack of dogs, Coco the jackal, and Mercury came galloping back at full speed. Poor little Mercury was most frightened to find us gone; he chattered his teeth in terror, and looked forlornly at the water. The dogs planted themselves by the fire, gazing landward with ears erect, occasionally barking or howling a challenge.

The horrid roars grew nearer. "Probably a couple of leopards or panthers scented the boar's carcass," I hoped aloud.

I was wrong in the extreme.

Soon a large, powerful animal sprang from the underbrush and bounded toward the fire. It was a lion—one much larger than any I had ever seen exhibited in Europe.

The dogs slunk behind the fire. Mercury shrieked and ascended a tree. The lion sat almost like a house cat on his hind legs, eyes alternating between the dogs and the great boar hams hanging nearby. His tail twitched in irritation. He got up and started pacing, giving a series of short, angry roars. I expected him to spring at any moment. When he noticed our boat, he crouched at the water's edge as if to leap at us. We had maneuvered it far enough away that I doubted he could reach us but near enough to give the dogs gunfire support. My sons held fire, awaiting my command.

While I tried to decide whether to open fire or retreat, the sharp crack of a rifle rang through the darkness.

"Fritz!" exclaimed everyone. The lion sprang to his feet with a fearful roar, then stood stock still. He tottered, sank to his knees, and rolled over motionless on the sand.

"We're saved!" I cried. "What a shot—right in the heart! Row for shore, boys, but stay aboard. I must join my brave Fritz."

The dogs were glad to see me, but they continued to whine uneasily and look toward the woods. This seemed good advice, so I kept careful watch along with them. Seeing nothing of Fritz, I lingered by the boat. Suddenly a lioness bounded from the shadows into the firelight.

She paused at the blaze as though startled, then padded around the edge of the lighted area and roared. When she came to her mate's body, she touched him with her forepaws, sniffed, and licked his bleeding wound. After a moment, she raised her head, gnashed her teeth, and gave forth the most dreadful sound I ever heard—a mingled roar and howl of grief, rage, and revenge all in one.

Crack! I saw a wound open in the lioness's right forepaw. I raised my gun, and the dogs gathered courage and charged. My shot wounded the lioness again, but not mortally, and the battle was on.

I reloaded but couldn't get a chance to shoot without endangering our dogs. In the black night, the fire shed an unnatural light on the dead lion and his wounded mate. The cries, roars, and groans of anguish and fury were enough to try the steadiest nerves.

The dogs circled, snarling and snapping at the lion. Old Juno had led the pack to battle. After a time, I saw her change her plan of attack and spring at the lioness's throat. The great cat raised her left paw and struck. The cruel claws laid Juno wide open. The brave, loyal companion of so many years flew across the sand, mercifully stunned in addition to her mortal wound. She would know no more pain.

Fritz then appeared from the trees, saw his opening, and fired. The lioness weakened, and I took two steps forward and shot. Soon the great cat grew feeble, and I dispatched her with a hunting knife deep in the chest. We called Ernest and Jack from the pinnace to see the results. Their joy at seeing us safe was matched only by their grief at the loss of faithful Juno.

It was now quite late, and we fed the fire. In

the renewed light we solemnly retrieved Juno's body and washed it in the stream. Wrapping her in canvas, we loaded her aboard the pinnace for burial at Rockburg the following day. Wearied and sorrowful, but grateful to God for our personal safety, we brought all the dogs aboard and went to sleep.

The next morning, before sailing for home, we landed to take the magnificent lion skins. Two hours later, we left the flayed remains to the mercies of vultures and other scavengers. "Homeward bound," sang out the boys, as they cheerily weighed anchor. Jack didn't complain, but I could see soreness in his stiff movements.

"You must pilot us through the channel in the reef, Fritz," I said. In a lower tone, I added, "And then it'll be 'farewell,' my son!"

"Yes, dear Father—and farewell to you!" he answered, a light in his eyes. He threw a cushion and a fur cloak into his kayak where Jack had ridden before.

"Thanks, Fritz," exclaimed Jack, "but I think I'll let Father and Ernest carry my battered bones in the pinnace. Very considerate of you, though," he finished, assuming that his brother expected him to ride back in the kayak.

"Good plan," laughed Fritz as he boarded the kayak and paddled for the open sea.

We followed carefully and soon passed the

reef, after which the boys got busy setting the sails for a homeward course. Fritz waved to me, turned in the other direction, and quickly vanished beyond the point. In my mind I named the point of land Cape Farewell.

When his brothers noticed his absence, I explained, "He wanted to go exploring, and said he might stay away for a few days if he found it interesting." No one suspected there was more to the story.

Toward evening we sailed into Safety Bay.

CHAPTER 20

Miss Montrose

My wife and Franz were delighted to see us return safely, though a bit alarmed at Fritz's absence. We told our tale, emphasized by Jack's still-pale appearance. Elizabeth trembled as we described the desperate encounter.

On hearing of poor old Juno's sad death, tears came to Franz's eyes. He said quietly, "Were you able to bring her body back? I would like the honor of burying our friend." The next day he did so, setting up a stone with Ernest's help:

JUNO
A true servant and faithful friend
who met her end fighting bravely in her
master's cause.

The boar's meat delighted my wife. I had promised Ernest the boar's head for the museum, so we took it and the lion skins to Whale Island for tanning and dressing.

As days passed, I grew increasingly anxious for Fritz. On his fifth day of absence, I announced to my family over dinner, "I'm taking the pinnace to search for him."

"I'd like to go," said Elizabeth. The rest felt likewise, and we began preparing for a major expedition.

The next morning dawned bright and breezy. We and the dogs boarded the pinnace and ran for Cape Cathedral. It was a beautiful voyage, with everyone in high spirits.

With the archway in sight, I saw a dark mass dead ahead, just below the surface. "Brace for a shoal!" I called out, and everyone took hold. As I steered to miss it, I thought to myself, "A sunken rock. Why didn't I notice it here before?"

I was too late. We felt the keel scrape over it, but fortunately it didn't tear a hole in the pinnace. When I glanced back to fix the spot in my mind, the "rock" was gone. Jack announced, "Another to starboard, Father!"

Sure enough, there lay what looked like another sunken rock. "It's moving!" shouted Franz. A great black body emerged from the sea, and from its top rushed a mighty column of water that fell like rain all around us.

Now the mystery was explained. As the beast emerged further, I recognized the distinctive form of the cachalot whale—a very dangerous animal known to sink larger boats than ours.

Apparently offended at being run over, the whale was lining up for a run at the pinnace. I sprang to one of the small swivel-mounted cannons, and Jack manned the other. We both aimed and fired without hesitation.

The whale lashed the water with its tail a few times, then plunged out of sight beneath the surface. I snapped orders. "Reload! Ernest, pilot us toward shore! Franz, keep a sharp lookout for him!"

Soon we sighted the great whale's death throes in the shallows near the shore. Ernest calmly lined up the pinnace within easy cannon shot, yet out of range of the furiously slashing tail. Both cannons boomed again, and after a few more moments of frantic struggle, the cachalot lay still in the shallows.

The boys were about to raise a cry of victory, but Franz hissed, "Quiet! I see someone! Look over behind that rock!" We all saw a figure in a boat far up the shore. He was quickly maneuvering his craft into hiding. Positive identification was impossible.

I feared the worst. "Load the guns, but don't attack except in self-defense," I ordered. "We won't be taken easily, but we won't start a fight." We waited and watched. Someone peeked quickly out from behind a rock higher up on the shore, then vanished. A few seconds later, another face popped out from behind the original rock.

Everyone looked anxiously at me for orders. "Hoist a white flag," I said, "and hand me the megaphone." Using the megaphone and speaking Maylay, I shouted, "We want to be friends! Please come out and identify yourself!"

There was no movement. Jack lost patience after a moment, grabbed the megaphone, and bellowed in English, "Come out, you coward, or we'll blast you! We're just—"

"Stop that!" I said. "You'll provoke a foolish fight!"

"No! See, he's coming toward us!" Jack cried. Sure enough, the canoe was rapidly approaching.

"Look! He's in Fritz's kayak! I can see the walrus head!" cried Franz. Again I thought the worst—but only for a moment.

Only Ernest remained calm. He took the megaphone and called out, "Fritz! Welcome back, old fellow!"

Before Ernest even finished speaking, I too recognized the well-known face. In another minute the brave boy was welcomed with a slew of questions: "Where have you been?" "Why were you away so long?" "Why did you hide from us?"

He smiled. "Right now I'll only answer the last question. The rest can wait. I didn't think you'd come out here in the pinnace, so I thought, 'Who else would have cannon? Malay pirates!' I hid and watched. Then, Father, you shouted in Malay, which seemed to confirm my fear. Only when Jack started yelling insults in English did I realize whose boat it was."

We then described our adventure with the cachalot whale, and I asked if he knew a good anchorage for us. "Certainly," he replied, with a meaningful glance at me. "I can lead you to one in Pearl Bay—and the scenery is lovely." Turning his kayak he piloted us through the vaulted cavern and over the calm water toward a pretty island in the bay.

Now that I knew Fritz had found the person he sought, there was no more reason to keep the story from my wife, and I quietly shared it. She was startled, yet delighted. "Another human being—and another woman to boot!" she whispered to me. "I love you all, but you can't know what it's been like, being the only female! Why didn't you tell me sooner?"

"Because if our hopes failed, you would have been terribly disappointed," I explained.

The boys were curious about our whispering but too busy sailing the pinnace to pay much attention. Fritz piloted us to a good landing spot on the island. Once we were ashore, we followed him in silence. He led us through a thicket and into a clearing where we discovered a hut made of branches.

Fritz disappeared into the leafy shelter. He reappeared a moment later, bringing with him a handsome youth in a naval uniform.

Fritz was radiant as he made the introduction. "Please welcome Edward Montrose! Mother, Father, will you accept him into our family as a brother?"

I could see that my wife was no more fooled than I was, but I assumed Fritz had his reasons; perhaps the girl was embarrassed at being seen in men's clothing. "Indeed!" I exclaimed, offering my hand. "Our wild life hasn't hardened our manners. Be welcome!" My wife heartily embraced the youth, and my younger sons and the dogs all joined in welcoming "Edward."

My sons ran back to the pinnace to bring provisions and cooking gear, and before long my wife set a fine meal before us. Soon "Edward" was laughing and chatting as gaily as the rest. Our celebratory feast lasted well into the evening, and everyone drank to the newcomer's good health.

When the youth grew tired, my wife led "Edward" to sleeping quarters aboard the pinnace. The rest of us were too excited for sleep just yet.

After Elizabeth returned, Jack threw some more wood on the fire, plopped down in his usual careless fashion and exclaimed, "Now, then, Fritz, let's have it. Where did you find him? Was it luck, or did you go looking for him?" We all waited to hear the tale.

Fritz hesitated a moment, then began. "You may remember me telling you that on my earlier voyage, I knocked down an albatross. That albatross brought me notice of a shipwrecked stranger, and I sent back an answering note with the same bird. I was full of hope, but I needed to add a second seat to the kayak. When the time was right, I took Pounce and went searching. After several hours of paddling, the weather got worse, and I found shelter for the night in a quiet cove.

"The next morning, I decided the weather was good enough to keep going. I was looking for smoke or any other trace of human habitation. At noon I came to a new area of coast, with sandy shores bordering dense woods. I could hear the fiendish laughs of hyenas, the cries of apes, and the death-bleats of deer. I felt very solitary and thoughtful. I paddled on for some hours more. There were river mouths, which I might otherwise have been tempted to explore, but the message had arrived by albatross. Whoever sent the message would not be found up a river. At nightfall I found a cove to moor the kayak, stretched my legs a bit, had dinner, then went back aboard for the night.

"The next morning Pounce and I again landed for breakfast. He had brought down a plump parrot, and I lit a fire to roast it. During this, I heard a slight rustle in the long grass behind me. I turned and found myself face to face with an immense tiger!"

Now Fritz's voice became solemn, and I noticed for the first time that he had come back without the eagle. He went on, "In another moment, I would have been dead, and our young guest would have been doomed to God only knows how many more years of solitude. There was no way I could reach my gun in time.

"Pounce saw my danger—and he attacked the tiger's face! His slashing and flapping distracted the tiger just long enough for me to grab my gun and aim. I put a bullet in the tiger's heart, and the beast's spring died before it began. Pounce lay motionless on the ground close by. The tiger had batted him down with one furious paw-blow. I checked for signs of life, but Pounce would never rise again!" Fritz's voice shook, and he was silent for a moment before continuing.

"I was as sad as I've ever been. I buried my friend where he died. Too sad to even care about the tiger skin, I paddled away. I felt a terrible loneliness, and I began to despair of success. Maybe the albatross had come hundreds of miles. Maybe the stranger was on faraway shores. Perhaps I was going the wrong direction.

"I wasn't discouraged for long. I paddled around a peninsula and came into a bay. The other side of the bay seemed to be another peninsula covered in thick forest. At the rocky tip of this peninsula I saw a column of smoke rising into the air.

"At first I just gazed at it, like in a dream. Then I began to paddle with all my might. I secured the kayak nearby and jumped ashore. The fire looked freshly built. I was about to shout, but before I could do so, I saw a slight figure coming toward me.

"I advanced a few paces and said in English, 'Welcome, fair stranger! Merciful God has heard your call, and has sent me to help you!' Miss Montrose came quickly forward—"

"Who? What?" interrupted the boys.

Amid the general hubbub, Ernest said quietly to his brother, "I wasn't going to spoil your secret, Fritz, but we no longer need pretend not to see through the disguise."

Fritz was embarrassed at his slip of the tongue, but he took his brothers' kidding in good spirits, and they all gave three cheers for their new sister. When the hubbub died down, he picked up the story again. "Miss Montrose took my hands and said, 'I've been waiting for you ever since the bird brought back your message! Thank God you've come!'

"With tears of joy and gratitude, she led me to a tree house she had built—sort of a small Falconhurst. Below it was a hut where she kept bows, arrows, spears, bird-snares, basic fishing gear, knives, and all sorts of other tools. Three years before, she said, she had survived a shipwreck on this coast. The tools and a trunk of clothing were all she had been able to salvage. It was immediately clear she is marvelously self-reliant, motivated, and intelligent. I knew Mother would be delighted to meet a woman as resourceful as herself.

"Imagine my surprise when a cormorant flew out of her hut as if to attack me! Miss Montrose called it off, then explained that she had captured it and trained it to catch fish—what a wonder! She had utensils as fine as ours, and she cooked me a most appetizing meal. While we ate, she told me her story.

"Her first name is Jenny. She was born in India, the daughter of a British colonel who had served there for many years. Her mother died of a fever when Jenny was three. Her father tried his best to teach her womanly arts but also instilled in her a great love of camping, riding, and hunting. By the age of seventeen she was as much at home on horseback in the woods as she was at her father's formal dinner parties.

"When Colonel Montrose was ordered home with his regiment, he didn't like the idea of bringing her aboard the troop-ship, so he booked her homeward voyage on another vessel. The separation pained father and daughter alike, but it was necessary. Miss Montrose sailed from

Calcutta in the *Dorcas*, bound for England. A week out, a storm drove their vessel off course. It grew too leaky to manage, and the crew took to the boats.

"Jenny was in the largest boat. They endured the open sea for many days, and further bad weather separated the three boats. When her boat sighted land, its occupants tried to reach it, but the boat capsized in the surf. She was the only one to reach shore alive—half-drowned. When she revived, she managed to find some oysters and crabs and began to recover her strength.

"Since that day I was the first human being she had seen. She always kept a fire going, to try to attract any passing ship. She began attaching messages to any birds that she could capture alive. The albatross she had partly tamed, but since it often went off on long flights, she decided to send a message in hopes it would return with an answer.

"Our dinner was over, and we were both weary from the day's excitement. She went to sleep in her tree house, while I slept in the hut below. The next morning, I packed her belongings in the kayak and we got aboard. She said goodbye to her familiar bay, and we set out. We would have reached Rockburg tonight, but the kayak developed a slow leak. We landed on this island so I could patch it. I was just finishing my work when I heard your first shots. As I mentioned before, my first thought was of Malay pirates, and I asked her to stay while I went to investigate. I was certainly glad to be wrong!"

All had listened attentively to Fritz's story, but Franz now gave out a great yawn, followed by others from Jack, Ernest, and Fritz. It had been our most exciting day since being shipwrecked. We went to the pinnace for the night, the men sleeping on deck and my wife joining Jenny below.

The next morning at breakfast, I asked Miss Montrose if we might address her by her true name. She smiled. "Of course; my disguise could hardly have worked for long. After all, I have no need to be ashamed of my clothing. It's all I've had for the last three years, and it has surely been more practical than dresses and hats."

After breakfast, I prepared to start for home, but Fritz reminded me of the whale. "While I'm not eager to go through the butchering process again," he suggested, "it would be a pity to lose out on all that oil."

"True. Let's do our best to get some and spend another night here," I agreed. Ernest, Jenny, and my wife stayed on the island. The rest of us boarded pinnace and kayak. It took little time to reach the sandbank where the monster lay at low tide.

No sooner did we come near than the dogs

leaped ashore. Before we could follow, they rushed around to the other side of the carcass. There was a great snarling and howling, and when we arrived we found our dogs disputing the whale with a pack of wolves. The battle didn't last long after we arrived. Two wolves already lay dead, and when our guns claimed three more, the rest fled. Among them were two jackals, and when Coco saw these relatives, his instinct took over. In spite of our shouts and cries, he disappeared with them into the forest.

It would have been useless and dangerous to pursue the deserter into the woods; we could only hope he would return. Fritz then climbed up the mountain of flesh with his hatchet and began the process of salvaging the whale oil. We had long been in the habit of bringing a few empty containers in the pinnace, and these were soon full.

We returned to the island to find dinner nearly ready. After we got cleaned up, we sat down to relate our adventures over the meal. There was much sorrow at Coco's desertion, but Jenny offered some words of hope. "He might still return. Wild animals usually won't tolerate one of their kind who has lived with people. Even though my poor albatross was never completely tame, he used to come back from time to time. Jack, if you were to go searching early tomorrow morning, you might find Coco eager to rejoin you. If you like, I'll go to find him, because I would very much love a paddle in the kayak all by myself."

Jack was delighted at the former suggestion but wouldn't hear of Jenny going alone. "How about if we go first thing tomorrow morning," he suggested.

"Then let's do so!" she agreed, and we all prepared to retire.

At sunrise they were off, armed with some meat and biscuit as a lure, plus a chain and muzzle Jack had brought to confine the renegade. They landed at the sandbar and entered the forest, calling "Coco! Coco!" until the woods rang. Soon the deserter came slouching toward them, looking miserable and ashamed. His torn ears and filthy coat testified to the accuracy of Jenny's prediction. Jack had neither the heart nor the need to use the muzzle and chain.

Back on the island, dogs and people were overjoyed to welcome back the prodigal, whom I doubted would ever leave us again. All was now bustle and activity, and after breakfast Fritz and Jack climbed into the kayak. The rest of us took to the pinnace, and we soon left the island and Pearl Bay far behind.

The sea's morning calm was broken only by the gentle breeze carrying us home. Once our kayakers piloted us past the rocks near the archway, they shouted that they were heading home in advance. Jenny was most amazed to see our island fortress, with its flying flag and battery of cannon, and we landed to show off our bastion before heading to Rockburg.

As we came into Safety Bay, a grand salute of twelve guns welcomed our expanded family to Rockburg. Ernest insisted upon replying with thirteen guns, explaining, "It's a matter of tradition. An odd number is absolutely necessary."

Fritz and Jack courteously helped their mother and Jenny ashore. They then led us through the gardens and orchards along the way to our dwelling. Jenny's surprise changed to wonder and delight as she neared the house itself—its broad, shady balcony, its fountains sparkling in the sun, the doves and pigeons, the fresh vines. "I can scarcely believe my good fortune," she exclaimed. "It's hard to imagine that I'm still far from any civilized nation, among fellow castaways and friends."

When I reached the porch, I got a surprise to equal Jenny's. The boys had laid out a sumptuous lunch on our best china: decanters of wine, a bowl of all types of fruit, a haunch of deer, some chicken, a ham, and other delicacies. In the middle were bowls of milk and great jugs of mead, plus a vase of pretty flowers. The lavish welcome brought tears to Jenny's lovely eyes, and Elizabeth took her inside to change into a fine dress.

Now our new daughter looked prettier than ever. Elizabeth and I gave her the place of honor between us, and Ernest and Franz also sat down, but Fritz and Jack did not. They did duty as our entertainers and servants, bustling here and there, carving meat, and filling glasses. "All the servants have run off in our absence, Miss Montrose," explained Jack. "For the next day or two, we'll just have to fill in for them."

When the banquet was over, and the waiters had also satisfied their appetites, they joined their brothers to show their new sister all the wonders of Rockburg—the house, cave, stables, gardens, fields, and aqueducts. They would probably have worn her out completely, but my wife came to Jenny's rescue and led her back to the house.

We had long put off several days of pre-winter repairs at Falconhurst, and the following day we started packing up the needed tools, provisions, and comforts. All our mounts were still in their stables except Hurry the ostrich, which Jack had gone and saddled. "Mother," he said, "you and Jenny mustn't walk the whole way." He leaped back on Hurry and fled.

Before we had gone a quarter of the way to the stables, we heard the thundering tread of many feet galloping down the avenue. Our entire troop of mounts was rumbling toward us: Storm, Lightfoot, Swift, Grumble, Stentor, Arrow, and

Dart, with Jack at their heels on his ostrich. At his saddle banged a cluster of harness equipment, the racket urging the excited animals to higher speed.

We stepped aside to evade the stampede, but a shout from Fritz brought the whole herd to a sudden halt, and Jack spurred toward us.

"Which shall we saddle for you, Jenny?" he shouted. "They're all as gentle as lambs. Mother has ridden every one, so you can be sure they're safe."

Jenny showed her keen judgment by picking out Dart, the fleetest and most spirited of them all. We all set to work harnessing and saddling the mounts. After loading the baskets and hampers on Lightfoot, we rode off toward Falconhurst. Jenny was so delighted with Dart that we all agreed to reserve him for her special use.

A week's hard work went swifter than it otherwise might have, for our adopted daughter proved a lively, good-humored, helpful companion. When we finished our repairs, we stayed a day or two longer in order to get chickens from Woodlands and collect acorns, grass, willows, and canes for winter food and projects. The showers grew more frequent, and we barely got our mounts back into Rockburg's stables when the real downpour came.

With Jenny around, this once-dreary season seemed shorter than ever before—and far pleasanter. Everyone quickly learned English from her. Fritz learned to speak it so well that Jenny declared he might be mistaken for an Englishman. For me, it was a winter of thanks to God for His beautiful young blessing.

CHAPTER 21

Partings

This happy winter of storytelling, hobbies, and crafts ended before we knew it. Spring brought us all back out of doors to attend to our various settlements. We visited Falconhurst, Woodlands, Prospect Hill, and Shark and Whale Islands in turn.

One day Jack and Franz, in charge of the island gun battery, had gone out to repair the flagstaff and test-fire the cannon. The rest of us were out for a stroll on the beach, idly watching them. They loaded both guns, then towed out an empty barrel as a practice target. Back they paddled in the kayak, trained their guns, and fired. We saw the barrel shatter and heard their distant shouts of triumph.

They had just begun to clean out the guns when three *booms* resounded across the water from the west.

We stopped, speechless. For a moment we all thought we'd imagined it. Certainly Jack and Franz hadn't fired a second time, and just as certainly they too had heard it, for they leaped into the kayak and paddled full speed toward us.

A tumult of anxiety, joy, hope, and doubt rushed over us. Was it a European vessel, our means of rejoining civilization? Or was it a Malay pirate, who would rob and murder us? Or it might be a stricken ship in dire need. Who could tell?

Before we could discuss our thoughts, Jack and Franz reached shore. "Did you hear them?" gasped Jack. "What should we do?"

"It must be a European ship," exclaimed Franz. "We're going home!" Only then did I realize how deeply my boys longed for civilized life. Since Jenny's coming, I had seen their behavior change, but I hadn't realized why. Now I knew.

All eyes turned toward me.

"It's almost dark," I said. "All we can do right now is make plans and pray for guidance."

No one slept much that night. All talk was of the ship and what it might mean. The boys and I took turns keeping watch, in case of further signals or hostile action.

About midnight the wind began to rise, and soon a fearful storm was raging—the sort of storm that had wrecked us all those years ago. A man-of-war could have fired all its cannons at the entrance of Safety Bay without our knowing.

The hurricane lasted three days. At last it abated. It was time to execute our plan. Jack and Franz would fire another signal from Shark Island, and the response—if any—would determine our next course. I kept reminding everyone not to get their hopes up. "She may have run for the open sea, never to return. She might be wrecked in the surf." I went with my boys to the fort. They fired both guns in sequence, then waited.

For some tantalizing minutes there was no reply, then another three *booms* sounded in the distance. The strange vessel was still near! We waved the flag to signal shore that all was well, then returned. Everyone was most excited, and it took some effort to be heard. "Remember, this visit may not be to our advantage," I said. "It's time we learned for sure. Fritz, get ready."

Fritz and I armed ourselves with guns, pistols, and cutlasses, and I took a spyglass. As we boarded the kayak, my wife urged us to be careful. Jenny said nothing, but I saw a special anxiety in her eyes. We promised to take all due caution. Then we paddled out of Safety Bay.

For nearly an hour we paddled along the western coast, seeing nothing. At Pug Nose Cape, we rounded the old bluff point. In that moment all our doubts were replaced with joy and gratitude to the Heavenly Father.

There, in the little sheltered cove beyond the cape, a brig-of-war lay at anchor.

At her mast flew the flag of Great Britain.

We halted the kayak without further exposing ourselves, and I peered through the spyglass. Figures were moving about on deck. On the beach were several tents and campfires. As I handed the glass to Fritz, I felt a sudden uncertainty. What was an English vessel doing so far off course? I remembered tales of mutinous crews running for shelter in some place like this. Such mutineers would be desperate men—no friends of ours.

"I can see the captain, Father!" exclaimed Fritz. "He's in English uniform, talking to one of the officers. Seamen are going about normal duties. It must be a Royal Navy vessel!" He gave me the glass again, to see for myself. Fritz was right—no mutineers would have maintained such order on board. The Royal Navy was here.

"Well, they aren't leaving any time soon, nor do they seem to need help," I said. "We have time. I'd rather not greet them dressed like this, in rough clothing and bristling with weapons."

"Then let's greet them in style," recommended Fritz. "This is our land. We are lords here, not beggars. Let's look the part." We paddled back to Rockburg to bring our family the

delightful news. Despite the all-around eager-
ness, they also agreed with our decision to better
prepare for the meeting—even Jenny, whose
countrymen the visitors were.

We spent the rest of that day making pinnace
and people presentable. The boys scrubbed the
pinnace's decks, polished her brass guns, and
unloaded all unnecessary cargo. Jenny had salvaged an English flag from her own shipwreck;
we hoisted it atop the mast. My wife brought out
our neatest clothes, worn only on special occa-
sions, including dresses for herself and Jenny.
Again it was difficult to sleep for all the excitement.

The morning finally came, the day we would set
eyes on our fellow men after many years of exile.
We wolfed down our breakfast in near-silence,
striving for calm. Fritz and Jack then slipped quietly out and soon returned from the garden with
baskets of our choicest fruits as presents for the
strangers. Ernest took the pinnace's rudder; the
other boys raised the anchor and set the sails.
With the kayak in tow, the little vessel bounded
merrily over Safety Bay.

We sailed for Pug-nosed Cape. We looked
around at one another on the verge of the fateful
moment. Then Ernest put the rudder about and
sailed us around the point.

It took only a few moments for us to reach

hailing distance. What a commotion! Every eye on board and on shore was turned toward us. Whatever sights the gallant crew might have expected on this coast, a pleasure boat was certainly not among them.

Fritz and I stepped into our kayak and pulled for the brig. In another minute we ascended to her deck and stood face to face with a dignified officer. "Welcome aboard *HMS Unicorn*," he proclaimed. "I am Captain Littlestone. To what good fortune do we owe your visit? We had believed this coast to be uninhabited."

After we introduced ourselves, he invited us to his cabin. There we gave him a brief outline of the wreck, our time ashore, and the rescue of Miss Montrose.

The gallant officer rose and gave Fritz his hand. "Then, on behalf of myself and Colonel Montrose, let me heartily thank you. We came in search of Miss Montrose. The disappearance of the *Dorcas* was a terrible blow to the Colonel, yet he has never given up hope. As we were preparing to depart Sydney for the Cape a few weeks back, I found three men who said they were survivors of the *Dorcas*. To their knowledge, theirs was the only boat from the stricken vessel to reach land safely.

"One was the sailing master, who remembered the bearings where the *Dorcas* met her doom. I received permission to divert to this area, in hope of finding survivors. What unlooked-for good fortune! Again, I thank you for making our search successful."

"And I thank you for your kind words," said Fritz. "However, I can take little credit for Miss Montrose's rescue. It was not hazardous, and we have been repaid ten times over for the effort by the pleasure of her company."

The captain's eyes and mine met in silent approval of Fritz's modest gallantry. "Quite," he said. "But might I meet the ladies and the rest of your brave family?"

"With pleasure, sir," I replied.

"I will send a boat at once," he said. Then he added to his hovering steward, "Pass my orders to Lieutenant Martin immediately. He is to take a boat over to Mr. Robinson's vessel at once, present my compliments, and offer to convey the others here."

"Aye aye, sir," said the steward before vanishing. We passed some minutes in pleasant conversation, and soon Elizabeth, Jenny, and my other sons were aboard.

At lunch, the captain told us of his passengers. A Mr. Wolston, an invalid gentleman, had sailed with him from Sydney with his wife and two daughters in hopes that the voyage would improve his health. Unfortunately, this hadn't been the case, and the storm had worsened Mr. Wolston's condition. He had been eager for a short rest on dry land, and the *Unicorn* had taken slight damage in the storm, so the two needs had coincided nicely. "We would very much like to meet this family," I said.

"Nothing could be simpler," replied the captain.

When we landed, we found Mr. Wolston seated by a tent in the shade. The captain introduced everyone, and we all had a friendly visit. Before we knew it the sun was setting, making it too late to return to Rockburg. The captain kindly offered tents for anyone who wished to sleep on land, and the boys accepted.

That night Elizabeth and I had a long, serious discussion. Would we return to Europe, or remain in New Switzerland? I felt it would be hasty and foolish to return simply because we could. We danced about the issue, neither willing to commit, each unwilling to pressure the other. It was the most subtle, fateful conversation of our marriage.

At length it became clear that both of us regarded New Switzerland as our home and had no real desire to leave. What relief to agree on such a matter! My dear wife had only one condition. "I'd be happy to remain, provided you and at least two of our sons will stay. If the other two wish to return to Europe, I don't object. But they must encourage hardy emigrants to join our colony."

"Very good, dear," I replied. "I'm sure they'll do their best. Perhaps if my journals were published, it would provide incentive."

"I don't doubt it," said Elizabeth. "I do feel, however, that this island ought to preserve the name of New Switzerland, even if in time we also have English colonists."

"Then it's settled," I said. "We'll consult our sons and ask Captain Littlestone about placing New Switzerland under British protection. After all, our dear native land lacks the small matter of a coastline, much less a powerful fleet," I added with a chuckle.

"I wonder what our sons will choose," she said.

"Given a few days to socialize, they'll probably tell us without prodding," I advised.

"You're right, my dear," she answered. "So long as I have my family, I'll be happy."

In the morning, after breakfast, we invited Captain Littlestone, his officers, and the Wolstons to visit Rockburg. I hoped that our comfortable residence ashore might help Mr. Wolston's condition. "By all means, sir," exclaimed the captain. "We'd be honored, and I'm sure the gentleman and his family will feel likewise." Fritz and Jack hurried off in the kayak to prepare, followed at leisure by *HMS Unicorn* and our pinnace. Of my family, only I remained aboard the English warship.

Words cannot express our guests' marvel as they rounded the cape into Safety Bay. This astonishment doubled as the sound of cannon fire began to reverberate across the bay: eleven guns from Shark Island, where the British flag floated majestically at the staff. Every face glowed with surprise and pleasure, and poor Mr. Wolston's spirits seemed to revive.

"Mr. Martin!" bellowed the captain. "Cause a salute of thirteen guns to be fired in honor of New Switzerland and its populace!" I swelled with pride as the reports echoed off the cliffside. The anchor cable roared; boats were lowered. Seamen gently carried Mr. Wolston into a boat, and soon all were ashore who were going ashore.

I had the boys rig our most comfortable bed for Mr. Wolston, with a camp bed alongside for his wife. My sons and Jenny led the officers and Wolston daughters on a friendly if disorganized sightseeing tour. It took considerable effort to round everyone up for lunch, but we eventually reined them in long enough to eat. After that we had planned a visit to Falconhurst, but it proved impossible to corral the young people. Only by dinnertime did the excitement begin to die down.

To my surprised pleasure, Mr. Wolston joined us at the table. "Your cheeks are showing a far healthier color, sir. You must be feeling better," I observed.

"Thank you, Mr. Robinson," he answered. "If so, I have your kind hospitality to thank. I begin to wonder whether you might welcome some of my family to remain in this beautiful country. My wife also loves it here, and my older daughter's health is as fragile as my own. In any case, our younger daughter will proceed to the Cape of Good Hope to visit her brother. It wouldn't surprise me if he too applied to join your colony—all with your consent, of course."

"You have it, sir!" I answered. "My wife and I intend to remain in New Switzerland for the rest of our days. May your family find it as pleasant as mine has."

"Hurrah for New Switzerland! New Switzerland forever!" shouted the whole company, glasses ringing together.

"Long life and happiness to those who make New Switzerland their home!" added Ernest to my great surprise, leaning forward to touch his glass to mine, his mother's, and Mr. Wolston's.

"Won't somebody wish long life and prosperity to those who go away?" inquired Jenny with a mischievous look. "Much as I long to return to England and my father, it seems all the cheers are for New Switzerland!"

"Three cheers for England, *HMS Unicorn*, her valiant officers and crew, and Colonel Montrose!" cried Fritz. "Success and happiness to us who return to Europe!" The vaulted roof of

Rockburg rang again with cheers, and I did not miss Jenny's appreciative glance at Fritz.

"Well," I said when silence was restored, "in that case, Fritz, to you I delegate the pleasant duty of restoring Jenny, whom I have come to love as my own daughter, to her mourning father. As for Ernest, we rejoice that he wishes to stay with us. We promise him all the opportunity for honorable study New Switzerland can bestow.

"And now what is Jack's choice? His greatest talent is that of comic acting, but for that he must go to Europe."

"Jack is not going to Europe, however," was his reply. "Jack will stay here, and when Fritz is gone, he will be the best rider and shot in New Switzerland, which is his greatest ambition. The fact is," he continued with a laugh, "I am awed by European schools. If I go too near one, and they captured me, I might never escape."

"A good school is exactly what I want," said Franz. "I long for education, to seek my fortune in the world. Fritz will probably return here some day, but one of us should plan to remain in Europe. I am youngest and can more easily adapt than the rest—but I will accept my father's decision."

"Then you are man enough to make your own decision," I said. "Go if you wish, my dear Franz, and God bless all your plans and resolutions. The whole earth is the Lord's, and wherever you live a good and useful life, He watches. And now that I know all your wishes, only one question remains: will Captain Littlestone kindly enable them to be carried out?"

All eyes were fixed eagerly on the captain. After a moment's pause the gallant officer spoke. "I think my course is perfectly clear. This diversion has been so fortunate I regard it as God-given. I was ordered to search for shipwreck victims; I have found survivors of not one but two wrecks. Three passengers wish to disembark here, while three others wish to go to England. Could anything be more suitable? Yes, Mr. Robinson, I will gladly carry the passengers to the Cape, or to England, as they prefer. I may help England to gain a prosperous colony, which serves the Crown's interests nicely. Three cheers for New Switzerland!"

Deep emotion stirred every heart as the party separated for the night, many on the threshold of new lives. As for me, I felt a great weight lifted from my heart, and I gave thanks to my Creator for the solution to a perplexing difficulty.

Beginning the next day, everyone got to work preparing for departures, for Captain Littlestone could delay only a few days. We sent along everything that we could think of to help our children while they were on board and in Europe. I sent along a large share of pearls, corals, furs, and spices, so that they might not arrive in poverty. I also sent along private papers, money, and jewels that had belonged to the captain of our ill-fated ship, in hopes that his heirs could be located.

To Captain Littlestone I entrusted a short account of the wreck, along with a crew list I had found, so that their families might finally know the fate of their loved ones. We gave the ship's company a large supply of fresh fruit, vegetables, and preserved fish.

I could not send Fritz and Franz away without guidance. I took them for one last cruise to Shark Island. There, relaxing in sight of Rockburg, I urged them, "Remember your duties: to God, your fellow man, and yourselves. You will meet many temptations along the way; many paths lead to bad results. I trust and pray that you will cling to the values and faith in which you were brought up." Two fine young men promised to do so. I knew they would keep their word.

"Fritz, as you've told me, you and Jenny have grown most fond of one another. You must mention this to Colonel Montrose as soon as possible after you are introduced to him. I know relatively little about romance, but I know rather more about being a father. Trust me: he will surely suspect. The brave young man who brought back his greatest joy will be of great interest to him. Be bold, just as you so boldly went in search of her.

Look him in the eye, ask for his blessing, and hope for the best.

"As for our blessing, your mother and I have already spoken, and I give it to you in both our names. We grieve to part with both you and Jenny, but we would rejoice to hear that you two were not parted."

The evening before departure, I gave Fritz my journal—the story that you, faithful reader, have nearly finished. Ever since the shipwreck, I had recorded our lives, in hope that the story might someday be published. "As you know," I said, "it was written to entertain and to teach my children. It may well be useful to other young people. On the whole, children everywhere are alike; you four lads represent many others. It would make me very happy to know that our example has helped other families to see what blessings can come to those who are resourceful, who persevere, and who are kind."

Night has closed around me.

For the last time my united family sleeps in my care. Tomorrow this closing chapter of my journal will pass into the hands of my eldest son.

Greetings to Europe!

Greetings to dear old Switzerland!

Like you, may New Switzerland flourish and prosper—good, happy, and free!

Afterword

About the Author(s)

*T*he *Swiss Family Robinson* has two authors, both of them named Johann Wyss. Johann David Wyss was a minister who lived in Switzerland from 1743 to 1818. He and his wife had four sons. When the boys were young, Johann David Wyss created a story to entertain and educate his children. The story was about a Swiss family— mother, father, and four sons—shipwrecked on an uninhabited island. At first, Johann David just told the story orally, making it up as he went along. Eventually, he wrote it down. When he was done, he had more than eight hundred hand-written pages.

The second author of *The Swiss Family Robinson* is Johann Rudolf Wyss. Johann Rudolf was one of Johann David's four sons. He lived

from 1781 to 1830. Along with his three brothers, he grew up listening to the story his father
made up. After going to college in Germany, he
returned to his hometown of Bern, Switzerland,
where he became a professor of philosophy. He
was interested in Swiss history and folklore. He
wrote several articles and books on these topics,
and he also wrote the words to the Swiss nation-
al anthem. In 1813, at the age of thirty-three, he
got permission from his father to edit and publish
the eight hundred page manuscript. The version
that he first published was quite different from
the version we know today. It ends after the family has been on the island for only two years. And
it ends with the father wondering if they will ever
see other human beings again. In later editions,
the story was revised to include the character of
Jenny Montrose and the arrival of the English
ship. Some of the changes were added by Johann
Rudolf and some by people who translated the
book from German into French and English.

Even though *The Swiss Family Robinson* has
gone through many changes since Johann David
Wyss first told the story to his boys, it remains a
good adventure story. It has continued to entertain and instruct readers of all ages for nearly two
hundred years.

About the Book

At the end of *The Swiss Family Robinson,* Robinson hands his journal over to his son Fritz in hopes that Fritz will publish it when he gets to England. Robinson says, "It was written to entertain and to teach my children. It may well be useful to other young people. . . . It would make me very happy to know that our example has helped other families to see what blessings can come to those who are resourceful, who persevere, and who are kind." This statement explains what has kept the book popular for almost two centuries: it entertains, but it also teaches.

There are four ways in particular that *The Swiss Family Robinson* entertains us. One is by including amusing moments: Knips riding on the back of Turk; little Franz as the great bull-tamer, Milo of Crotona; Robinson flapping his arms among the geese to create a musical accompaniment for the opening of the holiday games; impulsive Jack being chased by a land crab. One does not have to read very many pages to find an amusing moment in the family's life.

A second way the book engages us is through moments of tension and danger. In the very first chapter, the family is trapped on a wrecked ship in the midst of a raging storm. Later in the book, Robinson and Jack are nearly trampled by a herd of stampeding buffalo. Still later, the family is threatened by a huge boa constrictor. Not long after that, Ernest has a narrow escape from two angry bears. Besides all the specific instances of tension and danger, there is a constant undercurrent of potential danger. This is created by the fact that they are shipwrecked in an uncharted world. They never know when some threatening creature—or maybe even some threatening human—may appear.

Another way the book gives us pleasure is by creating moments of mystery and uncertainty. What lies beyond the rocky hills and cliffs? Who wrote the strange message that Fritz discovers tied to the albatross's leg? Who has fired the three cannon shots that answer the family's own cannon shots? These and other mysteries keep us wondering and keep us reading to find the answers.

The final way the book entertains is by showing us imaginative solutions to problems the family faces. How to get from the dangerous wrecked ship to the safety of the island? Build a boat from barrels cut in two. How to get the farm animals ashore? Make life preservers for them. How to get the pinnace out of the hold of the wrecked ship? Blow a hole in the side of the ship. Each time the family seems faced with a problem that is impossible to solve, they come up with an imaginative solution.

In addition to providing an enjoyable story, *The Swiss Family Robinson* presents lessons about aspects of life. The first of these three lessons is simply the information it teaches about the natural world. Almost every chapter introduces us to animals, birds, sea creatures, insects, and plants from every part of the world. In some cases, we are even told how to cook these and what they taste like: "The bears' paws [cooked in a stew] were delicious, despite their resemblance to giant human hands." In addition, Robinson tells us the basic principles of all kinds of practical and academic topics. From building a birch-bark canoe to using mathematics to determine the height of a tree, from catching and training an onager to using the physics of levers to lift heavy objects— the book is packed with information.

The book's second lesson is in its celebration of three qualities that people must have in order for a community to function well: resourcefulness, perseverance, and kindness.

To be resourceful means to be able to act effectively and imaginatively in any situation. We see repeatedly how Robinson and his family are resourceful as they make use of their knowledge and the objects around them to create whatever they need. Robinson figures out how to build a boat out of barrels. Elizabeth figures out how to make waterproof suits to protect her husband and sons from the rain. Fritz comes up with the idea of creating life vests to float the farm animals ashore. Ernest invents a woven basket to use for catching fish. Jack makes porcupine-skin armor to protect

Turk. Franz figures out how to tame Grumble, the bull. Almost everything the family does demonstrates the advantages of being resourceful.

To persevere means to persist, to hold firm to a task or a course of action. Every single project that the Robinson family takes on they see through to completion. When they are building the pinnace, they face huge obstacles—lack of space, lack of experience, lack of means for getting the boat out of the hold of the wrecked ship—but they keep at it until they have a wonderful and useful boat. When first attempting to chisel a shelter out of the rock cliff at Tentholm, their progress is agonizingly slow. But they keep at it until they have a safe, dry home for the rainy season. They are constantly building, improving, and inventing. They never become discouraged or overwhelmed in their efforts to make New Switzerland as comfortable and safe as Old Switzerland. They never waver in their faith. They teach us what perseverance is by the way they live.

Kindness is the third quality the book teaches. Robinson constantly reminds his children to be kind to one another. Early in the first chapter, Fritz speaks sharply to Franz. Robinson immediately tells Fritz to speak more kindly: "Well said, Fritz, had you said it kindly. You often speak more harshly to your brothers than you truly feel. Let your words reflect what is in your heart." Robinson does not scold Fritz. Instead, he compliments his son ("Well done, Fritz") and gently suggests how to speak more kindly ("Let your words reflect what is in your heart"). This example is typical of the way he teaches his sons to be kind: he tells them and he shows them. As a result, they learn kindness by experiencing it.

The final lesson in *The Swiss Family Robinson* is the need to increase our understanding of others. Robinson learns this lesson by discovering how to better understand Elizabeth.

From the start, Robinson respects and admires his wife. In the first chapter, he says he is "inspired" by her bravery. But in Chapter 4, we learn that he also worries about her when he must leave her alone. The first time he returns to the wreck, he tells us, "I could not sleep worrying about my wife and children, alone with only two wounded dogs to protect them." The next morning, when he sees the signal that they are safe, his reaction is, "What a weight that signal lifted from my heart!"

In spite of his respect, admiration, and concern for Elizabeth, Robinson has no understanding of how his wife feels. Every time he goes back to the wrecked ship, Elizabeth expresses her concern. In Chapter 5, she tells him, "I would rather lose the rest [of the cargo] than sit here and worry myself sick, as I do every time you even mention going to sea." Robinson hears her words, but he does not understand what she feels. In Chapter 5, she states the problem exactly: "Must you really go again to that dreadful wreck? You have no idea how nervous those trips make me." He really does have *no idea* how she feels.

Finally, in Chapter 9, when Robinson announces the last trip to the wreck, he begins to understand how strongly Elizabeth feels. "As we caught the outbound current, I thought to myself that I'd been very slow to realize how much she hated our salvage trips. I resolved to be a more perceptive husband." At last, he realizes that he must become more sensitive to what his wife feels.

Later in the book, he demonstrates that he really has become a more perceptive husband. In Chapter 17, a sudden violent storm comes up while Robinson, Ernest, and Jack are in the pinnace and Fritz is in the kayak. Robinson says, "I could only imagine how my wife and Franz felt, alone [on shore] in the storm with no news of the rest of the family." Now he *is* able to imagine how upset she is. This is the most important lesson taught by the book: the need to increase our understanding of others.

In sum, Johann David Wyss and Johann Rudolf Wyss succeed in entertaining us greatly with their story. They also succeed in teaching us important lessons in how to live successfully in a community and how to grow as human beings—lessons as valuable today as they were two centuries ago.